HUNGER FOR YOU

Praise for Jenny Frame

Unexpected

"If you enjoy contemporary romances, *Unexpected* is a great choice. The character work is excellent, the plotting and pacing are well done, and it's a just a sweet, warm read."—*Curve*

Royal Rebel

"Frame's stories are easy to follow and really engaging. She stands head and shoulders above a number of the romance authors and it's easy to see why she is quickly making a name for herself in lesfic romance."—*The Lesbian Review*

Courting the Countess

"I love Frame's romances. They are well paced, filled with beautiful character moments and a wonderful set of side characters who ultimately end up winning your heart...I love Jenny Frame's butch/femme dynamic; she gets it so right for a romance."—*The Lesbian Review*

By the Author

A Royal Romance

Heart of the Pack

Courting the Countess

Dapper

Royal Rebel

Unexpected

Charming the Vicar

Hunger for You

HUNGER FOR YOU

by
Jenny Frame

2018

HUNGER FOR YOU
© 2018 By Jenny Frame. All Rights Reserved.

ISBN 13: 978-1-63555-168-6

This Trade Paperback Original Is Published By
Bold Strokes Books, Inc.
P.O. Box 249
Valley Falls, NY 12185

First Edition: April 2018

Credits
Editor: Ruth Sternglantz
Production Design: Stacia Seaman
Cover Design by Tammy Seidick

Acknowledgments

A huge thank you to Radclyffe, Sandy, and all the team behind the scenes at BSB. You do so much great work to get our books out there, and it's very much appreciated.

Thank you to my editor, Ruth, who has infinite patience and restraint when it comes my grammar and spelling, and as always for her help in making my stories better and steering me in the right direction.

My biggest, loudest shout of thanks go to my two vampire, witch, and paranormal research assistants—my nieces, Robyn and Amy, who have helped me so much in my paranormal fact-finding missions. Thank you, girls!

Finally, to Lou and our Barney boy. You make my life happy and hopeful, and above all, make me feel very loved.

For Kayleigh
Always And Forever In Our Hearts

Chapter One

A melia Honey skipped upstairs from the cutting room of Grenville and Thrang bespoke tailors, one of the oldest on London's Savile Row. Her stomach was doing flips with excitement, as it always did when she spent any precious time with Byron Debrek. Her lover's international business commitments meant their time together was limited and unpredictable. That was the one and only thing that had troubled Amelia in the six months she had been dating Byron. She wasn't reliable, and as much as Byron apologized for the cancelled dates and missed phone calls, it was hard when Amelia found herself at home alone on a Friday night, while other couples were spending the weekend together, having fun and binge-watching all the latest TV shows.

When Amelia reached the top of the stairs and saw Byron framed in the doorway by sunlight, holding a single long-stemmed rose in her hand, with the sexiest smile she had ever seen, she let her worries fall away. Life wasn't perfect and she supposed that was part of Byron's attraction. She was unpredictable and brought flash and glam into her formerly dull, grey life. None of that mattered now. They were going on a holiday together for two weeks, and she would get Byron's undivided attention. She guessed Byron had suggested a holiday to make up for all the missed dates and appointments.

As she walked towards Byron, Amelia purposefully put an extra roll to her hips and got a thrill when, as always, her lover's eyes followed them intently. She felt powerful—she, Amelia Honey, a tailor, could keep the attention of the enigmatic, rich, stunningly good looking CEO of the Debrek banking group.

Byron took her hand and kissed it softly. "Miss Honey, you are beautiful as always. This is for you."

She took the rose from Byron and inhaled its perfume. "Thank you."

Amelia's heart hammered in her chest when Byron's lips touched her hand, and she inhaled the scents of the rose as well as Byron's aftershave. It was astonishing how much her life had changed since she had measured Byron for a suit for the first time six months ago. Byron had been coming to Grenville and Thrang since before she'd joined the staff. Amelia's Uncle Jaunty, the Grenville of Grenville and Thrang, had always dealt with Byron privately, and Amelia had admired her from afar for a long time, before her uncle had given her the opportunity to take an appointment with Byron.

The appointment had been nerve-racking, scary, and exciting, all at the same time. They had a powerful chemistry from the very first, so much so that during their second meeting, Byron introduced her to some of the darker pleasures she had only fantasized about, here, on her workbench downstairs.

She had never felt so physically attracted to anyone in her life. When they were near each other, everyone else around them melted away and it took every shred of control Amelia had not to give in to their passion. She felt almost compelled to touch her, or be touched. There was much more than passion, though—she was falling in love with Byron, and she hoped this time together could cement their feelings and Byron would give her some kind of commitment.

"Are you ready? Your carriage awaits," Byron said.

Amelia smiled and lightly traced a fingernail down Byron's inky blue tie with white polka dots. "I just have to see Uncle Jaunty first, then make sure Daisy has everything she needs, and then I'll be ready."

Daisy, her apprentice, was fresh out of fashion school and eager to fill in for Amelia while she was away.

She grasped Byron's tie softly. "I like this tie by the way."

"I have to keep you interested, Miss Honey. Why don't I come with you? Your uncle and I can share a drink while you get ready to leave."

As they walked through the shop hand in hand, the staff and the customers averted their eyes. Byron seemed to have the ability to make people nervous or intimidated with just a look. Those looks made

Amelia hot, excited, turned on, but never scared or intimidated. Byron had never given her any cause to be fearful—the opposite, in fact, she treated Amelia more like a fine piece of china, and sometimes Amelia really wanted to shake Byron up.

"Weren't you supposed to phone me last night?" Amelia said as they walked to the back office.

"Ah…yes. I'm sorry. I was in Zurich, and a business meeting ran over. I thought it too late to telephone you after I got back to my hotel suite, but I promise to make up for it."

Amelia stopped outside her uncle's office door, and looked at Byron carefully. There was a little voice, a little jealous voice that often questioned whether Byron was alone when she went back to her hotel rooms, as she travelled all over the world. As she looked into Byron's eyes, all she could see was passion and, she hoped, love—but Byron had never said the words.

She raised up on tiptoe and pecked Byron on the lips, deciding to ignore the nagging voice. "I hope so, no more business talk. We're going on holiday," Amelia exclaimed.

She knocked on the door and entered to find her uncle working at his computer. He stood and smiled when he saw them.

"Byron, wonderful to see you again so soon." Jaunty walked around the desk to shake Byron's hand. Jaunty was tall and impeccably dressed, never seen without a suit, his trademark bow tie, and the ever-present tape measure hanging around his shoulders.

"Good to see you looking so well, Jaunty. Is Simon well?" Byron said.

Jaunty put his arm around Amelia, and she immediately reciprocated, laying her head on his shoulder.

"Very well, thank you. I hear you are taking our little Amelia to Monaco. I hope you'll take care of her."

"Uncle Jaunty, don't. You know I can take care of my myself." Amelia nudged her uncle. She was secretly pleased he was so protective and cared so much. At eighteen, she had run away from her highly conservative and religious parents to stay with her uncle and his partner Simon.

She had always been forbidden from talking to or asking about her mother's brother, but she did her research and secretly communicated with him, and eventually ran to London to get away from her suffocating home life—and to pursue her dreams of becoming a fashion designer. It was only natural that after graduating from the London School of Fashion, she came into her uncle's business.

Byron placed her hand on her heart. "With my life. I promise you, Jaunty."

Amelia kissed her uncle on the cheek and said, "I need to speak to Daisy and get my things. Why don't you and Byron chat while I'm gone?"

"Of course, sweetie. Off you go."

When Amelia went off to get her jacket and freshen up, Jaunty poured them a drink.

"Have you ever done this before, Byron?" Jaunty handed her a glass of whiskey.

"What do you mean? Go on holiday with a woman?" Byron asked.

Jaunty nodded. Byron crossed her legs and took a sip of whiskey. "No, I've never even taken a holiday before, with or without a woman."

Jaunty sat back behind his desk, but seemed tense. "This must be serious for you, then?"

"Jaunty, if you have something to say, then say it."

Jaunty looked entirely uncomfortable talking this way to her, but she admired his strength for doing it.

"Byron, Amelia is like a daughter to me and Simon. She came to us hurt, alone, and with her confidence destroyed by my sister and brother-in-law. We got her through college and gave her a safe place to live."

"I know that, Jaunty. I know she thinks of you and Simon as her fathers."

"She's not one of those streetwise women I'm sure you meet on the European business circuit and at your glamorous parties."

"You don't think I'm toying with her, do you? I know sometimes I have to cancel our dates but—"

"You are my friend, Byron, and your father and I have been friends for years, and I know how difficult this kind of relationship will be for you and Amelia."

The way Jaunty looked at her and the way he was speaking gave Byron pause to think he knew what she was, what her father was. She leaned forward and put her drink down on the desk.

"What do you mean?" Byron asked.

Jaunty got up and walked to the safe in the corner of the office. He spun the lock and the door opened with a creak. He riffled through some papers and then brought a photograph over to show her.

"This was taken on the first day I bought into the business, after Albert Thrang died. Your father loaned me the money to buy the business."

Byron nodded. "I know—my father said he trusted you implicitly. That's why I came to you, Jaunty." Byron had lived her life as a man through the centuries when running an international business as a woman would have been difficult. As time went by, and the culture changed, she felt able to come out as her true self, but she was always naturally more masculine than feminine and expressed herself that way both in her clothes and sexually. Jaunty, as her tailor, gave her the discretion she needed, and never blinked an eye as he measured her up for her suits, and found her to be wearing a strap-on. This was just who she was, and he'd always accepted it.

"I know why you came to me." Jaunty showed her the picture and pointed at the tall man in the picture who looked so much like Byron, except for the artificially induced salt-and-pepper hair.

"This was forty-seven years ago, and your father hasn't aged a day."

Normally her family didn't keep up long-term friendships, so these difficulties didn't arise. But Michal was very fond of Jaunty, so was Byron, and now she was falling for his niece. She had never planned on this relationship, but after the first taste of Amelia's lips, she knew she could not turn her back on her, despite the many problems a relationship posed for someone like her, and despite vowing long ago to never ever care for a woman again.

Byron was reminded of that close friend from a long time ago who had prophesized that one day a young woman would come along and pierce her impenetrable heart. Byron had never believed it—until recently.

"I could never hurt her, and I would do anything to keep her safe, I can promise you that. This holiday is to work out what we can be together. I've never taken a chance like this, never let someone into my world like this."

Jaunty let out a breath. "You need to be so careful, Byron. My girl is head over heels for you."

This should have sent her fleeing in fear—it always had done before if any women she slept with got too close—but Amelia was different. She was her girl, shining with goodness, and that goodness lit up the dark parts of her.

Byron's hearing picked up the sound of Amelia's heels on the wooden floors. "She's coming. You don't have anything to worry about, Jaunty. Amelia is safe with me."

❖

Amelia gave her uncle a kiss goodbye at the door of Grenville and Thrang, and said, "Give Uncle Simon a kiss from me."

"I will. Keep in touch, okay, sweetie?" Jaunty said.

Amelia stepped back and allowed Byron to shake hands with her uncle, before saying, "I'll email you lots of pics, Uncle Jaunty."

Amelia looped her arm through Byron's and was escorted over to Byron's blacked-out Daimler. As always there were another two blacked-out limos parked behind Byron's. Byron had explained early on that she travelled with a lot of security, due to her business, but Amelia had always found it strange that a banker needed so much protection, especially the unusual people who headed up Byron's security team. Where other personal security people serving politicians or the rich and famous usually wore a standard uniform of a bland suit, Byron's team wore black combat trousers and black combat boots, as if they were ready for war.

Waiting by the car to open their car door was Alexis Villiers, Byron's personal bodyguard. Alexis was not quite as tall as Byron, with collar-length dark hair. She was stern, with a military bearing, and never smiled. Amelia had the feeling she didn't quite approve of her, but maybe that was just her imagination.

Standing at the car behind was Bhaltair, whom Byron called Bhal and described as head of her personal guard. Bhal was an extraordinary looking human being. Amelia was sure she was over six feet tall and built like a warrior ready for combat, but unlike Alexis always had a nod and a smile for Amelia. Her dirty blond hair was short and messily styled on top, with one strand of long braided hair hanging down. There was something about her that just seemed out of step with this time and place.

Alexis and Bhal, unlike the others, wore long black military-cut leather jackets, with epaulets and silver buttons which Amelia guessed denoted some sort of hierarchy.

Alexis held open the car door, and Byron helped Amelia into the car. When the door closed, she watched Byron talk in earnest fashion to Alexis before walking around to join her in the car. Alexis gave a signal to those in the car behind and got in the front seat.

Lots of Byron's life was strange if she thought about it for too long, but she chose not to dwell on it. Byron was here, and they were going on holiday.

Byron took her hand and kissed it softly. "Are you ready for an adventure?"

Amelia smiled and nodded enthusiastically. No, none of the strange little things mattered.

❖

They travelled fifteen minutes out of London to a former Royal Air Force base, now solely used for private planes. Byron's limo drove through the entrance and straight onto the private runway area. Amelia gasped as she saw a huge airplane sitting on the tarmac. When Byron had mentioned a private plane, she'd imagined a small jet with a few seats, but this was huge full-sized 747. Where the airline's branding would normally be, along the side and tail, it read *Debrek International Banking Group.*

Amelia looked at Byron and said, "That's yours?"

Byron smiled. "It belongs to the family, but I am the head of my family, so yes, it is."

Although she had known Byron for six months, her life was still largely a mystery to her. Byron never volunteered any information about herself or her family, Amelia always had to ask, and when she did she didn't get very fulsome answers.

Before Byron suggested this holiday together at her family home in Monaco, she had begun to worry that Byron was married and hiding a wife and family somewhere. She had done as much research as she could on the internet on Byron and her business, but there was virtually nothing. The Debrek International Bank was one of the oldest and most successful private banks in the world. The bank was established in

Venice in the fifteenth century, when the aristocratic Debreks settled there, but that was about all she knew.

"What are you thinking so hard about, Amelia?"

"That I've known you six months and this is the first time you've let me see your world. I know so little about you."

Byron's gaze met hers and then Byron caressed her cheek. "That's what this is about. I want to take you into my world. I've never brought anyone to our estate in Monte Carlo before. Apart from my London penthouse, this is my most private space. I live an unusual life, but I want to share it with you."

Amelia was genuinely touched by that. Byron was not used to showing emotion, she was used to dealing with black-and-white business information and figures, so offering to let Amelia into the privacy of her world meant everything to her.

"Thank you, I appreciate you letting me in. I want to know everything about you, Byron. I want there to be no secrets."

Byron's eyes flicked nervously ahead. "We are going to have a wonderful time."

CHAPTER TWO

They boarded the plane, and Byron showed Amelia around each part—the forward conference and meeting room, the large lounge area with comfortable couches, a full double bedroom to the rear, and Byron's private office. It was the ultimate in luxurious travel.

They finally got into the air. Byron unclasped her seat belt and turned to Amelia, who was pinned back against the seat, and was gripping the armrests.

She placed her hand over Amelia's and stroked her hair. "You can breathe now."

Amelia started to breathe normally. "God, I've never liked flying. I thought this might be different because we have more space but—"

Byron silenced her with a kiss that made Amelia moan, and when she pulled back from her lover said, "I'll take your mind off all your worries, *mia cara.*"

A smile broke out on Amelia's face. "I like it when you call me that."

"A vestige of my family's Venetian heritage. My parents always use that language for their terms of endearment, and that's what you are to me. Mia cara—my dear."

Byron saw that Amelia was thinking hard. "You never mention your parents much. Will you tell me about them?"

This was the start of letting Amelia have a small glimpse into her world, to assess how a long-term relationship could work with her many family secrets, the most important of which was that the Debreks were a royal family of immortal vampires, running an international banking and business group.

The six months they had spent together had never been in Byron's plans. She'd never intended to let anyone near her heart, because she knew what torment and pain falling for a human could cause.

At the start, Byron had kidded herself that it was just a bit of fun, showing Amelia a good time and teaching and opening a world of sexual pleasure to her, but if she was honest, Amelia had claimed a place in her heart from the very first look.

One summer evening two years ago Byron's Daimler pulled up outside Grenville and Thrang. She'd instructed Alexis to contact Bhal and have her ready her people and the plane to leave London by ten o'clock at the latest. She needed to be in New York for her North American and Canadian regional meeting first thing, and she'd promised her cousin Angelo she'd have breakfast with her first.

Her door was opened by her driver and she walked straight into Grenville and Thrang. The shop had closed to the public and there were only a few staff sweeping and tidying up. She was met, as always, by Jaunty her tailor, who'd held out his hand and given Byron a warm greeting. There were very few people in this world that she trusted, but Jaunty was one of them. He had proven his discretion and loyalty to both her father, Michal, and herself over the course of many years.

Byron was about to tell Jaunty how brief her visit would be when she heard the sweet lilt of a woman's laughter. She turned around and immediately felt her rarely beating heart thud like a drum. Coming up the stairs from the shop workroom was a beautiful young woman she had never seen before. She was naturally beautiful, not covered in make-up or wearing false nails like most of the women she met. She caressed the woman's face with her gaze, and then her focus fell to the woman's neck, where it zeroed in on her throbbing, vibrant pulse point.

She'd felt her mouth water and the pressure of her fangs as they threatened to erupt. In a second her mind was filled with a vision of making this woman moan as her teeth pierced her neck and she drank from her.

"Who is that, Jaunty?" Byron had asked without taking her eyes off the woman.

"That's my niece, Amelia. She's just graduated from the London School of Fashion, and she's come to work with us full-time. She worked weekends throughout her college days, so you wouldn't have seen her before."

As soon as Jaunty said the woman was his niece, the prospect of getting to know her better was brought to an abrupt stop. She would never disrespect Jaunty by trying to seduce his niece into a no-strings encounter, because that was all she would ever give a human woman.

"She's very beautiful, Jaunty. Look after her."

From that day forward, Byron never got the image of Amelia out of her head or her heart, it seemed. Any woman she slept with, or drank from, the image of Amelia floated through her mind, and each time she went to Grenville and Thrang for an appointment, her craving for Amelia got worse.

Byron's passion for the woman she had never even spoken to grew and grew, until she could not stop herself from meeting Amelia. The opportunity soon presented itself when Jaunty was in hospital and unable to make her appointment. Byron suggested meeting with Amelia. She thought perhaps when she met Amelia in the flesh, her hunger and attraction would wane, but she was so wrong.

"Byron? Did you hear me?" Amelia shook Byron from her thoughts.

"My apologies, what did you say?"

Amelia narrowed her eyes with mild annoyance. "Will you tell me about your parents?"

"Of course." Byron cupped her cheek and gazed into Amelia's bluish green eyes. She could get lost in those eyes for hours. In them Byron could see the light of Amelia's unblemished, untainted soul, not weighed down by centuries of taking blood and killing when the need arose. She saw pure innocence that she wanted to drown in.

"No one has ever looked at me like you do, Byron."

Amelia was pulled into her gaze, and the thought occurred to Byron, as it had many times, how easy it would be to compel Amelia to forget about her. Forget about what they meant to each other, and let Amelia go home and live a normal life. It would be the kindest thing to do for Amelia's sake—she deserved so much more than a dangerous life with a vampire. Somewhere deep inside she knew that the day might come when she would need to do that for Amelia and walk away, but it would destroy all the good inside Byron, and allow the monster that she feared lived deep down in her soul to take over. She knew that.

"I will tell you all you need to know. This is more than a holiday. I'm trying to open up my world to you. I know I've not been the most forthcoming about my life, but—"

Amelia silenced her with a kiss, and then rested her forehead against Byron's. "Shh, I know what it's about, and I appreciate you having faith in me, and going this far for what we have together. We have two weeks, plenty of time to talk about your family."

Byron sat back and smiled. "We don't have to have just two weeks."

Amelia suddenly looked concerned. "What do you mean?"

"I've cleared my schedule for a month. If you could be persuaded to extend your stay, we could have lots of time together."

"But I can only stay away from the shop for a fortnight—"

Byron took her hand and said with satisfaction, "I spoke to your uncle and asked if he could do without you for longer. Jaunty owes me a favour or two, and he said it was fine with him if you are agreeable."

Much to Byron's surprise, Amelia looked angry and pulled her hand back abruptly.

"You spoke to Uncle Jaunty behind my back?"

Byron was taken aback. She did not expect this reaction. She'd thought she was doing a good thing, and besides, very few people ever talked back to her.

"Amelia, I just wanted to give us more time together."

A fire that Byron hadn't seen before erupted in her lover's eyes.

"I don't think you respect my job or my schedule." Amelia's voice went high-pitched and angry. "Did you think about the projects and clients that would have to be cancelled because I'm not there, and all to suit you? I have Daisy, an apprentice I'm teaching, and she'll have no one until I get back."

"Amelia," Byron said firmly, "there really is no need—" Her lover's anger drew Byron's eyes to the throbbing pulse point on Amelia's neck, the same point that taunted and tempted her to bite when they were making love. Byron's mouth watered and she ran her tongue over her erupting teeth.

Her lust and hunger were disrupted when Amelia stood up abruptly. "I'm not some plaything who's there for you whenever it suits you, Byron. After all the times when you've cancelled dates, and I've sat alone on Friday and Saturday nights because"—Amelia made air quotes and said sarcastically—"you have more pressing business that can't be put off, and you don't give one thought to *my* job, *my* life. I don't want anyone making plans or decisions for me. I need some space."

Byron was dumbfounded. What exactly had she done wrong? She stood up and called after her lover but she never turned around. Then she heard the bedroom door slam shut.

The flight staff who had been preparing drinks and snacks for them looked at Byron nervously. She doubted they had ever seen anyone talk to her like that, and they were probably expecting anger from her. Instead she straightened her tie, and said, "Carry on."

❖

By the time Byron walked to her conference room at the front of the plane, some of her anger and annoyance had dissipated, as she took on board what Amelia had said. She did cancel plans and put the bank and clan business first, and realized she wasn't giving Amelia's job the same respect.

When she opened the conference room she found her Duca—the clan second in command—Alexis, and her chief of the Imperial Guard, Bhal, looking over security plans for the Debrek Monte Carlo estate.

They stopped talking immediately and both bowed their heads in respect. "Principe."

Bhal looked to Alexis and said, "I'll leave you both to talk, Duca."

"Thank you, Bhal," Alexis said.

Bhal bowed again on her way past Byron. Alexis must have felt the simmering frustration and anger from Byron, because she signalled to one of the human servants standing in the corner.

He walked over to Byron and without a word unbuttoned and rolled up his shirtsleeve and offered his wrist.

Byron shook her head. "Thank you, but no one has fresh while Amelia is so close, not until we get to the estate. Bottled will suffice, Francis."

While he went to get Byron a drink, she said to her Duca, "Sit with me. I'm sure you heard our first little squabble."

It was difficult to have secret conversations or arguments when you were surrounded by vampires with exceptional hearing.

"Yes, Principe." Alexis sat beside her and Francis placed two crystal whiskey glasses in front of them.

He poured out what to outsiders might have looked like dark red wine but was, in fact, human blood. Although the Debrek clan fed from their trusted human staff and consenting humans, they always needed a supply of freshly bottled blood to drink when feeding straight from a human was inconvenient or inappropriate.

She lifted the crystal glass to her mouth and closed her eyes, allowing the deep, sweet scent of the blood to fill her nostrils. Her hunger for blood was always bad, and was getting progressively worse, being in Amelia's company. The more she cared for her, the more she wanted to taste her blood. She had managed to cope and control her hunger and cravings so far by feeding from others, but it got harder every time. Amelia was like a drug, a temptation constantly laid in front of her, but one that she couldn't take.

Being with Amelia was like being a recovering drug addict, but living with and loving the one drug your body craves. If she did indulge, Byron didn't know if she could ever stop.

Byron tilted the glass and let the thick blood touch her lips. Immediately she could taste it wasn't fresh—it wasn't perfect but she would make it work. She imagined kissing her way down Amelia's sweet neck, her fangs erupting, but taking her time and only lightly grazing her lover's skin with her teeth, and licking and tasting the sweetness and smelling the scent of her neck.

Then, when she had held herself back as long as she could, quickly sinking her fangs into Amelia's throbbing pulse point that so tantalized her.

When the thick, warm blood from her glass hit her mouth, her imagination was bought crashing back to reality. Nothing could ever substitute for Amelia.

She opened her eyes to see Alexis watching her intently.

"You can't keep this up."

Byron signalled for her glass to be refilled. "Can't keep what up?"

"Stopping yourself from feeding from Amelia," Alexis said.

"I can't *ever* feed on Amelia. She is too perfect, too innocent to be ruined by the likes of me," Byron said sadly.

She heard Alexis sigh and take a long glug of blood from her own glass.

Byron sat back in her seat and looked at the human servant. "You may leave now, Francis." Once he exited she said, "I can feel you itching to say something, Duca."

"Principe, I owe you everything, my life, my sanity—you gave me your trust and made me your Duca, your second in command. I find it hard to sit here and watch you suffer. You told me a long time ago—humans break, and then they break our hearts. You know, I know how that feels. I understood your attraction to her at the start. She's beautiful, natural, so feminine, so gentle, but all I can see ahead is pain and hurt, just like I felt."

Byron gave a hollow laugh. "She is all those things and more, and as gentle as she is, she is fiery when she wants to be. You heard our argument? Have you ever heard anyone talking to me like that, Alexis?"

"Not if they didn't want their throat ripped out and every last drop of blood drained from their body," Alexis said only half jokingly.

"I'm falling in love with her, just like I promised I never would, not after—"

Both Byron and Alexis looked down at their glasses of blood, and Byron swirled hers around the glass.

"Anyway, I know how much it's hurting not to be my true self with her, but she's in my every waking thought and in my dreams. I simply couldn't walk away from her. This is why I've asked her to my estate. I need to work out how this can work, what I can tell her."

"How do you tell someone you are a three-hundred-year-old, fourth-generation born vampire? The most powerful vampire in our world?" Alexis asked.

Byron sighed. That was the question, and she'd pondered it over her long life. It was one thing to explain to a human you were a vampire, but the Debreks were vampire aristocracy. Not only the oldest clan, but the most powerful. "I never have found a way to explain, or a reason to. With anyone I cared about, I always ended up walking away when their suspicions became too much."

"You know what might happen if our enemies find out that you are close to someone?" Alexis said.

She was sure the end of that sentence was, *like Anna, like Rose.*

Byron finished her blood, savouring every drop. "We haven't heard of any moves by the Dreds in over a hundred years. I think now is the time to take a chance and see where this leads. I know this may end in pain for me, but I can't turn my back on Amelia. She deserves more than sporadic dinner dates and snatched time together while I lead another life that she knows nothing about. She deserves a normal relationship, something that is very hard for me. Amelia is worth the effort and the risk."

❖

Amelia's outburst of anger was now down to a simmer. She riffled through her flight bag, trying to find her small make-up kit.

As she looked around the lavish bedroom, she almost forgot she was on a plane. How could she, Amelia Honey from a little village in the south of England, fit in with an aristocratic, multibillionaire banking family? Everyone who was connected to Byron, even the plane staff, looked like they belonged in a Hollywood movie. She thought of the gorgeous air stewardess who had brought them drinks, with her perfect model's body and her perfect blond hair, and then looked over to the free-standing mirror in the corner of the room and saw an ordinary brunette with puffy eyes, and wondered what Byron could possibly see in her.

There was a knock at the door and someone walked in. She knew it was Byron without even turning around. When Byron was near she could feel her energy in the air and smell her cologne. It drew Amelia to want to kiss her.

"Amelia? May I speak with you?"

"You can do what you want—you do anyway," Amelia said with an edge to her voice.

She heard Byron sigh and felt two hands rest on her upper arms. "Please, look at me?"

Amelia's anger was already starting to waver at the sound of Byron's voice. That deep, low burr made her melt inside.

Amelia turned around, and Byron's hands slid to her waist. "Amelia, I'm used to thinking like a CEO. I don't rule by committee. I thought you would be pleased, that the idea of a longer holiday would be a nice surprise. I wanted to make up for all the times I've let you down, when I've cancelled our plans and you've had to stay at home on the weekend, when I should have been treating you like the princess you are."

"Byron, I left my mum and dad's house because they controlled everything in my life—what friends I had, what clothes I wore, what music I listened to—and I felt suffocated. I have a life when you're not with me. I think sometimes you forget that when you're jetting around the globe, doing trillions of pounds' worth of business. I have a job, I have friends, and you can't just fly in and make decisions, and disrupt my life."

Byron looked down for a few seconds and then cupped her cheek tenderly. "I've never been in a relationship before, Amelia. I'm following my instincts to try to make you happy. My instincts won't always be right."

The touch of Byron's hand made Amelia want to forgive her instantly, but she realized if she wanted a long-term relationship with someone who had such an alpha personality, she had to make a stand or they would never be equals.

"I'm not one of your employees or security people following in your wake. I'm…that's the thing, I don't know what I am to you, Byron. Am I just a lover? Am I your girlfriend, or something else? Whatever I am, you can't just disregard my thoughts and feelings."

"You are not *just* anything, Amelia. You are my shining girl, and I may be a novice at this relationship business, but I want to learn, and I never want to make you feel like your parents did."

Byron pulled Amelia closer, and heard her Duca's words ringing in her head. *Humans break, and then they break our hearts.*

She was hesitant to give a name to what they were together, because as soon as she did, Amelia would be marked by the enemies of the Debreks. In the past six months, she had tried to forget about the reasons she had never allowed herself to become emotionally involved, but her feelings for Amelia had momentarily blinded her to the risks.

"Amelia, I don't apologize. That's not something I'm accustomed to doing—my business and my family live and die by my decisions. But I can see why you were angry, and I promise to learn to do better. Forgive me? I'll take you home after two weeks if you wish."

A small smile crept up on Amelia's face. "I think I could survive a month with you, in the sun of Monaco." Byron went to speak, but

Amelia held her finger up to her mouth to silence Byron, and said firmly, "But I'll only consider staying as long as Uncle Jaunty says it's okay, and Daisy is coping alone."

Byron smiled and kissed Amelia's palm. "Consider me severely reprimanded."

"I should think so too," Amelia said with a small grin.

Byron felt such relief at Amelia's forgiveness, though she still had those nagging doubts at the back of her mind, but with the newly consumed blood in her system, all she wanted to do was touch her lover. Every sense of hers was heightened, matched by intense emotional and primal needs for love and sex, and hunger for blood.

"Thank you. I told you when we first met that I'd show you the world, and a new world of experiences, and I will."

Amelia slipped her arms around Byron's neck and kissed her on the lips. "How about the mile-high club?"

The corners of Byron's mouth crept up into a dangerous smile. "Why, Miss Honey, are you the same shy young woman I first met?"

Amelia unbuttoned the top button of Byron's shirt, while she kissed her lips and along her jaw. "She was corrupted by a rich, sexy international banker."

Byron kissed her lips softly at first, tasting everything she loved about Amelia, her goodness, her innocence, but their kisses soon became fevered. They were passionate with a great need to connect and touch and express that passion, and after not being together for two weeks, their need was desperate.

Amelia moaned as Byron pulled up her short skirt to touch and squeeze her thigh. Making love with Byron was different every time. As much as Byron liked to be in control and take Amelia on a sensual journey, pushing her limits for pain and pleasure, sometimes, and Amelia didn't quite know why, sometimes Byron lost that little bit of control and became hot, needy, and desperate. This felt like one of those times.

Byron lifted her, and Amelia wrapped her legs around her waist. Byron walked them over to the fitted chest of drawers that ran along the side of the bedroom, just underneath the airplane windows.

Byron placed her down and urged her to lie back, and she had a sudden panic when she realized she was looking out to blue sky and clouds, and seemed inches away from nothing between her and the ground.

"Byron, I don't—"

"Take my hand," Byron said.

Amelia gave her both her hands, and Byron held them over her head. "Look out the window and trust me to keep you from falling."

Amelia's heart was pounding with both arousal and fear. She closed her eyes and took a breath. She felt Byron's hand slip under her skirt, and cup her sex through her lacy underwear. Amelia opened her mouth and groaned.

Byron's massage stopped when she said, "Open your eyes and trust me."

Her flesh was hot and needy under Byron's palm, and she wanted to beg, but knew that Byron wouldn't waver. She held on, and on, while her hips moved trying to encourage Byron to continue touching her.

Byron's hand did move then, but only to trace her fingers over the lace that was getting wetter by the second. "Trust me. I will never let you fall."

Amelia couldn't take it any longer. Her eyes popped open and she was faced with clouds, blue sky, and hundreds of feet to the ground. She gasped in fear, but soon felt Byron's fingers slip past her underwear.

"Good girl, keep looking out." Byron stroked her clit and slipped down to tease her entrance with the tip of her finger.

Facing her fear of heights at the same time as being touched so intimately was exhilarating. She pushed against Byron's hand just to give herself the extra stimulation of knowing she couldn't move. It was so good, and her body demanded more.

"More, more, go inside." Amelia groaned.

"Anything you ask, mia cara." Byron slipped two fingers inside her, and started to thrust.

It felt so, so good. Like she was falling from the sky, but flying towards an orgasm at the same time. Byron kept holding her hands down tight. She knew how Amelia loved to feel out of control of her orgasm, and she was. It was rushing towards her so fast, and felt like it was going to be so intense she couldn't take it.

"Byron, I can't." Amelia moaned.

"Of course you can. I'm here. Let it wash over you. I won't let you fall," Byron said as her thrusts got faster and her thumb stroked her clit.

Amelia struggled as the intensity crept up on her, and she was helpless to resist the pleasure about to hit her. She was groaning continuously now, almost as if in pain.

"It's too much. Too much," she said desperately.

"Amelia, look at me," Byron said.

As soon as she looked in Byron's eyes, she knew she was safe, and her orgasm hit her. "Yes, yes, oh God."

Amelia had never experienced anything like that. She tried to calm her breathing, and as she did Byron released her hands. She immediately pulled Byron down into a kiss. Amelia wanted to say, *I love you so much*, but had to bite her tongue.

Byron pulled back and smiled at her. "Welcome to the mile-high club."

Amelia laughed and cupped her cheek lovingly. "Thank you."

"I'll always be here to catch you," Byron said. "Always."

Chapter Three

Victorija Dred groaned as the last of her victim's blood flowed deliciously over her tongue and down her throat. She pulled back from the young servant's throat, and let her body fall with a deadly thud to the floor of her bedroom.

She gasped inhaling the scent of blood as it ran messily down her chin and neck, dripped onto her bare chest, and began to seep into her crisp white shirt.

Victorija ran her tongue over her lips, determined to gorge on every last drop of warm blood. She heard footsteps heading towards her room, and knew who they belonged to.

The door opened and she said without turning, "Good morning, Lillian. You're up bright and early."

She turned around and smiled at her visitor. Lillian was a contrast to her messy state, and she always possessed the ability to look effortlessly well dressed, today looking extremely executive in a short-skirted business suit, her dark brown hair twisted into a bun.

Lillian sighed and Victorija followed her gaze to the bed where the other servant, a young male, lay with the last of his blood dripping onto the bed sheets, a breakfast tray left untouched beside him.

"Victorija, why do you insist on eating in bed? You make such a mess and your father will have no staff left if you continue to use them for food."

In a heartbeat, she flashed across the room and pushed Lillian up against the wall, her hand around her throat. "Remember who you are talking to, witch."

Victorija loved the shortening of Lillian's breath, the fear she could produce in her, even though she and the witch were allies, but almost instantaneously Victorija smiled again. "I had a late night and needed a pick-me-up. As for my father, it won't be his castle for long."

In her family's castle just outside Paris, the unwritten rule was not to use the human staff as food, so as not to alert the local population to their presence, but Victorija never liked rules. She let Lillian go and heard her gasp in relief. Victorija walked to her bathroom and said, "Is everything prepared for today?"

"Yes, my witches will be there for the meeting. Everything is set."

Victorija leaned over the sink and tutted with dissatisfaction at the sight of the servant's red blood all over her shirt. She quickly pulled it off, leaving her in only her black leather trousers, and ran her hands through her hair.

"Excellent." She could feel the effects of the fresh human blood starting to make her body buzz with energy and sexual excitement. Her body needed release, and soon. She wetted a white washcloth and cleaned the blood off her face and chest, and walked back into the room to find Lillian at the window looking out over the grounds.

She could hear the fast beat of Lillian's heart. She was clearly anxious, and it was hardly surprising. Today she was going to help Victorija and her supporters wrestle the crown from her father's grubby hands.

Gilbert Dred had clung on to the title and role of Principe of their clan for far, far too long. Succession in those vampire clans with royal blood, like the Debreks and the Dreds, was meant to be an orderly thing. Since before her father's immediate family was cast out from the Debreks five hundred years ago, the convention was that after a respectable number of centuries, or sooner if they wished, the Principe would hand on the leadership of the clan to their heir. It allowed the former leader to have a life outside the clan, a fresh energy to be brought to the clan leadership, and a different face to represent them in the human world. Unfortunately for Victorija, Gilbert was power hungry and didn't really care about his daughter's rights to the leadership, but removing a nearly indestructible born vampire was easier said than done. She was the only other born vampire in the Dred clan, and it would be dangerous to take him on by herself. That's where Lillian was so important.

Today Lillian and her coven of witches would help her put an end to Gilbert's tyrannical, old-fashioned regime. Victorija stepped behind Lillian and slipped her hands around her waist.

"I can feel you are tense, Lillian." Victorija moved closer, and whispered in her ear, "You're not having second thoughts, I hope?"

Lillian turned around, and answered a little too quickly, "Of course not."

The plan to remove her father had been long in the planning and the making. She'd built up support secretly within her clan, vampires who were frustrated at the Dreds' lack of expansion and control of the human population. Gilbert was content with what they had. He had become lazy and allowed the Debreks to grow stronger and stronger, while they stood still. The Dreds had been cut off from their Debrek birthright, and Victorija was determined to get it back.

Victorija had won over Lillian, a witch her father had importuned to his service, and who was leader of the French coven. For the plan to work, she needed her witch to remain calm. She looked into Lillian's eyes and projected a feeling of calm and well-being.

"Everything will be fine. There is nothing to worry about."

"There is nothing to worry about," Lillian said in parrot fashion.

Victorija smiled and began to run her hands over Lillian's body. "There, isn't that better, Mademoiselle Witch?"

She leaned in and gave her a hard kiss. Lillian moaned and threaded her fingers through Victorija's hair, apparently intoxicated with her.

Victorija prided herself on the fact that she rarely needed to compel the women she was interested in, only ever to calm them, as her charm was compelling enough.

She allowed one of her fangs to nip Lillian's lip. The drop of blood fuelled Victorija's excitement, and her sex demanded release, but first she had to get the plan clear. She and her vampires had worked too long and hard for anything to go wrong. Victorija placed gentle kisses on her neck and said, "Tell me the plan."

Lillian groaned and tried to talk through what Victorija knew was a fog of lust. "When we are gathered in the throne room, I wait for your signal, then begin the incantation."

She ran her hand up Lillian's skirt and grasped her thigh. "Then when he falls, you must...?"

Lillian's hands clutched at her bare back and shoulders, and she breathed heavily. "We keep him down until you have..."

When her voice trailed off Victorija turned her around, quickly raised her skirt, and dropped her own leather trousers. She could smell how turned on Lillian was, and proceeded to rip off her underwear and slip her fingers into her lover's wetness.

"Until I have pulled his heart out, crushed it, and cut his fucking, smug, sociopathic head off."

All Victorija could think about was coming and sucking hard on Lillian's pulse point. She opened herself up, and began to thrust against Lillian's pert bottom. Victorija groaned at the first touch of her hard clit on her lover's flesh. "Mademoiselle Witch, you feel so very good."

Her thrusting matched the thrust of her fingers, and the way Lillian was moaning and pushing back against her showed she was clearly enjoying it. She ripped open the collar of Lillian's blouse and tasted her pulse point.

"Oh God," Lillian cried out. "So good, but don't bite me and mess up my neck. You've already had enough this morning."

Victorija just laughed. She wasn't going to fuck a woman and not taste her blood. She thrust harder and felt her own orgasm, powered and amplified by the blood she had already consumed, build fast, until her groin and lower stomach felt hot, burning, and ready to erupt. When Lillian's walls started to grip her fingers, she sank her teeth into her lover's neck. The taste of human blood multiplied her orgasm, especially as Lillian wriggled beneath her, and she thrust wildly into her. She drank until her orgasm subsided then pulled her fangs from Lillian's neck, her lover's blood running down her chin.

Lillian turned and pushed Victorija away angrily, while clasping her neck. "You said you wouldn't."

Vic pulled up her trousers and got a towel that was hanging over the dressing table chair. She handed it to her lover for her neck, and said, "You said that—I didn't reply. I take blood whenever and wherever I want, Mademoiselle Witch. You should count yourself lucky you're not lying there with them."

She pointed to the two human bodies by the bed, and closed in on Lillian, holding the towel. "I didn't kill you." She smiled. "That means I like you."

More truthfully, Lillian knew, Victorija needed her. When she didn't... "I have your word that my witches will be safe when your father is removed?"

"You need me to say it?" Victorija said.

Lillian pulled the towel away from her neck and looked at her wound in the dressing table mirror. "Yes, I need you to say it."

Victorija lifted her hand and kissed her palm. "I promise, Mademoiselle Witch. Your coven will be safe under my rule."

And her control.

❖

After their flight, Byron's Daimler set off with them for her Monte Carlo estate, or so Amelia thought. When the car stopped at a harbour, Amelia turned to Byron in confusion.

"I thought we were going to your house?"

Byron smiled and took her sunglasses from her top pocket. "We are." She popped her sunglasses on, making her look even more suave and dapper. "Are you ready for another new experience?"

Amelia smiled. Everything about this holiday was a new experience, and she was loving every glamorous moment. On their journey from the plane, her gaze had been glued to the scenery and the people as they passed. It was like dropping into a world of a fragrance commercial. The sky was blue, the sun was shining brightly, the streets were filled with exclusive shops and boutiques, but the thing she noticed most were the people.

They were just how she'd imagined the rich and famous of Monaco to be. Sophisticated and richly dressed, and she admired the exquisite tailoring on show on the male population. Clearly bespoke tailoring was a big business here.

"What are we going to do?"

Byron winked. "I'll show you. Wait here for a second."

The car doors were opened by Byron's staff and she got out. Soon Byron was standing by Amelia's car door offering her hand, ever the dashing, dapper lover.

Amelia took her hand and stepped out of the car. She quickly had to hold down the hem of her dress as the gusty harbour wind tried to blow her dress up around her waist.

"Careful," Byron said with a smile, "I don't want to share you with any of my people."

Byron offered her arm, and she slipped her hand around it. She was led down to the edge of the harbour and a waiting line of varnished wooden powerboats, the kind she had always seen actors and actresses travel in at the Monaco film festival.

Amelia took her sunglasses from her handbag and put them on before they walked down the steps to the water's edge. Byron stepped into the boat, and beckoned Amelia to follow, but she hesitated.

Byron turned around and held out her hand. "Are you ready to get the wind blowing through your beautiful hair?"

Amelia was nervous, but as with all things she tried with her lover, Byron's complete confidence and control of everything around her gave Amelia the courage to take that extra step. She took Byron's hand and stepped in, and when she lost her balance, Byron was there to steady her.

"It's all right. I have you, Miss Honey."

She was led up to the seats behind the steering area, but Byron said, "It's much more fun if we stand."

"Where's your house?" Amelia asked.

Byron stood behind her, one hand wrapped possessively around her waist and the other pointing over her shoulder.

"You see the tip of the peninsula over there?"

Amelia nodded. "Yes."

"Just around there. It's completely isolated, and the front entrance is only accessible by boat." Byron kissed her cheek. "Very secluded, very private, and I hope you are going to love it."

Amelia gazed up at Byron lovingly. "If I get to be alone with you, it's going to be perfect."

"I hope you feel that. I've put a lot of thought into making this a special holiday for you."

Alexis cleared her throat, getting their attention. Amelia looked behind them, and Alexis and one other guard had joined them on the motorboat. Bhaltair and the rest of the guards filled the boats behind them. Again it struck her how much security Byron travelled with. Byron explained that financiers had many enemies, especially since the Debreks' money helped finance most countries around the world.

Byron nodded to Alexis, who then gave a signal to the driver of the boat, and they set off. It was a bit scary to start with as they picked up speed, particularly because they were standing, but she soon relaxed feeling Byron's arms wrapped around her middle, and her chin rested in the crook of her neck.

Amelia closed her eyes for a moment and enjoyed the refreshing wind in her hair, and the feeling of utter security in Byron's arms. The words *I love you* floated across her mind. If only she had the courage to say them. But knowing Byron's relationship history, or lack thereof, Amelia was not going to be the first to commit.

The boat jerked forward, and Amelia gave a little squeal and grasped Byron's arms tightly.

"I've got you. Look out and enjoy the view." Byron kissed her brow. "I won't ever let you go."

"Why do I feel like Rose in *Titanic*? There aren't any icebergs around here, are there?"

Byron gulped hard, an unreadable look upon her face. "No, you're safe."

The boat picked up more speed with every second, and the faster it got, the more her heart sped up, and she started to feel the exhilaration of the speed and the view. All around them boats and multimillion-pound yachts bobbed around in the blue water in the distance.

Amelia chuckled to herself.

"Why do you laugh?" Byron asked.

"I'm just thinking about how my life now resembles some sort of American TV show. You've brought flash and glam to my life, Byron."

"Flash and glam?"

Amelia nodded. "When I'm not with you, in London, everything is grey and drab, but then you come and bring colour, vibrancy, excitement, and my life seems full of possibilities. You see? Flash and glam."

"There's lots more of that to come. Look." Byron indicated for her to look forward and she saw they were approaching the rocky outcropping fast.

The boat got closer and closer, and then, there it was. Amelia gasped out loud at the sight in front of her. The Debrek Monte Carlo estate was hewn into the coastal rock, and the stone medieval-looking building appeared to be both part home and part fortress. There were at least four stories, and behind the building the rocky coastline was covered in thick green trees. Byron was right. This was completely isolated.

"It's stunning, Byron."

"I'm glad you think so. You can only get to this entrance by water, and I thought you would enjoy this view as much as I do."

As they got closer, Amelia noticed that beneath the walled lower level was the estate's own personal harbour with boats of all sorts, and over the side of the harbour was a private beach with a swimming area marked by buoys.

"You really live here?" Amelia said.

"Part of the year. I'm mostly based in London and I have other homes all over Europe and the United States, but this is special to me. I come here to be myself, secure in its privacy."

The boat pulled in at the harbour and Alexis and the crew disembarked. Byron whispered, "Come on," then kissed her tenderly on the cheek. "Let me show you my world."

Amelia felt that once she stepped into Byron's estate, it would be the start of something special, something serious, just like she wanted. She knew how private Byron was, and for her to bring her here was letting Amelia into her trust, and that meant so much to her.

❖

Gilbert Dred sat on his throne, set on top of a raised dais. Victorija stood by his side, looking out over the throne room, full of his vampires.

Gilbert had a slight build, and Victorija had always assumed his feeling of physical inadequacy fuelled his sadistic tendencies. Everyone was afraid of Gilbert Dred, but now was the time for Victorija to step out from his shadow and take control.

"My daughter says someone requested an audience. That they have problems with my leadership," Gilbert said.

Vic watched all the assembled vampires look to each other. Only some of her clan knew what was about to happen. She hoped that when they saw which way the wind was blowing, they would support her.

When no one was forthcoming, Gilbert stood and walked to the front of the dais. "Come on. Speak up. Does someone wish to say something? Hmm?"

His arrogant gaze ran over those assembled in front of him. There was an eerie silence as he watched and waited. Victorija looked to one of their vampires she had compelled to make a move, and nodded to him.

Gilbert bellowed, "Who amongst you is foolish enough to take on a born vampire?"

He laughed and turned his back to walk back to his throne. Just as he looked to his daughter, the vampire from the crowd shot to him in a flash, but Gilbert, being faster and superior to a turned vampire in every way, caught him easily, and held him up off his feet by the throat.

"You think you can attack me?" As he held the male vampire in the air he addressed the others. "I lead this clan, no one else, and there is no one who can stand against me."

He quickly plunged his hand into the vampire's chest and pulled out his heart, before crushing it and letting it and the body drop to the floor. His breathing was heavy, the veins on the side of his head protruded, and his eyes glowed red. Gilbert lifted his hand to lick the dripping blood from it.

"If anyone else would like to offer me their blood, I would gladly drain it from their body."

Victorija looked to Lillian and gave a brief nod. She started a low chant alone at first, but then voices from around the room started to join her.

Gilbert looked confused, and shook his head. "What is this?"

The chanting got louder and Gilbert started to stumble and sway. "Duca! Victorija!"

Lillian and her witches moved closer to the dais, all the time chanting louder and louder. Gilbert's Duca jumped in front of them, but Victorija's close ally Drasas launched at him and drove a stake through his heart.

Then Victorija knew it was safe to move forward. All those vampires not in on the plan looked confused and scared and Gilbert dropped to his knees and screamed. Victorija stood in front of her father and said in a low tone, "Anyone who interferes will be eliminated."

Just as she said that, the vampires in the ensemble loyal to her stepped forward with wooden stakes in their hands. Now satisfied everyone was subdued, Victorija turned to her father and saw the scene that she had played over and over in her head the whole of her life—her father on his knees in unbearable pain.

"Victorija, help me, help me, please!"

That stopped her momentarily. She'd never dreamed that Gilbert Dred would be begging her even as death stared him in the face.

Victorija knew she didn't have long. Her witches couldn't hold him forever. It was near impossible to kill a born vampire but she had planned everything meticulously, and her one shot was now in front of her.

She walked to him and cupped his cheek, taking a few seconds to enjoy the pain on his face.

"Victorija, help me, help me," he pleaded.

"Shh, Father. I will help you."

The few seconds of relief evident on his face disappeared when she thrust her hand into his chest and grabbed his heart.

"No, you!" Gilbert said with shock. "This…was you. Usurp my crown?"

Victorija's fangs burst through her gums. She squeezed his heart, but didn't pull it out yet. "I do this in the name of my mother, Alice, everyone I ever cared for before you destroyed my soul, and for the good of the Dred clan."

She pulled his heart from his chest and walked over to the fire altar on the dais, a place where Gilbert had burned the hearts of so many people, including her mother.

"Vic…don't…"

A million memories of his hurtful, sociopathic behaviour flashed through her mind, and with one last look to him, she dropped his heart into the fire. He screamed and his body started to blister with burns.

Drasas brought Victorija a long blade, and she took position in front of him, so that the last thing he would see would be her face.

His body was starting to blacken with the burns, and she held off another few moments enjoying his pain, then swung the sword through the air. Gilbert's head flew off and rolled down the steps of the dais.

Victorija's heart was pounding with exhilaration. She had done it. She had killed the man who had tormented her life, and now the Dred clan was hers. She felt the wetness of what must have been her father's blood. She touched her face and looked at the blood on her fingers before tasting it on her lips.

She roared and held the sword above her head. Her supporters roared in joy too, and Drasas stood by her side, and shouted, "Bow before your new Principe!"

All the vampires and the witches bowed, some more quickly than others, and Victorija knew she now had to practice a bit of diplomacy.

"Friends, comrades!"

The crowd calmed to a low murmur.

"For over a hundred years the Dred clan has stood still under Gilbert's leadership, while the Debreks have grown more and more powerful. He clung onto power longer than he should have and grew lazy. I am the last born vampire of this clan, and your rightful Principe. I ask that you join with me, and together we can make the Dreds the most powerful clan in the world. To do that we must regain the secret of siring new, stronger vampires, born vampires like me who can help us take back what is ours. It is my birthright, and I pledge to you that we will prevail. The Debreks will no longer be the ones with the secret that they greedily covet. We will learn it, and take it from them, and grow our clan until we are the most powerful royal vampire house. The Debreks will be nothing but a memory when we are finished. Are you with me?"

The crowd of vampires cheered and roared louder than the throne room had heard in hundreds of years.

The exhilaration was unlike anything she had ever felt. Now she needed blood and lots of it. "For tonight the city is yours—feed till you are gorged."

She looked to the side and saw a worried looking Lillian. Victorija would still need the services of the most powerful witch she had ever met, and her followers—for now.

"Everyone is fair game, except the witches, for they are under my protection. Go, and bring me back new turned vampires. We have an army to build!"

Chapter Four

Byron and Amelia walked through the huge doors of the Gothic Debrek mansion, perched in the rocky coastline. Amelia was awed as she looked around the grand entrance hall. She had seen from the outside that the castle was built from the bedrock, and now inside, Amelia could see that the exposed grey stone of the castle walls extended only to the ground floor. The marble staircase to the first floor marked the start of the more modern levels, which had obviously been renovated over the years, she supposed due to the family adding to the house as time and fashion moved on.

The older ground level had ancient looking tapestries, wall hangings, and oil paintings decorating the cold, grey stone.

"It's beautiful, Byron. How old is it?" Amelia asked.

"There has been a house here since the 1300s. We have added and rebuilt along the way."

Two members of staff were waiting for them, and they took their jackets.

Byron turned her attention to the female staff member. "Diana? Could you make sure Miss Honey's luggage is brought in carefully and taken to her room?"

"Yes, of course." Diana walked back out the doors.

Byron guided Amelia up a large black and white marble staircase. "You'll have to excuse our lack of staff—my butler and head housemaid are with my mother and father at the moment."

They stopped outside Amelia's bedroom, and Byron stuffed her hands in her trouser pockets to hide their slight tremor. She hadn't fed properly since before she picked up Amelia this morning, and the bottled blood on the plane just wasn't cutting it.

Just being in the same room as Amelia made Byron's hunger intense, and after making love on the plane, she greedily drank more bottled blood, but it only took the edge off. She needed to feed on fresh blood, and feed now.

This holiday was going to be a difficult juggling act, trying to sneak away to feed without Amelia noticing anything. Thankfully she had the excuse of business phone calls and urgent emails.

"I'll leave you here to settle, while I take care of some business matters."

Amelia folded her arms and raised an eyebrow. "I thought you were on holiday?"

"Sadly, the business of banking never takes a holiday. There is no rest for the wicked." Byron leaned in to kiss her cheek and whispered, "But the rest of the time I will be yours."

"See you soon, then?" Amelia said hopefully.

"Absolutely. Relax and settle in and I'll have someone bring you to me later." Byron finished by giving her a kiss to the palm.

Amelia smiled. "Okay, see you later."

As soon as Amelia was in the door, Byron turned and shot downstairs in a millisecond, certain that her lover wouldn't come back out of the bedroom and see her unusual speed.

At the bottom of the stairs, Alexis waited for her. "Alexis, I need to feed. Send someone to my office as soon as possible, and you and the rest of the guard must feed as well."

"Of course, Principe. I will."

After Alexis bowed her head and started to walk away, Byron stopped her again. "Oh, Duca, after I've fed could you ask Bhal to come and see me?"

"Yes, Principe."

Byron walked through some long marble corridors and came to her large wooden office doors. The electronic lock on the door frame was a contrast to the aged varnished oak door. She pressed her hand to the computer lock and it opened. Only a select few in the Debrek clan were allowed down in this part of the house. It was an act of trust to be given that kind of access to the private areas of the Debrek estate.

She walked in and let out a sigh of relief. It was harder than she expected covering up who she really was from Amelia. In their six-month courtship, the most they had stayed in each other's company was a day and a half at the weekend, and she'd thought that was hard enough.

This—a whole month together—was going to be another thing entirely, but Byron felt she had very little choice. Their relationship had gotten to the stage that she either had to say goodbye to Amelia or try to let her in.

Byron looked down at her hand and saw it tremoring still, so she walked over to her side table that had crystal decanters full of aged whiskey, and poured a large glass. The alcohol would help stave off her burning hunger for blood until her attendant arrived.

She glanced up at the screens covering two walls of her office. The screens played rolling news, financial market reports, and the Debrek bank's own internal channel, showing footage of every office around the world. The Debrek banking group split its interests into regions around the world, each region run by a Debrek born vampire or an older, trusted turned vampire. With a glance, Byron could check their numbers and investments from the comfort of her office.

Byron refilled her glass and enjoyed the burn as the whiskey ran down her throat. She hated to feel this jitteriness, this intense need for blood. It made her feel out of control, and that was something she didn't like.

A call came in on the screen in front of her. "Answer."

The face of her cousin Angelo came on the screen. Angelo ran the North American arm of Debrek International. She was unbelievably intelligent, worked hard, and played even harder.

"Principe." Angelo smiled.

"Angelo, good to hear from you." Angelo was younger than her, only having lived a hundred and fifty years. Where Byron was controlled, Angelo was the life and soul of the party, similar to Byron's sister, Serenity. She was incredibly distinctive looking, with dark looks and skin taken from her African American father, but with light blue eyes.

"How was your journey, cousin?" Angelo asked.

Byron grinned. "Pleasant, Angelo. Very pleasant."

Angelo laughed softly. Having spent many lifetimes in her cousin's company, she caught her meaning well.

"And Miss Honey? Is she well?"

"A bit overwhelmed, I think. There is a lot to take in," Byron said before taking a drink.

"I hope I will get the pleasure of meeting this mysterious Miss Honey soon. I've not known you to be taken with a woman in..." Angelo hesitated. "A long time."

Not since Rose, Byron thought, but she changed the mood by replying with a joke. "I would fear you would steal her away from me, cousin."

Angelo placed her hand on her chest. "As if I would, Byron. Do you have time to talk? There are a few investment possibilities I'd like to discuss with you."

Byron was now shaking inside for blood, but she tried to keep herself together. "Could we postpone till tomorrow morning? My time is rather limited at the moment."

"Of course. Enjoy the first day of your holiday. Till tomorrow then, Principe." Angelo smiled.

As soon as Angelo disappeared from the screen, there was a beep at the door, and Byron groaned. Her attendant was here.

"Come in."

When the doors opened, one of her human attendants walked in—a young woman with light chestnut coloured hair. Byron wondered if Alexis had chosen her because her colouring resembled Amelia's, and to help relieve her craving for her lover.

As kind a thought as it was, Byron knew no one would ever sate her hunger, except Amelia.

This human—Katie—she knew well. Her mother and father had served in her household, as their parents had done before them. Certain human families, who had gained the trust and respect of the Debreks long, long ago, served them generation after generation. Not by force, but by consent. It was a true, mutually beneficial, symbiotic relationship. Their human attendants were better paid than most executives, had all their healthcare, education, and other necessities paid for by the family, and generally were taken care of in every possible way. In return they served the Debreks both domestically and by supplying them with blood. A perfect marriage.

"Thank you for coming, Katie."

"You are welcome, Principe. May I feed you?"

Byron slipped off her suit jacket, and placed it carefully over her chair. "Yes, thank you."

Katie turned her back and unbuttoned the first few buttons of her blouse. Byron grinned, delighted that Katie was allowing her to feed from her neck.

For the last five hundred years, the Debreks had lived by a code of blood by consent, and it was their unwavering rule. Katie allowed her blouse to slip past her shoulders and waited.

Byron approached, zeroing in on Katie's throbbing pulse point, and her fangs erupted from her gums. Her hunger was so intense it was hard to keep her control for one second longer, but she had to. Byron was the most powerful vampire the Debreks had ever produced, born of two exceptional vampires, and as such her hunger was greater than any other, and something she had to learn to control over the years.

"Do you consent?"

Katie shivered. "I consent, Principe."

As soon as Byron heard those words she sank her teeth deeply into her attendant's neck. Katie gasped, but Byron knew it wasn't a cry of pain. The vampire bite infused a feel-good chemical to relax the human, and to help with healing and with pain.

Byron moaned at first taste of fresh blood since this morning. The feeling of the fresh, warm elixir rolling over her tongue was indescribable. It turned on every sense and need, especially for sex. Her sex started to throb, and she closed her eyes and tried to imagine this was Amelia she was drinking from. When she did, she took Katie's blood faster and faster, her mind clouded with bloodlust, and all she could think about was thrusting inside Amelia as she consumed her blood.

Katie started to wriggle in her arms, and the sound of Katie's discomfort penetrated Byron's fog of blood. She pulled away, gasping, blood running down her chin. Katie grasped at her neck, and Byron felt immediate guilt. She had lost control, and that was something she couldn't afford to do. She had not been present, but somewhere else, in her mind, feeding and making love with Amelia.

"Katie, forgive me for taking too much." Byron hurried to produce a dressing from the supply kept in every room of the house and gave it to Katie.

Katie smiled generously, even though she must be very light-headed. "That's all right, Principe. I know you haven't fed for a while."

But it wasn't all right. She could not lose control like this. It was too dangerous.

Katie buttoned up her blouse and placed the pad on her neck. Byron cupped her cheek, and she blushed.

"There's no excuse, but I have certain pressures on me at the moment that led me to become careless."

"I know. She's very beautiful, Principe," Katie said with a small smile.

Byron was surprised the young woman had connected the two things. Clearly even the staff had noticed how important Amelia was to her.

"I thank you for your understanding. You know, you are the first person to congratulate me on finding someone to care about. Everyone else is so concerned about the problems it may bring us. Alexis certainly thinks so."

She didn't normally talk this openly to many people, but there was something in Katie, an innocence, a goodness that reminded her of Amelia.

"Alexis—forgive me, Principe, *the Duca*—probably finds matters of the heart irrelevant."

She didn't always, Byron thought, and Byron was part of the reason Alexis had shut down that side of herself.

"I appreciate you telling me. Please tell Landon to take you off the blood service rota for a few weeks."

"It's okay. I don't—"

"Please. Those are my wishes," Byron said finally.

"As you wish. Thank you." Katie bowed her head and walked away.

Just before Katie left, Byron said, "One moment, Katie. Would you mind keeping an eye on Amelia while she's here? This will all be a bit overwhelming for her, and I think you are the right one to recognize that."

"Of course I will. I'll introduce myself once I've cleaned up."

"Thank you, and one more thing…" Byron walked over to her and ran her fingers over Katie's hair. "I won't feed from you again." She looked Katie directly in her eyes, and tried to convey her feelings clearly. Katie's looks and her gentle, caring spirit were too reminiscent of the woman who burned in her blood, and therefore too dangerous. "I hope you understand."

Katie gave her a sympathetic nod. "I understand completely, Principe."

When she left, Byron hurried into her private bathroom. She wet a washcloth and began to clean the blood from her lips and chin. Byron stopped and gazed at her bloody appearance. She could only imagine how horrified Amelia would be to see her like this. Would she see a monster?

The unnerving thing was, even though she had taken too much blood, it still wasn't enough. It had calmed her, but the hunger remained. She remembered her mother telling her about the intense hunger a vampire felt for another when they fell in love, as her mother had with her father. Sharing blood with a lover was a loving, intimate act. The most intimate act a vampire could share with another.

But then, Amelia would never want to taste her.

Was that where her unquenchable hunger was coming from?

Byron threw the towel into the sink, lowered her head, and let out a sigh. When she looked back up at herself in the mirror, she heard one question in her mind.

Was she in love? She had never, ever allowed herself before. There was only one other woman who had come close. Rose, the one woman who had understood her and tried to convince her there would be someone who would give her heart no option but to love.

Deep down inside Byron felt that someone was Amelia Honey.

Chapter Five

Amelia looked around her large, richly furnished bedroom, and suddenly felt quite lonely. The room was more than comfortable. A four-poster bed dominated the space, and French doors opened out onto a balcony where there were a table and chairs. At the other side of the room was the most sumptuous marble bathroom, with a walk-in wardrobe and dressing room. Her little flat back in London could probably fit into this bedroom.

So why did she feel alone and out of place? When her luggage was delivered, a young footman informed her someone would be along to put away her things, and then the door was shut and the lonely feeling set in. It was only when she was alone that she wondered why she and Byron were not sharing a bedroom. They did when she stayed at Byron's London penthouse suite, but now spending time together on holiday, they weren't.

Amelia sighed and told herself to stop being so needy.

There was a knock at the door, and Amelia opened it to one of Byron's staff.

"Hi, I'm Katie. Byron asked me to help you settle in."

Katie's warm, open smile immediately put her at ease. "Thank you. I'm Amelia."

She held open the door and Katie entered. She was similar in age to Amelia, and didn't come across as intimidating, like Byron's flight attendants did.

"It's so nice to have you here, Amelia." Katie walked over to her luggage and started to unpack it. "I know this place can be intimidating, and some of Byron's security a bit too serious, but it's really a beautiful place. If there's anything you need, just tell me."

Amelia walked over to the bed and started to help. "The large army of security Byron travels around with are a bit intense. I think Byron's guard Alexis doesn't approve of me."

"Oh, don't worry about Alexis," Katie said with a scowl. "She's a professional misery guts."

Amelia laughed and finally felt at ease. "It's not just me, then?"

Katie lifted two of Amelia's dresses over to the dressing room. "Believe me, it's not you. She scowls at me just as much."

Katie's manner and enthusiasm were infectious, so unlike the stiff, serious people she had met so far. Now that she'd met Katie, she felt like she had someone on her side.

"Thanks for coming to help me, Katie. I was feeling a little lost in this huge house."

Katie walked back and took her hand. "Don't worry. Byron wants you to be comfortable here."

"Thank you, I appreciate that," Amelia said. She knew it was rude, but she couldn't keep her eyes from the wound on Katie's neck. It looked well taken care of, but what an unusual place to have an injury. "Did you hurt your neck? Is it painful?"

Katie's eyes widened at the question but then soon were cool and calm again. "Oh, just a bee sting. Annoying, but it will heal. Now, what would you like to change into for the afternoon?"

Amelia felt like Katie was changing the subject, but decided to let it go. Another strange thing to add to the growing list, Amelia thought.

Byron was going through some figures at her desk when there was a knock at her office door. She knew who it would be. "Come in, Bhal."

Bhaltair stepped into the room and bowed her head. "You wish to see me, Principe?"

"Yes, take a seat, Bhal, and I'll pour us some good whiskey." Byron stood and made her way over to her decanters. She and Bhal shared a love of aged whiskey. Luckily, her family's longevity meant they had some of the oldest drinkable casks in existence in their collection.

Byron poured two glasses and brought them over. Bhal raised her glass and said, "Slainte, Principe."

"Cheers," Byron responded.

After each took a sip, Byron said, "I have a request to make of you, Bhal."

"Anything, Byron. You know that."

Byron felt so lucky she had Bhal to rely on, as had her father before her. Her relationship with Bhal was different than the one she had with Alexis. Even though they both had warrior backgrounds, Bhal's age gave her a wise, much more relaxed personality than Byron's intense, ordered Duca, and Bhal's counsel always gave her a different perspective.

She had known Bhal all her life. Bhal had tutored her in weapons, fighting, and military strategy, preparing Byron for her Ascension Day, the day when born vampires said goodbye to the last part of their humanity.

Bhal looked as young as Byron did but was so much older than her own three hundred years. Bhal was not a vampire, but something altogether different, and much more ancient.

"Amelia being here presents some dangers and difficulties, and I need to anticipate them, because she means a great deal to me."

Bhal smiled with the pride of a mentor. "I knew someone would make you take these risks one day, Byron. I can see the way you light up when she is in your company."

"I know I always told you that I would never care for anyone like that, but I just couldn't walk away from her. I've put my clan ahead of my personal life for three hundred years, and if I am to try to bring her into my world, I need to take precautions. The Dreds—"

Bhal leaned forward. "The Dreds have not made a move in a long time. Gilbert is lazy, selfish, and too paranoid about his clan members plotting against him to make a stand against you."

Byron sat back in her seat, and said, "That's true. If he remains Principe. Victorija is different. She is sadistic, cruel, without a sense of right and wrong, but she is clever and ambitious. If Victorija got her hands on the clan, things would change, and if she found out about Amelia, she would do everything in her power to use her against me."

Bhal said, "I was there when your great-grandfather exiled Gilbert and his wife. Gilbert split the Debrek family into two, simply because he could not accept the oath of consent. Gilbert was exiled. Victorija was only a child, and she saw her father's anger, his humiliation, but I doubt she would want to avenge that. Her main focus, if she ever gets her hands on her clan, would be making them powerful again, but shifting a born vampire is no easy task."

"If anyone could overcome that obstacle, it would be Victorija," Byron said and then leaned forward and fixed Bhal with her gaze.

"Bhal, I need you to make Amelia your top priority. No matter what I say, Alexis will always look out for me first. I need you to look out for Amelia no matter what is happening. If we are caught in the middle of a fight, I need to know that while Alexis and I are facing the enemy, you have Amelia safe under your protection."

Bhal finished her drink in one gulp and put the glass on her desk. "My tribe is sworn to protect your clan, and I will follow your orders to the letter, Principe, because I know Alexis will die to keep you safe."

"Let's hope no one will be dying…again." Byron smiled.

Bhal chuckled and stood, offering her hand to Byron. "I won't take my eyes off her."

"Thank you, Bhal."

Victorija pushed her last victim away and fell back onto her throne. Blood coated her shirt and hands. She had never gorged on so much blood before and the experience was exhilarating, what she'd heard humans describe when they got drunk.

She tried to regain her breath as she looked out over the throne room. The floor was littered with bodies. Some would wake eventually and return as vampires to help her build an army, and some were simply food. To turn a vampire was simple. If a person died with vampire blood in their system, and then revived and began to feed on blood, they were turned.

Her own vampires were littered around the room, some feeding, and some in states of undress, indulging their sexual desires. Some were doing both, and some were on the streets of Paris turning as many people as they could find.

Even her doubters were starting to see the benefits of her regime.

Drasas, her new Duca approached, her clothes as bloodstained as them all.

"You did it, Principe." Drasas smiled.

Victorija flourished her hand. "Did you ever doubt it?"

"Never."

She sat up straighter on her throne and said, "You need to keep everyone very disciplined, Drasas. We cannot achieve great things if we are not strong, not together. Make it known that anyone who fails me will find their heart on the burning altar."

A sly grin grew on Drasas's face. "You can count on me, Principe."

"Ensure everyone cleans up their messes out on the streets and doesn't draw us unnecessary attention, and pay a visit to the police department. A bit of compulsion should cover for any of tonight's festivities."

"I will," Drasas said, before bowing and starting to walk away.

Victorija stopped her. "Drasas, keep the witches safe and unharmed." She saw the look of annoyance on Drasas's face. "I know your feelings on the matter of the witches, but they are central to my plans. There will come a time when they are not, and we will dispose of them."

The smiled returned to Drasas's face, and Victorija repeated, "They are not to be harmed—yet. Quite clear, Duca?"

"Exceptionally clear."

When she walked away, Victorija's body reminded her just how much she needed to come to assuage the arousal the blood had caused.

She was just about to pick one of her female vampires when the doors to the throne room burst open, and her father's lover Eleanora strode in purposefully. As soon as her eyes turned on Victorija, a sexy smile erupted on her face.

Eleanora had been her father's lover for years, although not a permanent fixture in his life. She stalked across the throne room in her tight red dress and heels like she was on a Parisian catwalk. Gilbert had turned her into a vampire at her request a long time ago, but she had a more mature appearance than most vampires since she had been turned at age forty-five. If Victorija had expected anger from Eleanora at the recent events, then she would have been shocked. She hadn't, and she wasn't.

Victorija had always admired her buxom figure and could only imagine that she must be good in bed—otherwise her father wouldn't have kept her around so long.

Eleanora stopped at the bottom of the dais and put her hands on her hips, her long platinum-blond hair hanging down her back.

"I hear congratulations are in order, Principe," Eleanora said.

"I have killed my father and taken my rightful place at the head of this clan, if that's what you mean, madam."

"Yes, that's what I heard, and I cannot say I am sad. Your father may have been my lover, but a more evil, sociopathic person you could not meet. Now I am free, and I have you to thank for it."

When Eleanora said that, she looked directly at Victorija's fly. She immediately felt the ache inside her intensify, but she played it cool.

"Thank you, Eleanora. Please feel free to stay and partake of the celebrations. I was just on my way to my apartments."

She started to walk away and in a split second Eleanora was by her side as she walked. "May I accompany you and have a drink?"

Victorija almost growled out loud. She knew Eleanora's game. She wanted to retain her position close to the throne of the Dred clan. But despite Eleanora's intentions, Victorija did not show her excitement.

"If you wish," Victorija said coolly.

They reached her father's rooms in the castle, now hers, and walked in.

"Let me pour us a drink," Eleanora said.

Victorija took a seat on the couch while Eleanora took a bottle of blood from the ambient cooler in the room and poured them each a wine glass full of deep red blood. She handed a glass to Victorija, but remained standing in front of her.

"To new beginnings." Eleanora lifted her glass in a toast.

"New beginnings," Victorija replied and took a sip. Despite it not being fresh, this blood added to her buzz.

Victorija knew Eleanora wanted to seduce her, and that made her incredibly excited and turned on, but she sat back, relaxed and cool. Eleanora's tight-fitting dress accentuated her curvaceous body, and Victorija wanted to see it, but she waited for Eleanora to make the first move.

"I think you need to celebrate gaining your father's crown in a special way."

"Oh? And how do you propose I do that?"

Eleanora began to strip off her red dress. "By allowing me to give you pleasure," she purred.

As the dress came slowly off, Victorija's breathing hitched when she saw Eleanora had nothing on underneath. She threw the dress to one side, and left on her red heels.

It was no wonder her father enjoyed Eleanora.

"What better way to complete the end of your father's rule than to have *his* lover in *his* apartments?"

Victorija looked over Eleanora's shoulder to the large painting on the wall of Gilbert in uniform and fur-edged cape, the usual cruel, self-satisfied, smug look on his face.

"How right you are, Eleanora." She would never turn down sex after feeding but there was an added element of excitement about having her father's lover.

Eleanora walked forward slowly and teasingly, before kneeling in front of her. She placed her palms on Victorija's leather clad thighs and rubbed up and down.

"I always thought about you," Eleanora said.

"Is that so?" Victorija's eyes flitted between Eleanora's ample breasts, that bounced every time she moved, and her hands on her thighs. She doubted the truth of Eleanora's words. She clearly wanted the ear of the new Principe, but the idea that Eleanora's words were creating made her already burning sex desperate for release.

"Yes, I always watched you, Victorija. So much younger, so much more vibrant, and when your father touched me, I closed my eyes and thought of you."

Victorija grasped her hands and put them on her belt buckle. "Show me."

Eleanora smiled and licked her lips teasingly as she unbuckled the belt and then slipped Victorija's trousers over her hips. Now Eleanora had full access to her wet, throbbing sex. She opened Victorija up and lowered her head, but before she touched her, she looked up into her eyes and said, "The King is dead, long live the King."

Victorija groaned at those words and the first touch of her lips. She leaned back and sipped her glass of blood, watching Eleanora's blond head bob up and down between her legs.

She closed her eyes momentarily, and enjoyed the pure pleasure. Her father's lover was an expert at what she did. Her tongue licked all around her clit, before sucking it right between her bright red lips.

"Madam, you are so good at that," Victorija said, her hips rocking in response to her rapidly soaring orgasm.

The intensity made her want to grab, bite, and suck. She threw away her glass of blood, letting it smash on the floor. She grasped Eleanora's hair and groaned. Soon there would be no way she could stop coming. She needed it so badly, after everything she had achieved today.

Victorija looked up at the picture of her father and said out loud, "I took everything from you. Your crown, your castle, your clan, even your lover can't keep her hands off me. I'm superior to any man you ever wished I fucking was!"

Just before her orgasm exploded, she took one of Eleanora's wrists, and sank her teeth deep into her veins. A fellow vampire's blood was a different kind of high, and she came with such force that she knew her bite would become painful, even to a vampire like Eleanora.

Eleanora wriggled, but Victorija kept her in place until she had enjoyed her last ounce of pleasure, and of blood, all the while never taking her eyes off the picture.

Finally, she let go and Eleanora fell back against the couch, gasping. Victorija looked down at Eleanora, who was rubbing her healing wrist, and smirked. "Get up on the bed. I want to take everything he had."

Chapter Six

A melia stepped out of the large, luxurious shower and started to dry herself with the biggest, fluffiest white towel she had ever used. "Now, that is something special."

The Roman design marble shower enclosure had steam jets that came from all different angles. She would love to take Byron in there.

Amelia wrapped the towel around herself and closed her eyes. Her skin was still warm from the shower, and she could easily imagine the hot water massaging her body. Her heart started to beat as she imagined Byron stepping into the shower and circling her reassuringly strong arms around her waist.

Despite the heat of the shower she shivered when her lover kissed her neck and whispered, *I love you, mia cara.*

Amelia's eyes fluttered open, and she gave a little sigh. That was one part of the fantasy that wasn't yet believable. Would Byron ever tell her how she felt? She wrapped her hair in a smaller towel and had a final look around the marble bathroom. How the other half lived.

When she walked into her bedroom, she saw a white box tied with a thick red bow, and two smaller purple velvet boxes sitting on top. She chuckled. "I feel like the poor girl from a folk story."

Amelia made her way over to the bed and picked up a gift card, written in Byron's handwriting.

To my darling Miss Honey,
I would like to cordially invite you to dine with me this evening on the beach. I have left a few gifts that I hope you

may graciously wear for me this evening. I will send someone
for you at six thirty.
     Yours,
     Byron

The beach? That was not what she was expecting. She'd imagined a grand dining room with a long table and opulent furnishings. Byron was full of surprises.

Amelia opened the two velvet boxes and found a jaw dropping diamond necklace and earring set, with a matching diamond bracelet.

"Oh my God," Amelia said with shock.

She had never seen jewellery like this except in magazines about the rich and famous, but she supposed that was the world she was in now. But was she in it, or just visiting? That was the nagging doubt that lingered at the back of her mind.

"Is this a fairy tale, or am I…" Amelia didn't want to finish that thought.

Did Byron do this with every woman who piqued her interest? Did she shower them with gifts and show them the high life, before becoming bored and moving on?

Her heart said no, but her head was worried because she had fallen in love with Byron. Amelia set the jewellery boxes and her fears to the side and untied the red bow on the white box. She removed sheets of tissue paper and gasped as she lifted out the most elegant white evening gown, by one of Europe's most sought after designers, Edouard Bernard.

She ran the material over her fingers, and admired the cut and stitching. It was the most beautiful gown she had ever had or seen up close.

Amelia smiled and shook her head. Flash and glam.

There was a knock at the door and she said, "Come in."

It was Katie. "I wondered if you wanted a hand with getting ready."

"You're a lifesaver, Katie. I was just trying to work out how to pour myself into this dress," Amelia joked.

Katie laughed and walked over to her. "Oh, I'm sure you'll have no problem. You have a fabulous figure."

Once they had gotten Amelia in her dress and her hair dried and styled, Katie helped her with her make-up. The whole time she was getting ready, Amelia's eyes were drawn to the wound at the side of

Katie's neck. She'd detected Katie had been nervous when she asked about it before.

As Katie powdered her face, Amelia asked tentatively, "Are you sure your neck is okay, Katie?"

Katie's fingers immediately touched her wound, and Amelia could see nervousness in her eyes. "It's nothing. Just nips a bit. It'll be much better tomorrow."

Before Amelia got a chance to say any more, Katie took a step back and said, "There, finished. What do you think?"

Amelia suspected Katie was trying to distract her again, and it worked. Amelia was extremely happy with Katie's work. "It's perfect. Thank you."

"Why don't you take a look in the full-length mirror?"

Amelia stood in front of mirror, and a smile erupted on her face. "This dress is just exquisite."

"Told you—you have the figure to carry it off," Katie said. Katie took a lint brush over her dress, making sure everything was perfect. "Byron always has good taste."

That comment brought her nagging doubts back to the forefront of her mind. "Can I ask you something, Katie?"

"Of course," Katie said.

"Has Byron done this often? Does she do this often?" Amelia asked.

Katie didn't look as if she entirely understood the question. "What do you mean?"

"Bring women here. Shower them with gifts?"

"Oh no. I've never known her to ever do that. Maybe my parents have seen her bring people here, but I haven't. This is one of her most private spaces."

"Thank you. That's good to know."

Someone knocked at the door and Katie excused herself to answer it. She returned with a slight look of annoyance on her face.

"Something wrong?"

"Nothing. Alexis is here to escort you down to the beach—she said immediately, but I told her she'd have to wait."

"So, you really don't get along with Alexis?" Amelia asked.

Katie exhaled slowly. "Alexis gets on with few people, unless they follow her orders. She's ex-military, and tends to talk to you as if you are a soldier under her command, and that—well, let's just say it doesn't work for me."

Amelia laughed. She got the whole picture in that one sentence. "I get it." She took one last look in the mirror and said, "Will I do?"

Katie nodded enthusiastically. "You'll dazzle Byron."

❖

A golf cart driven by one of Byron's staff dropped her off at the edge of the beach. It was a part of the beach she hadn't seen when she arrived. A wooden walkway crossed the sand, and led to a stunningly beautiful platform out in the shallows, giving the impression you were dining on the water.

There was a wooden gazebo on the platform with a flat roof supported by intricately carved supports. The walls were long white silk curtains, now tied back, but presumably they could be closed for privacy. Along the roof and wooden supports were wound hundreds of fairy lights, like on a Christmas tree. It looked so beautiful, so romantic.

Even better was the sight of Byron waiting for her on the platform, dressed in dinner suit and bow tie, a sight that made her heart thud faster and faster. Byron was so gorgeous to her eyes.

When she got out of the cart and started down the walkway, Byron came forward to meet her. Amelia shivered when Byron's gaze caressed her body.

Byron took Amelia's hand and kissed it tenderly. "Miss Honey, you look absolutely ravishing."

The way Amelia's curves fit the dress made Byron truly wish to ravish her and taste her on the spot. She loved the way Amelia's cheeks flushed every time she gave her a compliment. Most of the women she had encounters with in the past—models, socialites, businesswomen—expected people to shower them with praise.

Amelia was different. She seemed surprised by every compliment she got.

Amelia tweaked her bow tie, making sure it was done properly. "You're looking very dapper yourself, Byron. Whoever makes your suits must be good," Amelia joked.

Byron ran her fingers over Amelia's collarbone, and her new

diamond necklace. "Oh, she is. That's why I like to keep her close to me."

She offered Amelia her arm and led her onto the platform. There waiting for them was a dining table, richly laid out with silver cutlery, crystal glasses, and sparkling white linens.

There were three waitstaff, one behind each of their dining chairs and a third holding champagne and glasses on a silver platter.

"This is just perfect. So romantic," Amelia said.

That made Byron smile. All she wanted to do was give Amelia a special time, a romantic time, and going by her hastening heartbeat, it was working.

Byron took her over to her seat and the waiter held out her chair. As soon as Amelia was seated, Byron quickly sat as well and nodded to the waiter to pour them each a glass of champagne.

"You really like it?" Byron asked as she reached across the table to take Amelia's hand.

"Yes, it's flash and glam just like you, but intimate, just you and me, just the way I want it."

It gave Byron such contentment and fulfilment to make Amelia happy like this, and this feeling was something she would never get tired of. "I'm glad." Byron picked up her champagne flute and said, "Let's have a toast to new experiences, new pleasures, and spending time together."

Amelia clinked her glass against hers, and gave her the small smile that melted her inhuman, centuries-old heart.

"Are you hungry?" Byron asked.

"Famished. I can't wait to taste what your private chef has made for us."

Another thing that made Amelia different from the models, actresses, and socialites she had dated casually. She would take them out for the most wonderful dinner and they would nibble a lettuce leaf, but not Amelia. She was as enthusiastic about food as she was about sex, and Byron loved that.

"Please serve," Byron told her waitstaff. She waved away more champagne, and instead poured herself a glass of Debrek Special Reserve the waiter brought to her. She knew Amelia had a dislike for red wine, so she could enjoy a glass of blood without her lover knowing a thing about it.

"Mm, this is delicious." Amelia hummed in contentment.

Byron had hardly taken much notice of her own food. She had spent the whole of the first and main courses concentrated on Amelia eating her food. Amelia savoured each bite, and moaned in pleasure at the taste. Each time Amelia closed her eyes for a few seconds when enjoying a new taste, the wetness on her lips from the wine, the way her tongue snaked out to lick her lips, all of these things were making Byron hunger.

For *Amelia.*

Quite a few times now, her gaze had fallen on Amelia's neck and her beating pulse point. She wanted to taste Amelia so badly…

"Byron? Byron?"

Byron quickly took a breath, in an effort to control herself. She had been so consumed with her own hungry thoughts she didn't even realize Amelia had been talking to her. "Sorry, you were saying?"

"Do you do this often? Dine out here?"

Byron shook her head. "No, this is my first time. My parents did quite regularly when they wanted some private time with each other, and I thought it would be a nice thing to do with you."

"That's very sweet. They must be a loving couple. Tell me more about them?"

Maybe some talking between courses would calm both her libido and her hunger for her lover's blood. Byron refilled her glass of blood, and dismissed the waitstaff.

Byron refilled Amelia's champagne glass. "So you wanted to know more about my family?" Byron had no idea how she was going to last the whole evening that she had planned, without going back to the house for fresh blood.

But she had no choice. She just had to.

"My parents are two wonderful people, and I don't just love them, I respect them greatly. They have strong morals, a sense of fair play, and an eagerness to make the world a better place around them. They brought me up with those same principles."

"My goodness," Amelia said. "They sound like wonderful people."

"They are."

"Do they still work in your business?" Amelia asked.

Byron took another big gulp of blood. She was calming slightly.

"They are…retired. It's a tradition in the Debrek family that the leaders retire early, and enjoy life while they are still young enough to do so. That is, as long as their children are of age, and competent."

"Where are they now?"

"New York actually. They enjoy travelling but do a lot of charity work, in the Debrek name, and are working with UNICEF in New York at present."

"How intriguing." Amelia picked up her glass and took a sip of the chilled rosé champagne. She shouldn't have been surprised. She knew that Byron had been to a lot of charity events over the last five months, although she had never invited Amelia as her date. Byron explained she liked to keep her private life just that—private. But it still niggled when she had seen the photographs in the media after of Byron surrounded by very glamorous and very beautiful women.

"That's a wonderful thing to do."

"It's part of what we do. It's a symbiotic relationship. Most of the world's population give business to the Debrek bank, directly or indirectly, and we give back. The bank funnels a lot of money into charitable organizations. One of the things my father did before he retired was to cancel a great deal of debt owed to us by many third world countries."

"That's wonderful, Byron. You constantly surprise me," Amelia said. She watched Byron take a drink of her dark red wine, while her eyes caressed her.

"Do you like your jewellery?" Byron asked.

Amelia touched the exquisite necklace and smiled. "They are beautiful. Where do you hire these kinds of things?"

Byron furrowed her eyebrows. "I do not borrow jewellery. I bought them for you."

"What?" Amelia squeaked. "You bought—"

Before she got a chance to finish her question, Byron stood and walked around the table to offer her hand. "Dance with me?"

Amelia looked around, slightly confused. "Here?"

"Yes, here. Join me."

When she rose more staff appeared and whisked the table and dinner items away in seconds, and a group of three violinists appeared already playing a beautiful tune.

Amelia was so touched by the romantic gesture that she had to stop herself from shedding a tear. "Byron...this is just—no one's ever done anything like this for me before."

Byron pulled her into her arms and cupped her cheeks tenderly. "Then I am here to change that. Dance with me?"

Amelia smiled and slipped in close to the crook of Byron's neck. They swayed together to the sound of the violins, and the sound of the waves, and under the moonlight. Amelia's heart fluttered. There had never been a more perfect moment in her life, and she had to physically stop herself from saying *I love you.*

As they swayed together, Byron's soft touches to her bare back became more like gentle scratches, and Byron's breathing became heavier. It sounded as if she was so turned on, but holding back.

Amelia pulled back and looked in Byron's eyes and saw fire and passion. "Kiss me, Byron."

Byron's lips met hers so softly, and her kisses were so tender, Amelia felt as if she was being worshipped.

Amelia couldn't stop from moaning into the kiss, and that sound seemed to loosen Byron's restraint. Her kisses became passionate, raw and hungry. Luckily the staff had left with the table, Amelia thought, or she guessed she would be on it, and she wasn't ready to explore sex in public quite yet.

This was the conundrum about Byron. Most of the time she was so restrained in their lovemaking, but sometimes it felt like she was overcome with emotion, and their sex would be on the edge of control.

Byron's desperate kisses moved from her lips to her neck. Amelia threaded her fingers through Byron's short hair, while she kissed along her collarbone.

Her lips felt so good, and Amelia's neck was such a sensitive area. She grasped Byron's head and pushed it into the side of her neck. Amelia's heart and her body thudded.

"Oh God, Byron," Amelia moaned. She felt Byron kiss and lick all over her neck, and then as she often did when they made love, Byron sucked on her pulse point.

"Byron, we need to go somewhere more private."

Then Amelia let out a little yelp and jumped back, and covered her neck with her hand. As she did she was sure she could see red in

Byron's eyes, but before she had gotten a good look, Byron turned her back.

"I'm sorry, darling. I didn't mean to hurt you."

Amelia immediately wanted to make Byron feel better. It had only been a nip, and hadn't hurt much, and her neck was so sensitive the bite turned her on.

She walked behind Byron and put her hand on her back. "It's all right. It didn't hurt, just made me jump. Don't feel bad. I actually liked it," Amelia admitted. "This has been a perfect night—don't spoil it now."

Byron turned around and the red that she had imagined she had seen in her eyes was gone.

"I'm sorry, I want you so much that I get carried away."

Amelia tenderly stroked her cheek. "It's forgotten. You know I like your passionate side."

There was still fire and confusion in Byron's eyes. She took Amelia's hand and kissed it before saying, "I need to go back to the house and deal with some business. I'll have someone escort you back."

"Business? Now?" Amelia said with annoyance. Byron was clearly running away.

"Yes, now," Byron said firmly.

"Who exactly is going to take me back?" Amelia said. She looked around the dining area then looked back to Byron, but she was gone. "What is going on?"

Amelia started looking all around the dining area, even checking behind the curtains, and couldn't find Byron anywhere.

"How could she have moved so fast?"

Just then, one of the waiters stepped into the space. "May I escort you back to the house, Miss Honey?"

Amelia's anger was simmering now. How could Byron give her the most romantic evening she'd ever had and then disappear?

"If you'd follow me, please."

Amelia sighed angrily, and set off at a fast pace, leaving the waiter needing to play catch-up.

Chapter Seven

Byron drained the blood of her male attendant more greedily than she had since her Ascension Day. After rushing back to her office, shaking with hunger, an attendant was called for and he was now servicing her appetite.

She stood by the desk feeding from the neck of one of the older male servants called Tom. As the blood flowed down her throat, she had to keep telling herself, *Don't take too much, remember to stop. You have to stop.*

As the most powerful Debrek vampire, she always kept tight control of her blood needs, but now she just couldn't seem to fill that monster inside of her. She could feel it slither around in her stomach demanding she *take more, take more, and don't stop.*

Byron used all her strength and pushed away from her attendant. She was gasping for breath, and fell into her desk chair. Blood ran down her face and chin. The smell of it was making that monster inside her crave for more.

"Thank you for your service, Tom. Once you attend to your wound, please send in the next."

Tom bowed. "Yes, Principe."

Byron was always patient and extremely thankful to those that fed her, but now she resented the time Tom was taking to care for his wound at the first aid station. She wanted him out and her next attendant in now.

She tapped her fingers on the desk repeatedly, trying to quell her frustration that was going to become anger any minute. Finally, Tom was finished, and he bowed and said, "Goodnight, Principe."

"Goodnight, Tom. Thank you."

Finally, he left and a young woman came in followed by the Duca.

"May I have a word, Principe?"

"Take a seat, Alexis. I need to feed."

The young woman went to unbutton her blouse but Byron said, "Wrist is fine."

When she held out her wrist, Byron attacked it in a millisecond, and the young woman let out a gasp, before the feel-good chemicals started to do their job.

Byron fed from her wrist like a starving dog, and all she could think was, *It's not Amelia. I need Amelia.*

After a few minutes her feeding slowed to a calmer pace. She pulled back and said, "Thank you for your service. That will be all."

When she left, Byron went into her bathroom to wash up, and just as it had earlier, her image in the mirror with blood drying on her face brought her shame. There was only one other time in her long life that Byron had felt shame for taking blood, and that was with good reason. But this? This was a normal occurrence. Why should she feel shame now?

Amelia. She was imagining Amelia seeing her like this, and how afraid and disgusted she would feel.

She washed and washed, but couldn't get the blood off her fast enough. To make matters even worse, the blood was starting to have an effect on her physically and emotionally. She felt an intense high and one that demanded touching and making love with the one her heart wanted most.

Byron dried off and combed her hair so it was styled perfectly, and sprayed on some aftershave. There was at least something she could control now, even if was only her appearance.

She walked back into her office and put on her suit jacket that was draped across the back of her chair. Byron never looked up, but could feel Alexis's eyes on her.

"Speak, Duca, because your silence is deafening me." Byron sat down and took out a cigar, one of her few vices. She offered one to Alexis, who declined, and lit her own.

"I only say this because only I or Bhal could say this to you without being killed."

Byron raised an eyebrow, and joked, "You're sure of that, Duca?"

Alexis didn't smile or respond to the joke. She just held Byron's gaze steadily and said, "I'm sure of that." Alexis tapped her fingers on the desk then said, "I saw how you were when you came back to the house. I know you were in pain, and struggling to control your hunger."

Byron blew out a long puff of smoke. "Of course I'm going to be hungry while spending time with my lover. Any vampire would."

"What if she sees the hunger in your eyes?"

"That will not happen," Byron said flatly, even though that had very nearly taken place earlier. "Enough questions, is everything ready for tomorrow?"

She was taking Amelia out on her superyacht for a few days, somewhere they could get real privacy.

"Yes, the supplies will be loaded first thing in the morning. Are you sure you won't take even a few guards on board?"

"Very sure. I want to be alone with Amelia, and I mean alone. It will be quite sufficient if you and your people follow up in the boat behind."

"And what about food? You're going to need a steady supply."

Byron stubbed out her cigar in the ashtray. Her desire for Amelia was growing by the second, as the blood took effect. It was pulling her upstairs, and her body wouldn't wait much longer.

"The crew will serve me well. Now, if that's all, I have a beautiful woman waiting for me." She got up and walked to the door.

Alexis followed until they were at the bottom of the marble staircase. "Goodnight, Principe."

"Goodnight." Byron took the first step upstairs, the blood in every cell of her body wanting, needing, and hungering for Amelia.

She heard Alexis say behind her, "I know how it feels, Principe, remember? I'm only thinking of you."

Byron stopped in her tracks and turned back around. She would never forget the night they both lost women they cared about. Nearly a hundred and seventy years ago, Victorija and her Dreds attacked Byron's London home. Byron lost her lover Rose, leader of her local witches' coven, and Alexis lost the woman she loved.

Alexis was cradling her girlfriend Anna's limp body. She looked up at Byron, distraught, tears staining her face. "It was too late. I couldn't—"

Byron gave Alexis her hand and pulled her up to her feet. She looked into her eyes and said, "Humans break, and then they break our hearts. There is no other outcome, Alexis. No one can ever get this close again."

"I know, Duca. I know you do. Then you should understand the reason why I can't turn my back on her." She wondered if there was any part of Alexis that still yearned for love after vowing to never love anyone again.

Her Duca didn't respond to the emotional question, but simply nodded and said, "Goodnight, Principe."

Before she went upstairs, Byron decided to take a detour and pick up a few things that might help her earn Amelia's forgiveness.

❖

Amelia sat at her dressing table taking off her make-up, rehearsing all the things she was going to take Byron to task over when she saw her.

She had changed into the cream and lace nightdress with matching dressing gown she hoped Byron would like, but she suspected that was a waste of time. Even kissing her under moonlight, with romantic violin music in the background, didn't seem to tear Byron's mind away from business.

She finished applying cream to her face and touched her fingers to the two tiny pinprick marks on her neck. She had no idea how Byron could do that. It was the strangest thing. She started to brush her hair a little more aggressively than normal.

"I mean, who needs to take care of banking business at ten thirty at night, after spending the most romantic evening with her girlfriend?" Amelia spoke to the mirror as if she was having a conversation with herself. "But am I her girlfriend?"

They had been together for six months, but never talked about commitment. They'd never even discussed being exclusive with each other. Amelia had just assumed.

Her mind started to whirl thinking of all the long business trips. Byron was so polite and noble that she never even questioned that side of things, but maybe she should have.

Was life always going to be like this? Running away to take care of business at all times of the day or night? Amelia always got the impression that a part of Byron's mind or attention was somewhere else.

Before she got a chance to think any more about that, there was a knock at the door. She opened the door to find Byron standing with a bottle of champagne, two glasses, and a single red rose.

Amelia's heart immediately wanted to forgive Byron, but she had to make her point. "Can I help you? I assume some big company has collapsed, or the financial markets have melted or something? Must be, to make you run from my arms on such a romantic evening."

"May I come in?" Byron said. "I'd like to explain, and beg your forgiveness, Miss Honey."

Amelia turned around and walked into the centre of the room, and crossed her arms defensively. Byron followed her in and put her things on the coffee table.

"I know I ran out on you, and I'm truly sorry. I suddenly remembered I had to return a signed contract to our American office."

She wasn't sure if she quite believed that. There was something strange about Byron's behaviour. Amelia watched Byron uncork and pour out the champagne, and noticed a slight tremor to her hands.

"Are you all right, Byron?"

"Me? I'm in perfect health, just anxious for your forgiveness." She brought over a glass for Amelia and held the bottle in her hand. "Would you take a sip and tell me what you think?"

Amelia couldn't help but show her annoyance with a sigh, and said, "Fine."

She took a sip and the bubbles and the flavour exploded on her tongue. It did taste really good, but then all Byron's wines and whiskeys were the best you could buy.

"Well?" Byron asked.

"It's really nice, but what's so special about it?"

Byron smiled and held up the bottle to her. "Everything."

Amelia scanned the label, not quite sure what she was looking for, and then she saw it. "That's the year of my birth. You opened one—just for me?"

With her free hand, Byron caressed Amelia's cheek. "The best year, in my opinion."

Amelia was torn between forgiving her, and her annoyance. She sighed audibly, and Byron said, "I'm sorry I keep letting you down. I...I will try to do better. Please forgive me?"

Amelia was surprised by the desperation in Byron's voice. That wasn't like her. She also noticed Byron's hand was still shaking. Amelia put down her champagne glass, and took Byron's hand. "Are you okay, sweetheart?"

"Of course," Byron said a bit too quickly. She put down her glass and pulled Amelia to her. "I just need to kiss you."

Amelia couldn't help but kiss her then, and after their lips came together, and Byron gave her a deep, frantic kiss, she realized how turned on Byron was. Amelia had a deep need to give Byron what she needed. It was part of Amelia's caring nature, but being the lover Byron needed turned *her* on sexually so much too, and satisfied her.

Amelia pulled at Byron's tie as they kissed frantically, and threw it to the side. Then she pulled back from the kiss momentarily, to unbutton Byron's shirt. She touched Byron's hand, and felt the tremor she had seen earlier.

"Is everything really okay? You seem—"

"I'm fine." Byron cut her off. "I'm so bad at this...relationship business. I keep trying to make you happy, and I keep failing." Byron rested her forehead against Amelia's and said, "I need you to help me, mia cara. *Need* you so much."

The way Byron said *need* chimed somewhere deep inside Amelia. She didn't quite understand it, but she sensed Byron felt out of control, not centred in some way. Amelia knew instinctively what Byron needed tonight, and she would give it to her.

Amelia stroked her cheek, and Byron pleaded, "I need to taste your innocence."

She kissed Byron so softly and lovingly that Byron moaned. She stopped her kiss but kept her lips inches from Byron's and said, "I understand. Let me give you what you need."

Byron looked at her, seemingly unsure of this turn of events. Byron always led them, and she still would tonight, but Amelia would take care of her along the way. Amelia had grown much more sexually confident since she'd met Byron. The woman Byron first encountered at Grenville and Thrang would never have initiated a sexual encounter she wanted, or admitted she liked control and domination. Now, Amelia revelled in their sexual energy.

She unbuttoned Byron's shirt and threw it on the floor, along with the compression vest she wore underneath.

She ran her hands over the hard body she so adored, her nails softly scratching down her shoulder and chest. It was one of the things that Amelia loved about Byron—underneath the business suit, she had the body of a sportswoman who worked out for a living. Amelia had no idea how she found the time to sculpt these muscles and build the incredible strength she had demonstrated on occasion. There was only one time she had seen Byron work out, at her London penthouse. After staying over the previous evening, and finding herself alone in bed, she followed the clatter of wood, and found Byron engaging in some sort of fight using short sticks, in her gym with Bhal. She'd watched the play of her muscles and the speed of her movements with awe, and fell in love with her body even more.

Now Amelia could see Byron was holding so much tension in her body, and she would enjoy helping her release it. She traced a fingernail around her pert nipple.

"Do you know how much I love seeing you like this, sweetheart?" Amelia said.

"Tell me." Byron pulled her close. She would probably take the initiative any second, and Amelia didn't want that to happen. She wanted to show Byron what she could be for her. How she could be everything she needed.

"I can tell you and show you." Amelia kissed her neck and shoulders and lowered her hand to squeeze the strap-on she wore.

Byron put her head back and closed her eyes. "I love it when you touch me like that," Byron said with a groan.

Amelia took a step back, and said, "Will you sit on the bed for me?"

Surprisingly, Byron complied. She turned without opening her eyes, and walked over to the bed.

Once Byron sat, Amelia pulled off her nightdress slowly, and knowing how much her lover enjoyed her full round breasts, she grasped them and squeezed.

"Come here," Byron said in a tense voice.

Amelia grinned, and gave her a look that was dripping with passion. Instead of walking over to her, she got down on her knees, and started to crawl slowly to her, exaggerating a sway to her hips.

She watched as Byron gripped the bed sheets tightly as she crawled.

When Amelia arrived at Byron's feet, Byron stroked her cheek, and said, "Oh, Miss Honey. How do you always know what I need?"

"Because it's always what I need. You are everything I need, Byron."

Amelia took a big chance betraying the depth of her feelings, and she could tell there was something going on behind Byron's eyes at that statement. Amelia wished Byron felt the same as her, and would one day say it back.

Amelia started to unbuckle Byron's belt and pulled down her trousers. Byron kicked them away.

"Do you remember the first time I measured you at the shop?" Amelia said, while caressing her strap-on through her underwear.

"How could I forget. It was a *night* I'll never forget."

"When I was down on my knees with the tape measure, I was so turned on, I thought about how I would do anything to be allowed to give you pleasure on my knees. Then I felt the hardness lying against your thigh, and I nearly melted on the spot."

Byron pulled her flesh coloured strap-on from her underwear, and held it in her palm.

"I know how much it excited you, I could sense it."

"May I?" Amelia held her hand close but didn't touch. Byron took her hand, and placed it around her strap-on.

"You may, always, mia cara," Byron said.

"I used to fantasize about a lover using one on me, but I never had the courage to ask. Then you come along, someone who wears one naturally, confidently, and without apology, and I was never so turned on in my life. All I wanted to do was unzip your trousers, and put my lips around it and suck it for you."

Byron let out a groan. She couldn't take it any longer—she needed Amelia now. "Do it."

Amelia grinned, held the base, and put her lips around it.

Byron couldn't remember ever feeling as turned on as this. Having Amelia near her, in her own private world, so soon after feeding was something new and so hard to control. She craved an orgasm, as much as she craved to drink from Amelia, but since the latter couldn't happen, all her cravings were now funnelled into her sexual craving for Amelia.

The little bit of sexual confidence Amelia was showing tonight surprised Byron and intoxicated her. She was showing confidence and demanding what she wanted in the softest, gentlest of ways, so it didn't take away Byron's need for control. Amelia Honey was just the perfect woman for her. She wished she could tell her.

Byron leaned back slightly, so she could enjoy the vision of Amelia's beautiful, full, wet lips sucking her. Byron thought of her strap-on as an extension of her clit—it was just who she was. She wanted to thrust inside her lover badly, but they could both enjoy this first. She closed her eyes for a second and groaned, as her orgasm started to build. "You're so good, Miss Honey." Byron moaned.

Byron's hips started to thrust with each bob of Amelia's head, and her steely control was starting to loosen. She would come if she wasn't careful, and she wanted to do that inside Amelia.

Just a little longer, Byron promised herself. Just a little longer to enjoy the sensation.

Byron knew she could stop, always regain control—she always could. As if reading her mind and responding to Byron's groans and thrusts, Amelia grasped the base of the strap-on more firmly and pushed the base more firmly down onto Byron's clit beneath.

This caught Byron by surprise. Her orgasm started to overtake her control, and as much as her mind told her to stop, she couldn't.

"Fuck, I can't—" As her orgasm became unstoppable, so was the vampire inside her. She felt her teeth erupt, and knew her eyes would be glowing red, and the veins on her temples would be protruding. Luckily Amelia's head was down, concentrating on giving Byron pleasure.

Bite, bite, drink from her. She hungered to reach down and grasp Amelia's wrist to drink, but the full force of her orgasm hit just in time.

"Fuck! Yes," Byron shouted and fell back on the bed as the exquisite pleasure hit her low in her stomach, and spread quickly all over her body, robbing her of her strength.

Byron lay there gasping, in the aftermath of her orgasm, staring at the ceiling in shock. She lost control. She couldn't stop. That never happened to her. Amelia made her lose control.

Byron felt a tiny spark of fear creep into her body, and the darkness, the demon she always kept at bay, stepped a little more into the light.

She covered her face with her hands when she felt Amelia start to climb on top of her. Amelia couldn't see her like this.

"Byron? Are you okay?" Amelia said as she sat astride her hips. She moaned when she felt Amelia's wetness on her stomach.

"Look at me," she repeated.

Once Byron regained her breath, and she was confident the vampire was gone, she took her hands from her face.

Amelia looked worried. Byron could understand why—she didn't normally display this kind of uncertainty, especially during sex. But losing control was a first for her.

"Did you not like that?" Amelia asked.

Byron had to reassure her and regain some of the control she felt slipping away. "That was sensational. You are such a good girl at being bad."

Amelia's smile was back. "I love making you feel like that."

Byron reached up and caressed Amelia's cheek. "I can feel it. You are so wet. Aren't you?"

Amelia smiled shyly and a blush rose to her cheeks. That was one thing Byron adored about Amelia—even after initiating and taking part in such an erotic act, there was still a part of the shy woman she met six months ago, who couldn't ask for what she wanted.

Byron sat up and flipped Amelia on her back. She started to feel calmer, taking control back. She stroked her fingers down Amelia's thigh.

"Tell me the truth or I won't give you what you want," Byron warned. "Are you wet?"

Amelia hesitated, and then whispered, "Soaking wet."

Byron grinned. "Oh, you enjoyed sucking my cock that much? How naughty you are."

It was Amelia's turn to groan. Byron knew how much Amelia loved that kind of talk, since it was something that went against all propriety and the way in which she was brought up. Byron loved to play up to that.

"Tell me what you want now. You want me to touch you with my lips and my tongue?" Byron ran her tongue around Amelia's lips teasingly.

"My fingers?" She traced Amelia's cheekbone with her fingers.

"Or…?" She left the question hanging.

Amelia was breathing so heavily. "Or?"

Byron thrust her hips. "Say it."

Amelia opened her legs further, and wrapped her arms around Byron's neck. "I want you inside me."

"My favourite place to be."

As she began to make love with Amelia, she felt alive, in control, and safe again, but she couldn't forget Amelia had the power to destroy her control. Love was making her lose control, and that was frightening.

Chapter Eight

Victorija was full of energy and excitement this morning. She was standing in front of her free-standing mirror getting dressed, her human dresser, Jacque, at her side.

She smoothed down her waistcoat, and popped her gold pocket watch into its place.

"Tie, Principe?" Jacque said.

He was a short balding man, who had been with the family for a long time, and Victorija was fond of him—as fond as she could be about anyone.

"No tie, Jacque." She fixed her collar so it was sitting to her satisfaction. "I don't think we need to be stuffy and old-fashioned. This is a new era."

"Very good, Principe." He held up her black suit jacket and she slipped in.

There was a knock at her bedroom door, and Drasas came in. "Principe—" Her words fell away when she looked around the bedroom floor, littered with bodies, all with their hearts and throats ripped out.

Victorija said, "Do excuse the mess, but I had to fire my father's loyal staff." She smiled cruelly. "They didn't take it too well."

Victorija perhaps appeared calm, but she'd noted every one of their deaths and their screams echoed across her mind. She imagined how happy her mother would be, looking from the other side. Every one of those turned vampires helped kill her, and now she was completely avenged.

Drasas pointed over to one particular body. "Is that—?"

She followed Drasas's gaze to the body of the blonde who had been her father's mistress. "Eleanora? Yes, she was becoming tiresome." She stepped over a few bodies and picked up her gold watch from the dressing table, and put it on. "Drasas, could you have this mess cleared up?"

"Of course, Principe. The newly turned vampires are wakened if you would like to address them."

"The cannon fodder you mean?" Victorija joked. Newly turned vampires were very green, and although powerful and nearly immortal, they had none of the skills her older vampires had gathered over the centuries.

"Yes, Principe." Drasas laughed along with her.

Victorija walked over to her Duca and said, "We need more. If we are going to take on the Debreks again, we need numbers to distract them while our more powerful vampires execute our plans."

"I'll make sure you get the very best recruits possible. I'll train them personally," Drasas said.

"If any show promise, let me know. Now let's go and address our new cannon fodder."

They walked down the corridors of the Dred castle, on their way to the throne room. Every human servant they passed and even some of her turned vampires shuddered in fear. That fear gave her a ripple of pleasure. After spending her lifetime in her father's shadow, now she was the one in control and no one could frighten her ever again.

She clapped Drasas on the back, and said, "We are going to cause some fear and terror, Drasas, make everyone remember who the Dreds truly are."

Drasas smiled. "Fear and terror? I can hardly wait."

"First things first, I want you to send your best vampires to do some reconnaissance on Byron and her clan. Where are they? What are they doing? Is there anything changed since we last crossed them, and is there anything we can use against them."

"Of course. It feels good to be back to what our clan should be."

"We have a lot of scores to settle, Drasas, and we are going to get the Debreks' secret, and my birthright. The royal house of Debrek and all the trappings that go with it are as much mine as Byron's. When my father and mother were exiled, our rights and privileges were ripped from us." And I was abandoned to the whims and ravages of my psychopathic father. Well, time to reap what they sowed, Victorija thought. She smacked Drasas on the shoulder and sneered. "Let's take back what is ours."

❖

As wonderful a time as Amelia was having, she was growing frustrated. She was trying her best to ignore all the strange things that went on around Byron—the disappearing, the strange actions of her staff, her unusual sexual appetites—but a week into her holiday, it was becoming harder and harder.

Soon after meeting Byron, Amelia realized Byron had a high sex drive, but it was only here in her home that she realized how high it was.

Could Byron be a sex addict? She thought back to last night, and how Byron had made love to her—passionately, yes, but generously. Byron always was an attentive lover and worshipped her body. Amelia didn't know for sure, but it didn't seem as if she was addicted to sex in general. Then the thought popped into her head: *More like she's addicted to me.*

One thing that was becoming clear was that Byron never wanted to go out in public with her. She asked to go out for dinner, to go to the theatre, anything just so she could see the sights and sounds of Monte Carlo, and Byron used every excuse not to go.

Last night, Amelia thought she had won her battle, when Byron agreed to take her out to dinner in town, but when they arrived she discovered that Byron had hired out the restaurant for the night, and they were the only two patrons.

It was starting to feel like Byron didn't want to be seen with her. She didn't want to believe it, but what other reasons could she have?

This afternoon Amelia was getting ready to have lunch on the beach with Byron, while Byron took care of some business. She stood and smoothed down her dress. "Not bad."

She was now sharing Byron's room, after she'd asked a few days ago why they didn't. Was she trying to keep her at a distance? Byron was slightly reticent at first, but then agreed wholeheartedly.

It was wonderful to sleep beside Byron at night, in her big oak four-poster bed, although she was still alone in the morning, more often than not. It was just probably one of the things she would have to get used to if she wanted a long-term relationship with an international banker.

The door opened and Byron walked in. "Are you ready, mia cara?"

"Yes. Did you finish with your business?"

Amelia saw Byron lick her lips, and she was sure her eyes grew darker. "Yes, all done."

She turned to spray her perfume and without any footsteps or sound, Byron was right behind her back. Amelia clasped her chest. "God, Byron. You gave me the fright of my life."

"Sorry." Byron rested her hands on Amelia's waist and leaned in to kiss her neck. "Oh God, you smell good."

Amelia shivered. The want in Byron's voice always made her melt and yearn for her touch. She turned around into Byron's arms and thought she saw little shards of red glint in her eyes. She was starting to notice this all the time—after Byron had taken care of some sort of urgent business, she returned hungry, passionate, and with a red glint in her eyes.

Amelia again began to worry that Byron was some kind of addict. A drug addict, sex addict, or both. Why else did she come back to her *desperate* for her? This was a completely different side to Byron, one she hadn't seen while they were dating in London. Normally she was so controlled.

Byron kissed her neck and collarbone while she slipped her hand up and under Amelia's dress.

"Byron, we have lunch waiting."

"I don't care—it can wait. I need you." Byron felt Amelia respond to her kiss, and she couldn't hold back any more. She lifted Amelia off her feet and carried her over to the old oak writing desk by the window. She balanced Amelia on the edge while she swept everything off the desk with her other hand.

Amelia grasped her neck and scratched her fingernails down it, and that stoked Byron's libido even more. Her blood and her body were on fire. There was no hiding from what she felt for Amelia. She loved her, and love affected her just as her parents had told her it would. She wanted to drown in Amelia, be inside her, taking her body, and tasting her blood.

Amelia broke from the kiss and leaned back on the desk. "I'm so wet, Byron."

Byron pushed up her dress immediately, and placed her hand over Amelia's sex. Her silky thong was soaked and she just had to taste. She dropped to her knees and pulled Amelia to the edge of the desk, pulled off her thong, and ran her tongue along the length of her sex.

One delicious taste of her lover and she couldn't hold back her erupting teeth. If she wasn't down here out of Amelia's gaze, Amelia would have seen her dark red vampire eyes, and the veins bulging on her temples, but Byron knew she was safely hidden. She relaxed and didn't force back her vampire features.

She started to suck on Amelia's clit and as her hips started to squirm, Byron could hear Amelia's blood rushing through her blood vessels. She imagined the fresh, hot blood rushing to Amelia's sexual organs. The sweet smell of Amelia was testing her control. Her hands trembled, and her body ached for just one taste of Amelia's blood.

Byron stopped sucking Amelia's clit and slipped two fingers inside her.

"Oh God, Byron. Please come up here." Amelia groaned.

"Not yet." Byron's sex burned and she wanted to go back to Amelia and make both of them come, but she was enjoying not holding back the vampire in her. She hastened the thrust of her fingers and kissed her way over to between the edge of Amelia's pubic hair and her hip, where Amelia's artery ran. She rested her lips on the soft skin there, and felt the beat of her blood pumping through her. Her fangs started to ache with the want of blood.

Byron moaned loudly, and rested her cheek on the pulse. She felt almost dazed—her need for Amelia's blood was so strong.

"Amelia, Amelia, I need you so much. I'm so hungry, so, so hungry."

She felt Amelia sit up and stroke her head. "Then come and take me, Byron. I'm all yours. I'll be yours as long as you want me."

If only it was so easy.

She ran her tongue along the pulse point, and then dragged her teeth, allowing herself to imagine what it would be like to sink them into her fleshy thigh.

Byron wanted to weep, for the temptation was so strong. It would be so easy to feed, just a little, and compel Amelia to forget.

So easy.

The dark part of her soul, a part she always fought hard to keep control of, egged her on. *Take her blood. You won't harm her, and she'll never know. Do it.*

"No!" Byron shouted out loud.

"Byron? Are you okay?" Amelia asked with concern in her voice.

She wasn't okay, and worried if she would be able to control herself forever. She could only think of one way to control her craving, and that was to lose herself in sex, but Amelia would see her face and realize there was something she was hiding.

She tried to take some calming breaths, but they didn't help the way they usually did.

"I need to fuck you, and make us come. Turn over onto your stomach."

Amelia gave her a breathy *yes*.

Luckily that was one of Amelia's favourite positions, so it worked out perfectly. As soon as Amelia was lying on her stomach, Byron stood.

Amelia placed her wrists behind her back and said, "Byron, please?"

Byron couldn't help but smile. Amelia loved to be restrained, and it suited Byron completely. "You are very naughty."

"Yes, Byron, I am. That's why I need you."

"Well, since you asked so nicely…" Byron started to undo her tie, and then wrapped it around Amelia's wrists. Amelia gasped when she pulled it tight. "I've got you now, Miss Honey."

"Yes, I need you inside me."

It was working. Byron's need to be inside her lover and make them both come was distracting her slightly from her need for blood.

Byron pushed Amelia's dress up around her hips, and unclasped her belt and trousers quickly. She pulled her strap-on from her tight designer jockey shorts and rested it against Amelia's sex. Amelia opened her legs further in response, and Byron saw the wetness that awaited her.

"Byron…" Amelia moaned.

She pushed the head inside her lover, and teased her with just a few gentle strokes.

"More, I want to feel you," Amelia said.

"Oh, you think you deserve that?" Byron was desperate to thrust inside Amelia, but tried to keep a semblance of control, knowing how much Amelia liked it.

"I don't deserve it, but you do, Principe."

Byron immediately stopped. "Where did you hear that?"

"That's what those under your command call you, isn't it? I heard your guards saying it."

Byron ran her hands down the small of her back and grasped her buttocks. "Yes, it is."

"May I call you by that title?" Amelia said breathily. "I'm under your command too."

Byron closed her eyes and groaned. This woman couldn't be any more perfect for her. She was everything. "Yes, you may." Byron was done waiting. She needed to come now, or she was going to have to take blood.

She pushed her strap-on fully inside Amelia and got a ripple of pleasure at the noises her lover was making.

"Ask me nicely, Miss Honey."

"Fuck me, Principe."

Restraint was over. Byron thrust into Amelia in long strokes, enjoying every little sound she made and the rush of blood inside her that only Byron could hear.

"Oh, Principe…" Amelia tested her bonds, as she always enjoyed to do, and reminded herself that she was under control. It was such a turn -n, and even more so in this position. She felt so bad, so naughty. Byron had caught her by surprise with the depths of her passion at the start, but as always when Byron touched her, she was soon ready to beg for whatever Byron wanted to give her. She'd taken a chance and called her *Principe* to test her reaction. She seemed taken aback at first, but then it appeared to arouse her.

Byron's thrusts were getting faster, and her sex was nearly ready to explode. She loved Byron's strap-on inside her. It was part of who Byron was, and gave Amelia such satisfaction to nurture that, to be what Byron needed, and to give her the pleasure she craved.

This dynamic that they shared was what she secretly longed for. Amelia had always known she wasn't straight, but she couldn't quite sort her sexuality out in her head. That was until she moved to London and a friend took her out to a gay bar. There she saw a butch swagger towards her, and the scales fell from her eyes. *This* was the kind of woman she longed for, but no other butch could have prepared her for Byron Debrek.

Byron's cock thrust fast and hard inside her, and her orgasm was seconds from exploding. "Principe, I'm going to come!"

Byron leaned over her, holding the back of her neck, and said in a desperate, breathy voice, "Come now—with me."

Even though she had permission, she tried to hold on a few more seconds so she could hear Byron gasp and shout out her release. Then something different happened. Byron called out, "Fuck, fuck, your blood. Can't stop." She ripped the top of Amelia's dress and nipped the same place on her neck as she had before. The shock of the little nip set off Amelia's own orgasm, the waves of hot pleasure rippled right down to the tips of her toes.

"*Byron*," she groaned.

As soon as the last of Amelia's orgasm had left her with a feeling of love and warmth throughout her body, she became aware of Byron rambling, as if speaking to herself.

"It's okay, It's okay. I didn't—I stopped, I stopped." Byron gasped.

Amelia had never heard her distressed. "Byron, untie me," she said firmly.

The tie was taken off and Amelia turned around quickly to find Byron breathing hard and looking so worried.

"I didn't bite—I just nipped again," Byron said.

Amelia could now feel a slight discomfort, like a scratch, where Byron had bitten her slightly before. This was obviously something Byron did unconsciously when she lost herself in passion. Amelia fixed her dress. She attempted to cup Byron's cheek, but she pulled back. Amelia would swear that she looked frightened, and that was not a word that she associated with Byron Debrek.

"Byron? Don't run. Everything is all right." This time Byron let her cup her cheek, without flinching.

"I'm sorry, I don't mean to bite, it's just something—" Byron struggled for the words.

"You get lost in our passion. It's all right, sweetheart. You don't hurt me."

"I could," Byron said with anger in her voice.

Byron pulled up her trousers, and began to frantically fix her shirt and tie, but her hands didn't seem to be working.

Amelia placed her hands on Byron's chest. "Stop and listen to me."

Byron's hands dropped to her sides, and Amelia started to fix her tie for her slowly. "You're not doing anything wrong or bad. I think we both like sex a little rough sometimes. I know I like it when you lose control of your passion. It's exciting and exhilarating to have you show me that much desire."

Byron sighed, and dropped her gaze to the floor. Amelia obviously wasn't getting through to her. She put her fingers under Byron's chin and lifted her head.

"Look at me," Amelia said, but Byron wouldn't. "Byron? Look at me now." This time she said it more forcefully, and Byron did indeed look her directly in the eyes.

Amelia cupped both Byron's cheeks tenderly. "I want you to understand and believe me, so there can be no misunderstandings. There is nothing you could do or *want* that could hurt me. I love everything you want to give me."

Byron's eyes were awash with confusion and uncertainty. "You don't know that."

Amelia took Byron's hand and placed it on her own chest. "I know that in my heart. Can you feel it?"

Byron nodded. "I can feel it."

"Then believe me, sweetheart. I will always be everything you need, if you let me."

Byron surprised her by kissing her passionately, and then she pulled back, and leaned her forehead against Amelia's. "Thank you. I don't deserve you, my shining girl."

"You do. Why don't we take a shower and enjoy a nice lunch, like you planned?"

"Yes. I'd like that."

CHAPTER NINE

After sharing a shower together and getting ready all over again, they made their way down to the beach for lunch. This afternoon, Byron was taking her to meet the other woman in her life.

Byron was content for the moment. She hadn't tasted her lover's blood, but she had just made love with Amelia, and she had accepted Byron's passionate side unequivocally. But would she if she knew what Byron truly wanted from her?

Her feelings for Amelia were growing more intense every day, but because of that her body was demanding her lover's body more and more too. She couldn't not touch Amelia, but at the same time it was painful not to taste her blood. Every time Byron kissed her neck, she heard her lover's strong steady pulse pounding in her ears, daring her, challenging her to take the blood, but she had to resist, had to keep strong.

"Are you all right, sweetheart? You seem miles away," Amelia said.

Byron quickly pulled herself together. "Of course." She pointed up the walkway. "Look, our guest is here."

"Who?"

"Come and I'll introduce you."

Amelia held Byron's hand tightly as they walked up the walkway. There was a beautiful young woman with wavy shoulder-length blond hair, dressed in cute designer jeans and a tight little string top, wearing designer sunglasses. As they got closer the woman took them off to reveal the same dark eyes as Byron's. She pushed her glasses on top of her head, and looked over Amelia thoroughly, before breaking into a big smile.

"Introduce us, Byron," the woman said.

Amelia was nervous. This woman was very familiar with Byron and completely gorgeous—fashion model gorgeous.

"Amelia Honey, this is my sister, Serenity Debrek. Sera, this is my"—Byron looked at Amelia and hesitated for a second before saying—"my girlfriend."

Amelia's heart soared. This was Byron's sister, and she was introducing her as her girlfriend. She did take this relationship seriously.

She was surprised by Sera throwing her arms around her.

"I'm so happy to meet the woman who inspired my sister to have a relationship," Sera said.

"It's nice to meet you too. I've been really looking forward to meeting Byron's family."

Sera took her hand and pulled her over to the table. "Come and tell me everything about yourself and, Byron, crack open the bubbly. This is a celebration."

Byron smiled at her sister and shook her head. "Everything is a celebration with you."

Amelia was delighted with Byron's sister so far. First impressions were that she was open, lively, and full of fun. This was going to be interesting.

They enjoyed a wonderful lunch where Amelia chatted incessantly with Sera while Byron sat back, apparently content to let them get to know each other. Later in the afternoon Byron went to attend to business while Sera took Amelia for a walk.

They walked along the beach wall until they came to the stairs. "Let's get sand between our toes, shall we?"

"Yes, that would be fun," Amelia said.

Sera looked behind her to the tall, dark-haired man following them at a distance. "We're going onto the beach, Henri. You stay here—we'll be fine as we are."

Henri looked as though he was going to protest but then nodded, and stopped where he was.

"Is he your guard?" Amelia asked.

Sera kicked off her shoes, and jumped down onto the sand. "Yes, he's my Alexis, unfortunately."

Amelia didn't jump. She carefully walked down the four steps to the beach. "Why unfortunately?"

"Henri is dull as dishwater. Byron won't let me have female guards. She thinks I'll either seduce them, or if they're not my type, have too much fun partying with them. So I get Henri the reliably dull."

Amelia laughed. Sera was like a breath of fresh air. She was easy-going, open, funny—not intense and controlled like her sister—and she and Sera had a love of fashion in common.

"Is Bhal around? She's usually helping guard me, and making sure I don't get up to any mischief," Sera said with annoyance in her voice.

"No, I haven't seen her for a few days. She's not quite as intense and gruff as Alexis," Amelia said.

"Hmm. Maybe not to you. I've had a lifetime of her trying to mould me into a Byron, Mark 2, but I'm not."

Amelia laughed. "So I see. You are quite different from your sister."

"I love my sister, and she is the perfect heir to lead the Debrek dynasty. I, on the other hand, like to have fun." Sera stopped for a second and took in the scenery around them. "It's so good to be back. I miss the old place when I go away. Tell me, what exciting things has my sister shown you while you've been here?"

"We've had some beautiful, romantic dinners on the beach, and we took an amazing cruise on her yacht."

"What about in the town? Surely, she must have taken you to her favourite restaurants, gone dancing—there's so much to see and do in Monte Carlo."

Amelia let out a breath, and kicked a shell at her foot. "No, I'm not sure why, but Byron hasn't wanted to be around other people with me. She just wants us to be alone."

Sera put her hands on her hips and shook her head. "She's doing her *I shall be all noble and protect you from every foe, young Amelia* thing, is she?"

What did Sera mean? She followed Sera down to the water's edge, and they paddled in the shallow waves. "I don't understand. What foes?"

Sera turned around and had a mischievous smile on her face. "How would you like to have some real fun?"

❖

A few hours later, Sera zoomed along the costal roads in her Ferrari at a high speed. Amelia clutched her handbag with a death grip, a huge knot of worry turning inside her.

"Sera, maybe I should call and let Byron know where I am. She'll be worried."

Sera glanced at her quickly before turning her eyes back on the road. "Don't worry. She can do without you for one evening. Katie is going to tell her that we've gone for a drive and will be back for supper. Relax."

But Amelia couldn't relax. Byron had been so emotionally fragile for some reason this afternoon, and she didn't want to do anything to cause distrust in their relationship. At the same time, it was important to get to know the Debrek family if Amelia wanted to became a permanent fixture in Byron's life. So she kept quiet and followed Sera's lead.

They arrived in town, and pulled up outside the club Sera had told her about. It must be popular going by the long line of people waiting to get in.

"It looks busy," she said.

Sera turned off the engine. "Don't worry about that. The Debrek name opens any lock."

She winked at Amelia, and her car door was opened by a valet. A club security officer helped her out.

"Ms. Debrek. A pleasure to see you again."

Another large man opened Amelia's door and she got out gingerly, and walked around to Sera.

"Thank you, Troy," Sera said. "This is Byron's girlfriend, Amelia. We want to have some fun."

Troy looked at Amelia with surprise. Everyone seemed to be surprised Byron was in a relationship. She didn't know how to feel about that. Troy escorted them into the foyer of the club. As soon as Amelia walked through the doors, the thump of the music and the sounds of the electrifying atmosphere excited her. She hadn't had a night out like this in a long time.

They walked into the main room of the club. It had a huge dance floor in the middle of the space, a bar running down one side of the room, and tables, chairs, booths, and couches all around the perimeter of the rest of the room.

About half of the clubbers were dressed up in costumes, mostly elaborate and scary, but the others angels.

A woman wearing the sexiest, skimpy outfit as well as two horns and claws walked up to them, and took Amelia's hand. "Would you like to dance with the devil, beautiful?"

Amelia looked at an amused Sera in panic. "I—"

Sera stepped in to save Amelia's stuttering refusal. "She's spoken for, darling." Then she leaned in closer to say with a smirk, "By someone who would eat you for breakfast."

The sexy devil seemed to take the message and departed quickly.

"Thanks," Amelia said. "I'm not really used to being chatted up."

Sera laughed. "You're adorable. I can see why my sister likes you."

"Why is everyone dressed up?" Amelia asked.

"It's Angels and Demons night. They have it once a month. Let's go."

Troy led them to the VIP area, where a bottle of champagne in an ice bucket was beside them within thirty seconds.

A young woman dressed in a revealing costume complete with angel's wings poured them a drink. "Thank you, Ms. Angel," Sera flirted.

Amelia chuckled. Sera was flash and glam just like her sister, and had immense confidence. She took a sip of her drink and watched Sera start to dance in her seat to the music. The next song started and Sera's eyes lit up.

"I love this song." Sera took her hand and pulled her to her feet.

"Where are we going?" Amelia asked.

"To dance, of course."

❖

Byron sat at the head of the table in the conference room. It was filling up with her guards, as they hurried to the basement for the quickly called meeting. Alexis had received some intelligence about the Dreds, and was about to inform them of the details.

"Sit down quickly, everyone," Byron said.

As everyone settled, Alexis leaned over to her and whispered, "Where is Bhal?"

"She won't be joining us. I gave her a separate assignment. Let's get this meeting under way, shall we."

Byron knocked on the table to bring the meeting to order. "Quiet, please. Alexis? If you would."

"Thank you, Principe." Alexis turned to face the rest of her people. "I received intelligence this evening that there has been a change at the top of the Dred clan."

One of the older turned vampires, Alexis's lieutenant, Neva, said with disbelief, "Gilbert finally stood down?"

"No, he was removed by Victorija forcibly. He is now dead."

There was an audible gasp around the room. Even though Gilbert was their sworn enemy, he was still a born vampire, and the death of a born vampire was greeted with shock.

Turned vampires looked up to borns. They were their royalty, and were nearly impossible to kill. If Victorija could kill Gilbert, then they certainly weren't safe.

Alexis continued, "We don't know how it happened, only that it did and Victorija is now Principe."

It was Byron's turn to speak. She leaned forward and clasped her hands. "You all know that Gilbert was not interested in expansion in the latter days of his reign, but Victorija is a very different beast. She is sadistic, cruel, and hungry for power. Gilbert kept her down so long that I believe she will be wanting to make a big display of power."

Alexis nodded and continued, "Our information says they are building their numbers, building an army, turning humans without consent." A look of fury came across Alexis's face. "She has no care for what humans want, or whether they live or die."

Byron, seeing the emotion this was bringing up for her Duca, took over. Alexis and Victorija had a difficult history.

"Consent is what we live by, and so this is a threat not only to us, but to the innocent humans that they will snatch blood and life from. I shouldn't have to tell you that security will have to be heightened. My sister will be staying here under our protection, and I will inform my parents. They should have adequate security, but they may return to us. You must be on your guard at every second. We may have quality in our clan, superior soldiers, guards, and protection, but they will have numbers. We must be careful."

Byron felt total fear inside when she thought of Amelia being anywhere near Victorija. Given the chance, Victorija would use her to get everything she wanted.

Alexis said in a low voice, "Miss Honey will have a target on her back now, if Victorija finds out about her. You know that, don't you?"

Byron knew that only too well. Just as she had decided it was safe to have a life and let herself fall in love, this had to happen. "I know, Duca—"

Byron's answer was interrupted by Sera's guard Henri running into the room. "They've gone, Principe!"

Byron had a sick, sinking feeling in her stomach. "Who has gone, Henri?"

"Sera and Miss Honey. Sera compelled me to let them have an hour's head start."

"My God," Byron said in disbelief. The two women she loved most in the world were out on their own at the worst possible time. "Find out where they are," Byron roared.

Byron's mobile rang. It was Bhal. After a brief conversation, she said to Alexis, "Let's go. One day here and my sister causes mayhem."

Chapter Ten

Amelia relaxed and enjoyed the dancing. Sera had an infectious personality. She seemed to enjoy every second of life and not worry about the next day. Amelia laughed when Sera started to dance provocatively with one of the club dancers, dressed as a demon.

The dance floor filled up even more, and Amelia started to feel a little crowded. People were starting to push and shove. Sera stopped dancing as if she had just heard something, and Amelia felt someone next to her grab her wrist.

She didn't even get the chance to shout for help before Sera pushed him off her, and he flew a few feet from just one little push.

Sera took her hand, and said, "We have to go, right now."

"Sera, what's going on?"

"Remember we talked about all those foes my family had? They're after us," Sera told her.

"I had no idea the banking business was so dangerous," Amelia said.

Sera sighed loudly. "You have no idea."

When they got out of the throng on the dance floor, Amelia noticed two people in dark suits talking to Troy at the VIP area, then point over to them.

"Amelia, we have to move now. We'll head out of the club through the back. No matter what happens, don't look back, and keep holding my hand, okay?"

Now Amelia was worried. If the easy-going, life of the party Sera Debrek was concerned, then it was time to panic.

Sera guided her quickly to the back of the club and through

double doors marked *Private*. They walked into what looked like a staff kitchen, with staff members looking perplexed. One man jumped in front of Sera and said, "You can't be in here. You have to leave now."

Sera looked him right in the eye and said, "You're going to let us by, and go about your business."

"I'm going to let you by, and go about my business," the man repeated back and stepped out of their way.

"How did you—?"

"Come on, we have to move," Sera said.

How could this be happening? Sera got that person to move with just her words. This was just one more strange thing about Byron's family.

They burst through the back door and found themselves in a poorly illuminated back alley.

"Okay, let's go and get a cab. They are probably waiting with the Ferrari," Sera said.

Amelia stopped dead, and pulled her hand from Sera's. "Stop, just stop, Sera. What is going on here?"

"We need to keep moving. Please, Amelia. Byron will kill me if anything happens to you," Sera said.

"Tell me what's wrong first. And who are these people?" Amelia said firmly.

"We don't have time. I'll explain later."

Amelia crossed her arms in defiance. She was sick of being treated like a child, and not being told what was going on. "No, explain now. You're behaving just like Byron, not telling me the full story."

Sera rolled her eyes. "Amelia…" Just as Sera spoke, five people dropped from the roof above and circled them. "Get behind me, Amelia."

The five were all dressed in black, and looked extremely menacing. Amelia stepped behind Sera, and whispered, "Sera, why do these people want to hurt us?"

"Because they are jealous of what the Debreks have," Sera said loudly.

The ringleader took a step forward to Sera, and she said to him, "You really want to do this? You know who I am."

"I know only too well. Your heart will be a perfect present for my new Duca."

Duca. There was one of those strange words again.

"If you know who I am, you know you cannot beat me," Sera said firmly.

Amelia was astonished. Sera was actually going to fight these people?

The first assailant lunged at Sera. She dodged him easily and threw him across the alley, where he smashed into the wall. How could Sera possibly have strength like that? Amelia wondered.

Sera smiled at the rest of their attackers. "Who's next?"

They all looked to each other, and then ran forward at once. Sera began to dispatch them one by one, in a way that astonished Amelia. Sera must have been some sort of martial arts expert, and so quick, their attackers couldn't keep up with her movements.

Suddenly, someone grabbed Amelia from behind. Sera soon got him off her, but with her back turned, the others got the advantage.

As Amelia looked on, terrified, Sera was knocked from her feet. But just then, Bhal jumped from the roof above, and landed beside them with a large, ancient, scary looking sword—like ones she had seen in the British Museum, only this one had no erosion or rust, and had a flashing green emerald on the end of the hilt.

Amelia squealed in horror as Bhal swiped one assailant's head from his shoulders, and the blood spattered everywhere.

"Sera, get Amelia out of here now. I'll take care of this lot."

"I'm handling it, Bhal. I don't need you to fight my battles."

Bhal thrust her sword though the chest of the woman Sera was fighting, and she fell to the ground.

"Byron will want Amelia home, Sera. Do as I ask for once," Bhal urged.

Sera sighed and grabbed Amelia's hand. "Let's go."

When they got to the end of the alley, one of the Debrek limos pulled up, and Byron, Alexis, and some of her guards jumped out.

Byron gave Sera a hard stare, and said coldly, "Amelia, get in the car."

Amelia's anger was already at boiling point, and now Byron was ordering her around like a naughty child. She got in the car and slammed the door, her anger simmering. Out the window she saw Byron giving Sera an angry lecture. Byron got in the car, and Sera got into the car behind with some of the other guards.

Byron never looked at Amelia, and Amelia never said a word. Her mind was a mixture of anger and confusion. Anger at Byron, and to a lesser extent, Sera, at the way they were ordering her around. The Debrek family was strange and dangerous, and there was a big part of Byron that she was hiding behind a façade, and Amelia didn't know if she could live with it.

❖

When they got back to the house, Amelia ran upstairs to their room without saying a word or looking back at Byron.

Alexis got out and opened her door. "What are you going to do, Principe? She's seen things she shouldn't."

"What I always do, Alexis. Put the needs of my clan first."

She walked upstairs with a heavy heart and knocked on their bedroom door. When she received no welcome, she walked in and found Amelia standing by the window, looking out absently.

"Amelia, we need to talk about what happened."

Much to her surprise, Amelia spun around with a look of fury on her face. "Yes, we do need to talk, and talk now. Why are people trying to harm you and your family? How can Sera fight like she did? She was so fast and so strong—fighting off those people was easy for her, not to mention your bodyguard, Bhal, who wields a medieval looking sword like some kind of ancient warrior. It's *crazy*. Everything about your life is strange and you are not telling me the truth."

This was what Byron was frightened of—Amelia finding out some of the things she was hiding for her own protection. But if she thought those things were strange, what would she think of the fact Byron and her family were immortal vampires?

Maybe she can't handle the truth, Byron thought sadly. She walked over to Amelia and cupped her cheek, but Amelia batted her hand away.

"No, Byron. I need answers. I've been driving myself crazy trying to work out all these strange little things about you, and about everyone around you. Where do you disappear to all the time? It can't be business every time. We get close, you run, and then come back to me as if you were high almost. Are you into drugs?"

"Amelia, please, don't be—"

"Don't tell me not to be silly. You have people coming and going from your office at all times of the day, staff walking around with injuries all the time—it's…weird. And why don't I know anything about your past? It's like you have a double life. Do you have a wife somewhere that I don't know about?"

This was the argument Byron had always feared would come about. "Don't be ridiculous. I have no other woman but you."

Tears started to roll down Amelia's cheeks. "Then why don't you trust me? I trust you, Byron. I love you. Do you love me? You've never said it."

Sadness enveloped Byron. Everything was unravelling in front of her. Amelia loved her and that felt wonderful, but it was also terrifying, because if she told Amelia the truth—that she loved her—it would destroy Byron when Amelia rejected her. And she was sure Amelia would reject her when she found out she was a monster that humans feared. A vampire.

The time she had always known might come had arrived. Her heart was breaking at the thought of manipulating her lover, but she had no choice. Byron grasped Amelia's head in her hands and looked deeply into her eyes.

"Amelia, I want you to forget about everything that happened tonight, and all your confusion, questions, and worries. We will have a wonderful end to our holiday, and you will go home happy."

She was shocked when Amelia pushed her off. "What are you talking about? You think I'm just going to forget everything that has happened tonight? You're off your rocker."

Byron staggered back a few steps, stunned and confused. She had just tried to compel Amelia and she couldn't. That had never happened before to her. She was the strongest vampire in existence and could compel humans and turned vampires with ease, except…

There was one person the leader of the Debrek clan couldn't compel, so her father and mother explained, and that was her Principessa, her destined spouse.

She thought of Rose, and her prediction that her Principessa would find her one day.

It couldn't be. Byron felt out of control. She had to get out.

"I have to go. I'll talk to you later."

When she walked away, Amelia said angrily, "That's it, run away like you always do. I can't live like this, Byron. You have to be honest with me."

Byron didn't look back, but paused at the door and said, "Later. I'll try."

"There may not be a later."

❖

Byron walked into her conference room and found Alexis, Bhal, and a moody looking Sera waiting for her. She calmly walked over to where her sister was sitting and stood behind her chair. "Could you give my sister and me a few minutes, please?"

Alexis got up straight away, but Bhal looked more reluctant. "Principe, I—"

Byron merely said coldly, "Bhal, leave us."

Bhal bowed her head this time and said, "Yes, Principe."

When they were alone, Byron walked to the head of the table but still remained silent. She could feel Sera's pulse and her rarely beating heart thud.

"Byron? Please talk to me."

Byron flashed over to her in a millisecond and slammed her hand down on the table sharply. "Do you have any comprehension about what you've caused, Sera?"

"I just wanted to show Amelia a good time. I know she was feeling hidden away here. I thought we'd have fun."

"She was meant to be hidden away here, Sera. If no one knew we were together, then she wasn't in danger. This holiday was to find out if I could let Amelia into our world, into my life. The first time I've ever let someone so deeply into my heart, and in one evening you expose her to the Dreds, and your vampire abilities."

Sera held her face in her hands. "I just wanted to bond with her and have fun. I realized how much you cared for her when we had dinner, and I wanted to get to know her, and make her feel welcome."

"You never think about the consequences, Sera. Immortality is just one long party to you."

"I enjoy my abilities. What's wrong with that? You always act as if you are ashamed of them. You always keep your vampire side and your emotions locked up so tight, that you let life pass you by. That's why I was so happy you found Amelia."

Byron said nothing, but her thoughts were filled with the reasons why she kept such strict control on herself. Only Bhal knew that pain, and she did not want to share it with her sister. She didn't reply, just shouted for Alexis and Bhal to return. When they did Alexis laid out photographs of the dead vampires, and they showed the black Dred tattoo on their shoulders.

Byron said, "They are Dreds. There's no doubt Victorija is making her first moves."

"There's something else, Principe," Bhal said.

"What?"

Alexis laid out a picture of Amelia and Byron together.

Byron sank to her seat, almost in defeat. "They know."

Sera jumped in and said, "Can't you just compel Amelia to forget about what she saw and lie low for a bit?"

Byron closed her eyes for a moment and said, "I can't compel her. I just tried."

Bhal and Alexis looked at her in disbelief, then lowered their heads, knowing what this meant.

"I have to end it," Byron said, gulping down her growing emotional distress.

"You can't," Sera said. "You love her, Byron."

"That's exactly why I have to let her go. I should have known never to let anyone close, because humans break and then they break our hearts."

Sera had tears rolling down her cheeks, but Bhal and Alexis looked at Byron with admiration.

"You're doing a noble thing, Principe," Bhal said.

Byron got up and walked to the door. "Alexis, get Miss Honey a first class ticket to London for tomorrow. One way."

"Yes, Principe."

Byron walked out of the conference room fighting to stop her emotions from overwhelming her. Somewhere inside she'd known this was inevitable. She wasn't good enough for Amelia, and if Victorija ever hurt her, she knew she would lose her perfect control and destroy everything that the Debreks stood for. She had to make the hard choices to put Amelia and her clan first, and that meant walking away.

❖

Amelia lay in bed, her eyes puffy from crying, praying that Byron would come back to her, apologize, and tell her the truth. Everything she had seen and heard whirled around her mind and she just couldn't make sense of it. It had crossed her mind that perhaps the Debreks weren't bankers after all. Maybe they were criminals? Why else would they need security armed to the teeth, and fear being attacked? But then she dismissed the thought. Debrek banks were everywhere.

She jumped when the bedroom door opened and Byron walked in sheepishly. "May I talk to you?"

"If you want." Amelia got up and saw Byron's eyes devour her body in the new lingerie she was wearing, and despite everything that had gone on, her body responded to Byron, as it always did. It was like she had no control.

Byron appeared distressed, tense, and emotional, not her usual controlled demeanour. Amelia stopped in front of her and said, "Well?"

Byron gulped hard. "I came here to tell you that whatever happens from now on, whether you forgive me or not, everything I've done or will do is because—" Byron looked down.

"Because what, Byron?"

She watched Byron take a breath, stand a little taller, and say, "Because I love you. I think I've loved you since I first set eyes on you."

Amelia's heart soared, and she momentarily forgot about all their other trouble. She had dreamed about Byron saying those words. "I love you, Byron. I wanted to say it for so long, but I was worried I'd scare you away."

Byron raised her hand and cupped her cheek. "You're so beautiful."

Amelia melted into Byron's touch, and her overwhelming emotions couldn't be stopped. They came together in a desperate passionate kiss. Byron kissed her like it was her last, and Amelia met her with equal passion.

They pulled at each other's clothes desperately, needing to feel skin. Byron walked them to the bed, tasting and kissing all the way. Amelia lay down on the bed, and Byron frantically pulled off her trousers, and joined Amelia.

Amelia pulled Byron back into a passionate kiss. She wanted to lose herself in their passion and not think about everything that was so confusing and worrying. She grasped Byron's hand and put it on her breast. Amelia groaned into their kiss as Byron squeezed. Byron pulled back and said emotionally, "I love you—I love you, mia cara."

"I love you, Byron. I've loved you for so long."

Byron licked and kissed around the mark on her throat, while she gently grasped Amelia's sex. Every time they made love, Byron concentrated on her neck, and Amelia wondered why. She pulled Byron's head up and was sure she saw the red glints she had seen a couple of times before.

"Sweetheart, tell me why you like to kiss and bite me there."

Byron looked almost dazed as she thought about her answer. "I want to taste you. I always want to taste you."

"Taste me, then. Tonight, we're holding nothing back."

"I can't. I would hurt you," Byron said.

"How could you hurt me? Taste me like you want to. I want you to be free. I won't break," Amelia said firmly.

Her words must have hit home because Byron pushed two fingers inside her making her gasp. In return she pulled Byron's head down into the crook of her neck.

"Taste me. Like you want to," Amelia said, wrapping her legs around Byron's thighs.

"Want to...*can't*." Byron groaned.

Amelia didn't know why, but as her orgasm built it seemed to be important for Byron to taste her skin.

"Just a little, Byron."

Amelia felt a sharp scratch and Byron give her neck a long lick. Her sex responded and she grasped at Byron's short hair.

Byron groaned. "Need to stop."

"Kiss me. I'm going to come," Amelia begged.

Byron raised her head but she had her eyes closed, and some blood smeared on her lips. She appeared dazed.

Amelia didn't know what to think. All she cared about was Byron's lips on hers while she came. Byron licked her lips, and Amelia said, "I'm coming, kiss me now."

She pulled Byron's head down, and their lips and teeth clashed. Amelia didn't stop the kiss. She held Byron tight between her legs, and came with a force that she had never experienced. Her whole body tingled, and it didn't seem to end for minutes.

As she came down from the high, she heard Byron whisper, "Don't ever doubt I love you."

❖

Amelia woke up and stretched her pleasantly sore muscles. She grimaced slightly when she felt the slight sting on her neck. Last night had been so intense, so real. Byron had even nipped her lip in their desperate kisses.

She looked to her side and didn't find Byron in her bed, as usual, but that didn't matter. Byron had said she loved her, and spent the night showing Amelia what was in her heart.

The strange events from last night started to return to her mind, and threatened to ruin her happiness. Flashes of Sera fighting with those men and women who attacked them made a knot of worry twist inside her. If she thought too hard at the almost inhuman strength and skill both Sera and Bhal had used, she would have to face truths about Byron and her family that would change everything Byron had shared with her last night.

Amelia closed her eyes and thought hard. She could go downstairs, find her lover, pretend like nothing out of the ordinary happened, and enjoy a loving, happy day, or she could demand answers to the questions she had asked Byron last night, and risk ruining everything. Their love, their happiness, their future.

Her heart gave her the answer. *Let it go.* If she wanted a future with Byron, she had to let it go.

Amelia had grown unaccustomed to sweeping thoughts and feelings under the carpet. But at home when she was growing up, she'd ignored the feeling that she was unwanted and unloved by her mum and dad, and most of all, she'd hidden her sexuality that was screaming at her to get out of the stifling religious home she was living in.

Let it go. She let the memory of Byron's declaration of love drive out all her worries and concerns.

She got up and walked to the wardrobe to get her dressing gown, and found it half empty. Byron's suits, shirts, and ties were gone. A feeling of dread crept upon her. Amelia ran to the chest of drawers, and yanked open the drawers. They were empty too.

"No, no." Panic was starting to overtake her, and then she spotted it—a white envelope sitting on the writing desk. She rushed over and read the front: *Miss Amelia Honey.*

Amelia picked up the letter and started to open it, her hand shaking as she did. When Amelia pulled out the paper an airline ticket came tumbling out with it. She was so scared of what the letter would say, she had to force herself to read.

Amelia,

First of all you must believe that the time we have spent together has been the happiest of my life, but I have come to the decision that it is best for both of us to part ways. A relationship is incompatible with my way of life, and I could not give you what you need.

Amelia felt the blood drain from her body and she sank to her knees. Her heart felt like it was being crushed and she could hardly breathe. Tears tumbled onto the paper as she read the rest.

I thought it best for us to make our parting as quick and painless as possible. Early this morning Sera, I, and the rest of my household decamped to my New York residence. You will find a first class plane ticket home with this letter.

I hope you will one day realize that this was for the best, and make a life of your own. I will always remember you fondly, Miss Honey, my shining girl.

Byron

Amelia ripped the letter into pieces in a frenzy and collapsed onto the floor, her heart painfully breaking.

"I love you! How could you do this?"

Amelia convulsed in tears, while hugging herself tightly. Byron's letter felt like she had ripped Amelia's heart out with her bare hands, and crushed it before her eyes.

The bottom had dropped out of her world, and she had no idea how she could go on.

CHAPTER ELEVEN

London
Six months later

Amelia finished dressing and sat at her dressing table to put on her make-up. It was the last thing she wanted to do at six thirty on a Monday morning, but she had to at least make an effort to look her best at work. The things she always took pleasure in—fashion, make-up, and looking good—held little appeal any more.

She gazed out her bedroom window and saw grey skies and the rain bouncing off the window. Perfect.

The weather could have been a metaphor for her life. Miserable, grey, and depressing. This morning gave Amelia even more reason to feel depressed. Six months ago this very day, Byron, the love of her life, unceremoniously dumped her and sent her on the first plane home.

For what seemed like the billionth time, she felt tears filling her eyes. "No, don't do this again."

She was sick of feeling sad, unloved, not good enough, all the things that her break-up with Byron had caused her to feel.

Amelia tried to remember the advice her Uncle Simon gave her: *When you're in pain, put on your sexiest shade of lipstick, smile your best smile, and show the world it can't keep you down.*

She wanted more than anything to move on and get rid of this pain, but it seemed impossible. Amelia started to put on her make-up as quickly as possible. She picked up her powder case and dabbed her face, but then her eyes were drawn to her neck. She let out a sigh.

"Will this bloody thing ever heal?"

The nip Byron had given her on her neck the last few times they made love never seemed to clear up. It remained red and raised and the two pinprick wounds that she had never quite understood refused to heal.

As time went by she began to resent it and its very sight made her angry. Every time she looked in the mirror, she was reminded of Byron—her secrets and her strange life that she never could quite understand. She never did allow herself to dwell on the catalogue of strangeness that she had seen and heard in Monaco. If she did, she knew it would only make things worse, so she shut it out of her brain.

The only thing she couldn't avoid was the bite mark on her neck. People commented on it all the time. She had made lots of excuses, but the truth was she didn't understand it herself. She had come to look at it like a symbol. It wouldn't heal just like her heart.

Stop it, Amelia chastised herself. She was getting lost in her melancholy thoughts again. She quickly powdered the wound, as she did every morning, to try to make it less noticeable, and finished getting ready.

Amelia stepped out into the cold, bleak morning, and put up her umbrella. She used to enjoy this little time to herself in the morning. She would put her earphones on, listen to her favourite songs, and read all the morning news on her iPhone as she travelled by Tube into central London.

Now every song reminded her of love, and her broken heart, so she got on the Tube and sat in silence until she arrived at her stop. As she walked out of the station, she was sure she could feel someone watching her. She quickly looked around but saw nothing. It was a strange feeling, and she had felt it often over the past few months, but had just brushed it off as her overactive imagination.

The London streets were busy, and people around her rushed as they tried to get to their destinations and out of the rain. Up ahead she saw the only slightly bright part of her morning, the little coffee stand on the corner that she stopped at every morning before work.

It had been taken over by a new owner six months ago. The new owner, Wilder, was a lesbian and tried to chat her up and make her smile every morning. Nothing much made her smile these days, but Wilder tried her best.

She walked up to the stand, and funnily enough, despite its popularity amongst the office workers around here, she never had to wait in line.

Wilder had her back to her, cleaning her machine and singing along to a song on the radio. She stopped as if she could sense her, and said without turning, "It's my sweet little ray of sunshine." She turned around and gave Amelia a bright smile.

"I'm no ray of sunshine, Wilder."

Wilder leaned on the van in front of her and winked. "Of course you are, so how's tricks?"

"Just the same as any other morning. How's business?"

It was such a shame. At any other point in Amelia's life she would have been more than happy to return Wilder's flirtations. She was a well-built, gorgeous butch whose slouchy jeans hung just the right way on her hips, and her sandy-blond hair and blue eyes would melt any girl's heart. In fact, she was everything Byron was not.

Where Byron was dapper, precise in her dress and manner, Wilder was rumpled and looked as if she had pulled on whatever clothes were on the floor that morning, but somehow the look was perfectly endearing on her, and the black ink Celtic tattoos on her arms were very sexy.

Daisy had encouraged her to go out with her, even if it wasn't anything serious, but after Byron she couldn't imagine anyone else ever touching her again, and what's more, she would never let anyone into her heart again.

"Business is always good. Everyone wants a wink and a smile from Wilder with their coffee."

Amelia smiled for the first time in a while. "I bet they do."

Wilder gave her another wink for that. "So, usual, darlin'?"

"Yes, please." Amelia took out her purse and lifted two packets of sugar and a plastic spoon from the counter in front of her.

"So, when are you going to come for a drink with me?"

Every morning Wilder would ask her out. It had become a running joke, and each morning Amelia had to come up with an excuse, but today on the half anniversary of her heartbreak, she had to tell the truth.

"I'm sorry, Wilder. I don't know if I'll ever want to go on a date with anyone. I'm damaged goods."

Wilder lost her bravado, and looked almost sad. She handed her the coffee and said, "I'm sorry to hear that. Whoever broke your heart must need their head tested."

"Thank you for making me smile every morning, Wilder. I appreciate it."

"You're welcome, darlin'. If you ever change your mind—"

Amelia stirred in her sugar and smiled. "I know where you are. Have a good day."

"You too, darlin'."

As she walked away, she wondered if she would ever be able to move on with her life. She was quite sure Byron had.

❖

The bright Monaco sun shone through Byron Debrek's bedroom windows, but it did nothing to heat her cold, empty heart. She had managed to stay away from her family estate in Monaco for most of the past six months. She didn't want to revisit the place where she had broken the heart of the only woman she would ever love, but business had forced her back eventually.

She couldn't sleep in this bedroom any more, as she could almost feel the pain Amelia must have felt. The first time she set foot back in here, and found the ripped pieces of the letter she had left, and the jewellery she had bought Amelia sitting on the pillow, it almost destroyed her. She had ordered the room left untouched, and now she came here most days to think of Amelia.

Byron walked over to the bed and picked up the pillow from Amelia's side of the bed. It was her daily ritual. She might not be able to hold her ex-lover, but at least she could feel close and inhale her beautiful scent. She put her arms around the pillow and pulled it to her face and smelled—nothing but laundry detergent.

Her fury rose in an instant. She dashed out of the room to the top of the stairs, and bellowed down to the staff going about their business downstairs, "Who washed this? I ordered my bedroom remain untouched!"

She felt a mixture of anger and panic. It was the last thing she had of Amelia, and now it was gone. The attendants looked up at her with worried faces, as she ripped the pillow apart and all the feathers fell lightly through the air. She dropped what was left of the pillow and sped downstairs at unbelievable speed. The staff stood still and nervously waited for her to enter the lift.

Byron gazed at herself in the mirrored interior of the lift. Her eyes were blood red, her fangs had erupted, and blue veins protruded from her temples, giving her a wild and dangerous look.

She leaned her forehead against the mirrored surface and smashed her fist into the wall, making a big dent in the metal. It was bad enough to feel the pain of losing her lover, but to feel the guilt of hurting Amelia was destroying the last goodness inside of her.

In the last six months she had been changing, every day that passed without Amelia. She had become harder and less emotionally connected to the humans around her. When she took blood, she was inconsiderate and bad tempered and took too much a good deal of the time. She had even started having dreams about hunting down her prey, and gorging on their warm blood until they were drained.

In essence she was scared she was losing herself to the darkness. The monster Byron believed rose inside her, and that she had spent centuries keeping in check, was winning the war of control.

The lift reached the basement and she walked into her office. She needed some connection with Amelia, something just to calm her soul.

Byron sat at her desk and said, "Call Bhaltair."

Bhal's face appeared on one of the screens on her wall. She bowed her head to Byron and said, "Principe."

"Good to see you, Bhal. How is London?" Byron asked. London was another place she avoided like the plague. For any pressing business there she sent her cousin Angelo.

"Cold and rainy as usual, Principe," Bhal said.

Byron sighed. "I miss it. There's nothing quite like a British rain."

Bhal smiled. "Too true. How can I help, Principe?"

Byron took a cigar from the oak box as her side and tapped it against the desk, trying to seem as nonchalant as she could be. "How is your assignment?"

"How is she, you mean?" Bhal said.

She lit her cigar and sucked the calming smoke into her lungs. "How is Amelia?"

Byron had not just dumped Amelia and run. She had assigned Bhal and a few of her warriors to watch over her and protect her if any Dreds turned up looking for her. Byron tried to call as little as possible, because any contact with Amelia, be it direct or indirect, caused her pain, but today she needed to be closer.

"Amelia is safe. I watch over her and I have someone make contact with her each day. It's six months today since you sent me on this assignment, you know."

"What do you mean by that?" Byron said.

"Simply that if the Dreds were going to target her, they probably would have by now. Maybe it's time to bring this assignment to an end."

"No!" Byron insisted. "If I ask you to watch her, then that's what you will do."

Bhal bowed her head. "Of course I will, Principe. You know that. I'm simply trying to make a point."

"And what is that?"

"That you can't let her go," Bhal said.

Byron stubbed out her cigar and went over to pour a large glass of whiskey. That was exactly what she feared. As long as her people were watching over Amelia, Byron was connected to her, but if she pulled them out it really would be goodbye, and if she said goodbye, then Byron might lose herself completely.

She gulped back the fiery malt whiskey and immediately poured another, her hand shaking and clinking the glass. *I need to feed, need to feed.*

"Are you quite well, Principe?" Bhal sounded concerned.

"Of course. I just need to feed," Byron said more harshly than she meant.

There was a heavy silence for a time. Byron was quite aware that Bhal knew her struggles with the darkness in her youth, but she did not want to worry her, or admit to that.

"She still has your mark on her neck." Bhal filled the silence. "It never healed. You know what that means?"

Every sign was pointing to Amelia being her Principessa. Her inability to compel her, and her mark, her bite, not healing. She hadn't even fully bitten Amelia, only tasted her blood, but still her mark stayed upon her neck. That meant their DNA was compatible. Unusual for a human and vampire.

"Whatever it means, Bhal, I can't explore it. Her life is more important to me than my feelings."

"Maybe if you spoke to the Grand Duchess—"

"No," Byron said firmly. "Keep a close eye on her. I'll be in touch."

Byron ended the call and opened the photographs on her mobile phone. She skipped to the pictures of them on the beach. Her body, her heart, her blood, every fibre of her being called for Amelia, and she couldn't have her.

Byron stared at the picture of them in a tight embrace, and felt her anger rising. She threw the phone against the wall. It hit so hard, it smashed a hole through the plaster. Byron looked down at her shaking hands and had the sensation of the monster, the darkness inside her, spreading through her veins. She was shaking apart inside, and she needed blood.

There was a knock at her office door. "Come."

Katie came through the door with a concerned look on her face. "I heard a crash. Is everything okay, Principe?"

Byron's gaze went straight to Katie's pulse point, and her teeth erupted. *Feed.* She reminded Byron so much of Amelia, that when her eyes were clouded with the need for blood, it was dangerous for her to be around the human woman. *I want to drain you.*

"I need to feed."

Katie walked in and undid the top button of her blouse.

"No, not you. Get me someone else, now!"

Katie looked a little hurt. "I can help—"

Luckily Alexis walked into her office at the right time. "Principe—"

"Get Katie away from me."

Byron was fighting her hunger hard. The monster inside her wanted, no, was demanding Amelia, but since she didn't have her, Katie would do. She knew if she started to feed on Katie she might not stop.

Alexis took Katie by the arm and pulled her away. "Katie, move now."

Katie looked angrily at Alexis and stormed off.

"Duca, I need to feed, and don't send a female."

"Of course. Byron, there is something happening to you, isn't there? I've seen you change since—"

"Get me food!" Byron roared, and then immediately held her head in her hands. She never referred to humans as simply food.

"I'm sorry, Alexis," Byron said with desperation in her voice.

"Let me help, Principe."

"You can. My hunger and my darkness are getting harder to control. Don't let me feed from Katie. No matter what the consequences are. She and her parents mean too much to my family. Promise me, Alexis."

Alexis walked up to her desk, and said with complete certainty, "Principe, I will die before I let you feed on Katie. I promise you that."

Byron breathed a sigh of relief knowing Alexis understood the darkness she was fighting. As Alexis was leaving, Byron said, "I should have taken my own advice, Duca."

Alexis turned back and said, "What was that?"

"Humans break, and then they break our hearts."

The household was sent into a tailspin when, in an unprecedented move, Victorija Dred arrived at the harbour seeking a meeting with Byron. Victorija hadn't set foot in the Debrek estate since she was a child, five hundred years ago. While Alexis advised against meeting, Byron decided they should meet again.

Byron made do with bottled blood.

Sera and some guards were keeping their guest company in the drawing room. When Byron got up there and walked into the room, she found Sera giving a grinning Victorija a deadly stare. The silence was deafening.

When Victorija saw her she smiled and said sarcastically, "Byron, thank God. You have saved me from your sister's sparkling conversation."

"Victorija, to what do we owe this pleasure?"

Victorija stood and opened her arms in an apparently warm family greeting. Byron ignored her and simply took a seat in the armchair by the fire. Sera stood by her left hand side in support.

"Is that really the way to greet your cousin?" Victorija said with mock hurt in her voice.

Victorija was her cousin twice removed and her senior by several generations, but the difference in the way they presented themselves made Victorija appear younger than her.

Byron crossed her legs and fought every urge she had for blood to appear calm and in control. "Forgive me if I don't find the family concern sincere since we haven't had so much as a Christmas card in centuries."

Victorija took a seat, and a human female, whom she had brought and who looked dazed and was probably compelled, sat on the arm beside her.

"Byron, please, I come here in good faith, without my Duca or any protection, simply to talk."

Byron flourished her hand and said, "Then talk."

"Very well, firstly I must apologize for not coming to see you sooner after my ascension to Principe, but my father's passing was such a shock and strain on the clan."

"I can quite imagine." Byron played along, but she knew from her own intelligence that the Dreds had spent the time building up their vampire army and resources.

Victorija continued, "Secondly, I see no reason why we have to have the same family hostility as our elders. We may have branched off and gone our separate ways, but we are family, we share the same DNA, the same history."

As conciliatory as that statement was meant to sound, what Victorija was really saying was, the Debreks were her family too, and she had as much claim to the Debrek birthright as Byron. In other words, their secret of reproduction.

That one tool gave the Debreks an edge over every vampire clan on the planet. Each new generation of born Debrek vampires was more powerful than the last, making Byron stronger than her older cousin.

"As you say, we have a history in common but different ideals," Byron said.

The issue of taking blood by consent had ripped apart the Debrek clan, and two brothers—Byron's great-grandfather, Antoine, and Victorija's father, Gilbert.

Upon becoming Principe, Antoine vowed to continue the clan tradition of taking blood only by consent, but Gilbert did not agree, and thus started a civil war, leading to Gilbert's ousting from the Debrek clan.

Victorija took the arm of the human beside her and let her fingers trace the veins in her arm. "Different ideals. Quite so."

Byron couldn't help but stare at the young woman's pulse, and felt her mouth start to water. She was so hungry that it felt like pain.

Victorija smiled. "I had heard some disturbing rumours that the great Byron Debrek had met a woman and fallen in love. True?"

Byron's heart started to pound, and it took every inch of her strength to seem uninterested. "A woman? Good God, no. You know what some women are like? You sleep with them twice and they think they are in a relationship with you."

"How true. I tend to drain them of blood and then they become less annoying." Just as she finished her sentence, Victorija sank her teeth into the wrist of her human.

Byron gripped the arms of her chair tightly when the blood started to drip down Victorija's chin.

Keep control, keep control.

Victorija released the woman's wrist with an exaggerated "Ahh!"

Her mouth was gloriously red, and blood dripped off her sharp fangs. The sweet, iron smell was overwhelming. Victorija took a pressed white handkerchief from her pocket and dabbed her mouth.

"Where are my manners?" Victorija said. She held out the woman's arm in Byron and Sera's direction, and said, "Would you care for a bite? She is my portable lunchbox for the day."

Take it, take it now, Byron's darkness screamed.

Sera almost snarled, and obviously sensing her sister's discomfort replied, "No, we do not feed without consent, and we will not take advantage of an innocent woman on our estate."

Victorija pushed the human's wrist away and licked the blood from her fingers slowly. "So sanctimonious, Sera. It makes me want to retch." Turning her attention to Byron she leaned forward and gazed in her eyes. "Are you feeling quite well, Byron? You seem stressed, and dreadfully hungry."

Byron was sure Victorija sensed her struggle with the darkness inside, her deep hunger that couldn't be sated. How she was keeping control she had no idea.

"I'm quite well. Thank you for coming and re-establishing communication between our two clans, but we mustn't keep you."

Thankfully, Victorija got up and buttoned up her black suit jacket. "Very well, places to go, humans to kill, you know how it is." Then she leaned over and whispered, "I can see into your soul, Byron. You're just like me inside, we share the same DNA, and deep down you're scared because you know it's the truth. The need to kill and to drain the life out of a human's body, it's all in you."

Byron felt sick. She used every ounce of control she had left and stood, her height towering over Victorija. "I'm nothing like you, cousin. Now leave my home, and leave the human behind. She doesn't deserve the ending you have planned."

"Take her, you need her more than I do."

In a blink of an eye Victorija was gone, and Byron fell to her knees.

Sera had her arms around her in seconds. "Byron, tell me what you need."

"I need blood—I need lots of blood. The hunger is tearing me apart."

"Duca?" Sera shouted.

Alexis came straight in. "Yes, Sera."

"Bloody Victorija. She did this on purpose. Byron is beyond hunger. I'll take care of our human guest, but please take care of Byron."

"Of course."

CHAPTER TWELVE

The workroom of Grenville and Thrang was alive with the noise of sewing machines and the chatter of the staff. Amelia smiled as she walked towards her apprentice, Daisy MacDougall. This was the one part of her life where she could find solace and some kind of happiness.

She had thrown herself into her work in the past six months. Amelia thought if she kept busy, she might just keep her sanity, and her hard work was paying off. Her new ideas and clients were keeping Grenville and Thrang a thriving business.

This morning she and Daisy had been cutting and then pinning together material for a new VIP client, and Amelia had volunteered to get the coffee.

"Here you go, Daisy. Let's take a break."

"Just a sec," Daisy said through a mouthful of pins.

Daisy pinned the top part of the sleeve on the mannequin, then set her tape measure and things aside. She took a seat next to Amelia and kicked off her heels.

"You've done really well today, Daisy. Your cutting is excellent, and I don't think you need me standing over you any more."

Daisy eyes lit up. She was so enthusiastic and fun to have around, and she brought laughter to the stuffy male-dominated workroom. She sat down beside Amelia and took her mug of coffee from her.

"How was your weekend?" Amelia was always interested to hear about Daisy's adventurous private life, since she had none.

"It was great fun. My friends and I took our cameras to an old graveyard and recorded all night."

Amelia chuckled. "I'm sorry, Daisy, but that sounds too cold and scary for me."

In Daisy's spare time she and her group of friends ran a YouTube channel that tried to find evidence for the paranormal. It was popular from what she gathered, and she could understand why—Daisy was so intelligent and fun.

"You would love it really. You'll need to come ghost hunting with us sometime. We got some strange noises on tape at the weekend."

"I'll take your word for it."

Daisy picked up her phone and opened her YouTube app. "Look at our trailer for this week's interview. This man works at the local hospital, and says he sells blood bags to vampires."

Amelia nearly spat out her coffee. "Vampires? You mean—"

"The blood sucking kind that live forever? Yeah." Daisy nodded as if it was a completely normal thing to say.

Amelia's stomach flipped for some reason, and her hand went to her neck. "You believe in them?"

Daisy adjusted her thick-black-rimmed glasses, and said simply, "Uh-huh. I have an open mind. Do you never wonder where all these paranormal myths come from? Vampires, werewolves, witches, ghosts—there has to be something in them."

Amelia never really thought about it that way. She had been brought up in a strict Christian household, so anything paranormal, or pagan, was viewed as evil. "I suppose when you put it like that… My parents believed in witches, certainly—they were forever going on about covens of women meeting in the New Forest National Park, and all their evildoing. I always assumed they were just well-intentioned New Age people."

Daisy became animated. "Oh no, they are definitely witches. Not evil, but witches. We filmed a show on the New Forest witches for my channel."

"Good God, you learn something new every day." Amelia couldn't shake this uneasy feeling she had. "I'll need to have a watch of some of your videos."

"You should. Have you never seen something you just couldn't explain?" Daisy said.

"No," she said a little too quickly. "Never."

Even as she said that, she saw herself standing in the alley in

Monaco, watching Byron's sister fighting like some kind of superhero, and the deep red hunger she had seen in Byron's eyes.

"Well, I bet you would enjoy the subjects. I'll email you the link. So? Did Wilder try her luck again this morning?"

Amelia sighed. "Yes, she's so sweet and persistent. I hate letting her down every day, but I just can't any more."

Daisy covered her hand and gave it a squeeze. "It was half a year ago, wasn't it?"

Amelia nodded. She hadn't told anyone the details of what happened with Byron, not even her uncle Jaunty. All he and those closest to her knew was that Byron broke it off, and she was heartbroken.

Daisy cleared her throat and said gently, "Amelia, I know I don't have a lot of experience in these sorts of things, but maybe you should use this day as some sort of closure."

Closure…was that even possible when you had lost the love of your life? She doubted it, but one thing she knew was she was not the same gullible, innocent girl Byron Debrek met, and had falling at her feet. No, she was never going to be made a fool of with her heart again, because she was never going to give her heart away again.

Her hurt had turned to anger, and it was the anger she was sure wouldn't allow her to move on. Maybe Daisy was right. Maybe this was a sign.

Amelia took a final sip of her coffee and slammed the cup down on the workbench, then stood up purposefully. "I think you might be right, Daisy. I think I need to start living again. Byron Debrek is in my past and I need to leave her there."

Daisy stood up just as enthusiastically, and was just about to say something when Amelia bent over clutching her neck.

"What's wrong? What's happening?" Daisy held Amelia in her arms.

"My neck, it's hurting." Amelia had felt discomfort coming from the mark on her neck since returning to London, but never this hot, searing pain before. She took a huge breath and staggered over to one of the workroom mirrors. Everyone in the room had stopped what they were doing, and had their eyes trained on her.

She looked in the mirror and saw the mark on her neck had become red and angry.

Daisy's face appeared behind her in the reflection. "What are you loo—" Daisy must have seen the mark because she stopped midsentence and then said, "You still have that?"

"Yes, it never healed properly, but it's never hurt like this—"

Another wave of pain hit her, and all she could hear was Daisy saying, "I'll get your uncle Jaunty."

❖

Byron had been watching her prey from the back of the dimly lit bar for the past twenty minutes. After slipping from her home, and evading her security, she'd spotted her prey and followed her into a bar.

The provocation from Victorija and her hunger had driven Byron to the edge. The monster inside her was demanding blood and a kill, but she still had some control in her foggy brain, so she thought going through the motions might calm her need to hunt.

She finished her drink in one gulp, and walked over to the bar, where the woman was sitting. She had Amelia's colouring and was close to her build, but was not Amelia.

"Excuse me, may I buy you a drink?" Byron asked.

The woman turned around, and she smiled shyly at Byron. "Uh, hi. Yes, thank you. A vodka and Coke, please."

Byron got that tingle in her stomach that she had felt long ago, the feeling of hunting prey. She looked over to the barman and said, "A vodka and Coke and the same again for me, please."

"Right away, Ms. Debrek," the barman said.

That was the drawback of fame, when you wanted anonymity. Everyone knew who she was in this town.

"You're *the* Byron Debrek? The billionaire?"

What was the need to lie? She could compel her to forget anyway. *Or to die*, the voice inside her said.

"The banker, yes. May I know your name?" Byron asked.

"Angelica," she said, blushing.

Who could be better prey than an innocent, sweet girl? After all, that was what she was craving—her own innocent, sweet girl, Amelia.

Their drinks arrived, and Byron said, "To you, Angelica."

The tingle inside her was growing and growing. She caressed Angelica's face and neck with her gaze. She could hear the blood rushing around her body, and she could almost taste how sweet her blood would be.

On a whim, Byron cupped Angelica's cheek and looked deep into her eyes to compel her. "Tell me, Angelica, what brings you to a bar midafternoon?"

Angelica stared right back at her, slightly dazed. "I've just come from a job interview. I didn't get the job, and it was my last hope to pay the rent this month."

"How long since you've had a job?" Byron asked.

"Ever since I got pregnant last year. I was a dancer at a club, and as soon as they found out I was pregnant, they let me go."

Not her. It can't be her, Byron told herself repeatedly. This woman already had enough difficulties, but Byron's hunger was demanding.

"Tell me, who do you have at home?" Byron asked. Maybe if she kept talking she could stop herself.

"Just my little girl," she said.

Byron was fighting her hunger, and losing. She reached out and grabbed Angelica's wrist, then pulled it to her lips. *Bite, drink her. Drink her blood now.* She felt the pressure in her gums as her teeth started to erupt. "I don't want to do this," Byron said painfully.

"What don't you want to do?" Angelica asked.

"Keep talking to me—tell me everything about you. Stop me from hurting you," Byron pleaded.

Under Byron's compulsion, she began to babble about her life like an automaton. The painful hunger Byron was feeling began to take over her senses, and she no longer heard the words Angelica was saying. All she could hear was the blood pumping in her veins.

Byron couldn't stop herself any more. She quite calmly said to Angelica, "You'll stand and quietly follow me out of the bar. You won't look back and you won't struggle."

"I won't look back and I won't struggle," Angelica repeated.

Byron got up, peeled off some money from her wallet, and left it on the bar. She buttoned her jacket, straightened her tie, and walked away from the bar with complete confidence her prey was following.

She walked out into the Monte Carlo afternoon and walked down a side alley of the bar. Angelica arrived beside her, but when she looked at her, she saw Amelia.

"Amelia? You came back to me?"

Now free of compulsion Angelica said, "Who's Amelia?"

In a flash Byron pushed her up against the wall, and she started to struggle and cry. "Please don't hurt me."

But Byron couldn't see through her lust for Amelia's blood. She held her by the throat, and said, "I need you so much, mia cara. I'm so very hungry."

"Please don't hurt me. I have a child—" Angelica's worlds turned into a scream. Byron quickly brought her under control and compelled her to calm.

As soon as she was quiet, Byron was about to strike when she heard a familiar voice through her fog of bloodlust.

"Principe, don't do this. She's not Amelia. You need to fight for control." It was Alexis.

Byron looked at her Duca then back to the woman, who didn't look like Amelia any more, but a stranger.

She released the woman and staggered back. Alexis caught her in her arms, and Byron said, "God, what did I nearly do?"

"You didn't. We'll let her go. I have two male attendants in the car waiting for you. You need to feed, but not on her."

Byron took some deep breaths, and stood up straight. The horror at what she had nearly done made her feel sick, especially remembering the woman's sad life story. Byron closed her eyes for a second, then stood up straighter, fixed her tie, and willed her vampire features to recede.

"Alexis, thank you for finding me. I'm back in control."

"Go back to the car and feed, Principe. I'll take care of the human."

Byron nodded but her guilt twisted in her gut. "Alexis, her name is Angelica. She has a child. Find out her details, pay off her debts, and make sure she has a very healthy bank balance by the end of the day. Make sure she and her child's future are secure. I am in her debt."

"She will be taken care of, Principe. Go and feed."

As Byron walked to the car all she saw in her head was Amelia. How could she control this unstoppable urge to feed from Amelia? The blood of others only took the edge off her hunger, and the hunger was driving her to darkness.

Byron couldn't risk another day like today. She had to find a way to conquer this.

Maybe Bhal was right. Maybe she needed to visit the Grand Duchess.

❖

Amelia sat on the couch in her Uncle Jaunty's office, holding an ice pack to her neck. Daisy brought her a cold bottle of water. "Here, drink this."

Uncle Jaunty was kneeling in front of her, holding her hand. "How is the pain now, sweetie?"

"Better," Amelia said.

The burning in her neck wasn't exactly simply pain, but she couldn't quite explain the ache inside that accompanied it. The impulse, the need inside to fulfil something she couldn't understand.

"Is it a burn? How did it happen, Amelia?" Jaunty asked.

"It looked to me more like a bite," Daisy chimed in.

Jaunty pulled the ice pack away from Amelia's neck, and gave her a serious look. "Daisy, could you leave us, please?"

Amelia gave Daisy a nod. The last thing she wanted to do was explain this.

As soon as Daisy left, Jaunty started with his interrogation. "When did you get this?"

What could she say? She couldn't tell her uncle the truth. He wouldn't understand this wasn't something bad. So far she'd managed to cover and conceal it from Jaunty and Simon.

"I can't remember—"

"Did this happen in Monte Carlo? Did Byron do this to you?"

"Uncle Jaunty, it's just a little—"

Jaunty cupped her cheek and looked her right in the eye. "Did Byron ever hurt you?"

Why was her uncle connecting an injury on her neck with her ex who she had broken up with six months ago?

"No, she never hurt me. Not physically anyway. She's your friend—you know she wouldn't do that."

Jaunty stood up abruptly, and started to pace. "I thought she was. She gave me her word she would never let her—" Jaunty hesitated. "You never told me why and how you broke up."

Amelia threw the ice pack onto the couch beside her angrily.

She didn't like talking about this and she didn't like lying and making excuses for her neck as if she was an abuse victim. "Because I didn't and still don't want to talk about it, Uncle Jaunty. Don't you think I've been made to feel enough of a fool by Byron without recounting it to everyone?"

She got up and walked to the window. The rain had stopped and the midafternoon sun was shining down on the wet pavements. She was sick of feeling like this. Stupid, hurt, broken-hearted. Maybe Daisy was right. It was time to move on.

Amelia felt Jaunty's hand on her shoulder. "I'm sorry, sweetie. I know she broke your heart."

"Broke it, smashed it, pulverized it—well, not any more." She turned around quickly and looked at the clock on the wall. It read half past three. "I'm going home early, Uncle Jaunty. I've no other appointments today."

"Of course. Go home and get some rest," Jaunty said.

Rest was the last thing she wanted. Amelia wanted to live again.

Amelia walked out of Grenville and Thrang with new determination. She was going to have fun, and kick Byron Debrek and the pain she brought out of her heart. It was a busy time of day in central London. The pavements were packed with shoppers coming and going, and office workers, and business people rushing from one appointment to another.

Where would she go? She thought of going to a local gay bar and then she thought of Wilder and her coffee truck on the corner.

"Time to tell Wilder I've changed my mind."

Amelia took her sunglasses from her handbag and popped them on. She was filled with new determination to start her life afresh. Whatever was going on with the wound on her neck, she was sure there was a rational explanation. In the meantime she wasn't going to sit at home pining after someone who broke her heart six months ago.

She started to walk down the street, heading to Wilder's coffee stand. After a few paces she heard a scream behind her and turned to see a car driving out of control and coming straight for her. She closed her eyes knowing there was no chance of moving, and then something pushed her clear across the pavement and she crashed to the ground.

She had no idea what had quite happened, but as she came to her senses, pinned down by a body on top of her, she heard the incessant noise of a car alarm, and saw the out-of-control car now crushed into the wall of a building.

She could have been killed.

Panic started to grip her chest and she struggled to get out from under the heavy body on top of her. "I need to get up. Let me up!"

"Shh, I have you, mademoiselle." The vaguely European accent surprised her and she stopped struggling.

The owner of the voice lifted her head and gave her a crooked smile. "That was a rather close one."

Amelia was struck dumb for second or two. Her saviour was female, with a tumble of collar length straw-blond hair, but dark, almost black, eyes. She was unbelievably striking, but there was more. Something about her looks, her bone structure, chimed inside her heart.

The woman stood and offered her hand to Amelia. "Are you unhurt, mademoiselle?"

Amelia allowed herself to be pulled up, all the while trying to work out the puzzle of her recognition.

"I'm okay, I think." She looked down at her body and brushed off the dirt. It was only then that she noticed the mayhem around them— police cars, an ambulance, and they were surrounded by onlookers. "You saved me."

"I'm only too happy to aid a damsel in distress. May I know the name of the beautiful woman whom I have saved?"

Amelia felt dazed, and perceived she must be in some sort of shock, but she couldn't take her eyes away from this striking looking individual. She was dapper, but in her own unique way, wearing a clearly bespoke black suit with a pressed white shirt, no tie, and a wide, open-neck collar.

"Honey—Amelia Honey, sorry," Amelia babbled.

Her saviour gave her the most charming smile, and bowed with a flourish. "Victorija Dred at your service, Mademoiselle Honey, but you can call me Victorija."

CHAPTER THIRTEEN

Victorija waited patiently while Amelia dealt with the police and was checked over by the paramedics, before accompanying her to a local wine bar. Everything about her plan had worked perfectly. One of her turned vampires ran a car straight for Amelia, and Victorija, like a gallant knight, came to her rescue.

The wine bar was cosy, and had an intimate atmosphere. Victorija chose a booth at the back to maintain the utmost privacy. So far her time with Amelia Honey had been pleasant. She could quite see what Byron saw in her.

"I can't believe the driver didn't have a scratch. I mean, he smashed into a wall and—" Amelia blushed and looked down at her wine spritzer. "I'm rambling, aren't I?"

Victorija laughed softly and covered Amelia's hand with hers. "Not at all. You've been through quite a shock. It's not surprising you need to talk, and I find your voice quite delightful."

"You're just being far too polite, I'm sure." Amelia finished her second large glass of wine.

Surprisingly, Victorija wasn't being polite. She had expected Byron's love to be some annoying, tedious woman, but she was delightful, sweet, and innocent. She would take great pleasure in feeding from her.

What folly it was for Byron to leave her unprotected.

Victorija poured her another glass of wine. "Not in the slightest. So, tell me, Mademoiselle Amelia, I know you work for your uncle's tailors, but tell me all about you."

"There's not a lot to tell really," Amelia said.

So bashful, so sweet, I'm going to enjoy this. "There must be. A beautiful woman like you must have an active social calendar."

Amelia's hand went to the bite mark on her neck. Victorija could have laughed out loud. The sanctimonious Byron Debrek couldn't even keep her famous blood control around this woman. Byron didn't simply love this woman. She was her weakness.

"I'm afraid not. I go to work and I go home. Very boring."

Victorija pulled her seat closer, so she was looking directly into Amelia's eyes. She could have so easily compelled her, gotten all the information she wanted, and had her willingly leave with her, but for some reason she wanted this encounter to be real.

"You've been hurt?"

Amelia looked surprised and pulled back.

"I'm sorry, that's very personal, isn't it?" Victorija said. While Amelia contemplated her response, Victorija said, "I know what it's like, you see. I can recognize every shade of pain it's possible to feel."

Victorija's gamble on Amelia's empathy worked when she covered Victorija's hand in sympathy.

"Someone hurt you, Victorija?" Amelia asked.

"A long time ago." *Before I had my heart and humanity beaten out of me.*

Amelia sighed. "Yes, I was very hurt by someone I loved more than anything."

"How long has it been?"

"Six months today. I had just left work early, determined to go out and start afresh, move on, when you rescued me. I'm so sick of feeling miserable and hurt."

Victorija clapped her hands together and smiled. "Then that's what we must do. Allow me to take you out to dinner, and dancing."

"I'd love that, but I think the accident is really hitting me now. I'm exhausted. But could we make it another day?" Amelia said.

"Of course, you name the day and I will take you out and treat you like the lady you are."

She saw Amelia visibly shiver and rub the bite mark on her neck, as if she was in some discomfort.

"I'd like that. How about tomorrow night?" Amelia suggested.

"Perfect."

They exchanged contact details, and Victorija escorted her out and into a taxi, and paid the driver chivalrously. Before she closed the door of the cab, she took Amelia's hand and kissed it softly. "Wonderful to meet you, Mademoiselle Honey. I look forward to taking you out tomorrow."

Amelia gave her the sweetest smile, a smile that stirred something in the blackness of her soul.

"I can't thank you enough for saving my life. I'll be forever grateful."

"You're most welcome."

Amelia tilted her head to the side and said, "There's something so familiar about you, Victorija. I just can't think what it is."

"Really? Strange." Victorija was happy the slight family resemblance was making Amelia more relaxed with her. If only Byron could see her now.

"Goodbye then, Victorija."

Victorija watched the taxi drive off in the early London evening. Almost immediately her Duca was by her side.

"Principe, did everything go well?" Drasas said.

"Perfectly. She is Byron's weakness."

"Why didn't you just compel her and take her?"

Victorija had been asking herself the same thing. "Patience, Drasas. I want Amelia Honey to come to me of her own free will. That will destroy Byron more than simply taking her."

"As you wish, Principe." Drasas signalled and Victorija's limousine pulled up. "You were watched the whole time by Bhaltair and her warrior, Wilder. The Debreks will know you've made contact."

Victorija got into the back of the limo and Drasas sat in the front, beside the driver. There was a human waiting in the back seat for Victorija, and she started to unbutton her blouse. "Just what I want, Drasas. Now I need to feed."

Her hunger was intense after being in Amelia's company, and she needed to lose herself in blood. Her fangs erupted, and she sank them quickly into the compelled human's neck. She imagined what it would be like to feed and drain the woman she had just left, and the mere thought was intoxicating.

❖

The Debrek plane and its crew waited patiently while Byron said goodbye to her sister on the tarmac below.

Byron enjoyed the warmth and comfort of her sister's hug. Apart from her mother, Sera was the only other woman who could safely give her that intimacy now.

Sera pulled back and cupped her cheek. "I'm so happy you're doing this, Byron. I know it's not easy for you to admit there's something wrong, but the Grand Duchess will help you."

Byron nodded. Sera only knew that she was struggling with her hunger and emotions. She didn't know the darkness that was inside her, and how she had struggled against it when she'd ascended and said goodbye to her humanity. That was what she feared, that her bond, her need for Amelia was going to destroy her control and let the monster inside her out.

"I know what I need to do, for the family, the clan, and the business. I'll be as good as new in no time." Byron forced a smile on her face.

"You need to do it for you, Byron."

Byron gave her a final kiss on the cheek and said, "Don't leave here. I can't be worried about you with Dreds swarming all over Europe."

"I promise. I told you, I've learned my lesson."

"Good girl. Goodbye, Sera. *Et sanguinem familiae*—blood and family," Byron said seriously.

Sera smiled and repeated the Debrek motto. "Blood and family."

Byron boarded the plane, followed by Alexis, and they were soon in the air, headed to where it all began for the Debreks—Venice.

❖

The Grand Duchess was as grand as her title. She stood with the aid of her walking stick, gazing at one of the many paintings on the wall of her drawing room, and surrounded by some of the most precious antiques and rare antiquities money could buy, her strings of pearls cascading over her ample bosom. Byron stood by the door, and waited for her to summon her. There was no one in the Debrek clan more revered than this small, white-haired, and richly dressed woman.

"Principe," she said without looking around. "Come here."

Byron walked to her and looked at the painting the Grand Duchess was gazing at.

"Beautiful, isn't it? One of Leonardo's earliest works."

"Yes, his talent was unsurpassed," Byron replied.

"I often wonder what advances we would have made, if he was still alive today. He was the cleverest man I ever knew."

She turned around slowly, leaning on her walking stick, and smiled. "Little Byron, you have grown to be such a strapping, intelligent, moral vampire, what your great-great-grandfather always envisioned for this family's future."

"Thank you, grandmother," Byron said.

The Grand Duchess gave her a pointed look, one that would be enough to frighten most people who were not her close family. Lucia was Byron's great-great-grandmother, but she did not like to be reminded of her age.

Byron smiled and corrected herself. "Sorry. Thank you, Lucia."

"That's more like it. I don't need to be reminded how very, very old I am."

Lucia looped her arm though Byron's, and Byron said, "Please, you look no older than two hundred years."

Lucia pointed her stick to the couch. "Enough flattery, young vampire. I need to sit."

Once they were seated comfortably, Lucia looked deeply into her eyes and said, "You are terribly hungry?"

Byron nodded, and Lucia rang a bell on her side table. A tall elderly man came into the drawing room.

"You rang, Duchess?"

"Yes, Archer, could we have a pot of tea, and a bottle of Debrek Special Reserve?" Lucia said.

Archer bowed his head and smiled. "Of course, Duchess."

"Tell me what's wrong, Byron. Why are you struggling with your hunger so much?"

Byron looked down at her clasped hands, unsure of where to start.

As if reading her mind, Lucia said, "Start at the beginning—start with your young woman."

Lucia always seemed to know everything without being told, which made her the matriarch she was.

"Amelia Honey. She is the niece of my tailor. As soon as I laid eyes on her, my heart was hers."

"Just as Rose always told you," Lucia said.

Byron looked up sharply. "You knew about that?"

"Of course." Such a statement from the Grand Duchess needed no further explanation.

"I tried for the longest time not to go near her. I knew somewhere inside that my love for her would cause hurt and pain, and it has."

"Love is all those things, but if you try to outrun love, she will always catch up with you," Lucia said.

Byron stood and walked over to lean on the fireplace. "My mother told me if I ever fell in love, I would have hunger like I'd never experienced before, but this is different. I had one taste of her blood, just before I left her, and it's been calling me like a drug ever since. Now I can't think of anything else, and it's breaking down my control."

"How so?" Lucia asked.

Byron was quite sure that her great-great-grandmother knew exactly what was happening to her, but thought she needed to verbalize it. "I have an unquenchable hunger for her and her blood, yet my attendants' blood only takes the edge off, never sates it. The hunger is making me want to hunt, to drain, to kill, and my mind is getting so clouded I nearly did. I see Amelia in every woman I see, and I'm going to hurt someone if I can't conquer this."

"You can't conquer love, Byron. This family was born of love."

"It's more than love!" Byron felt her fangs erupt and the veins on the side of her head pop out. "It's a form of madness."

Lucia hit her stick on the floor, and commanded, "Sit."

She sat just as Archer came in with the drinks. He poured out the blood in a glass and served the tea, then left them alone.

Byron drank the blood greedily. "I need you to help me, Lucia. You know what I did the last time I lost control. I don't ever want to hurt people like that again."

Lucia took her hand and squeezed it. "I know. Tell me about her."

"Amelia is beautiful, good. In fact, I think her goodness and innocence are what attracted me to her. She is my shining girl, or was. I can't compel her, and the small bite I gave her won't heal."

Lucia took a sip of tea. "So, her DNA is compatible with yours. She could be your Principessa."

"She could be, but she isn't. I can never take her as such. The Dreds have resurfaced and have been building an army of turned vampires. If they knew I loved this woman—" Lucia seemed quite unperturbed by the news. "Forgive me, Lucia, but you must know all this already."

"Of course. I know everything, as I always told your father when he tried to hide something from me. You tasted her blood?"

Byron hung her head low. "Yes, I didn't mean to, and I didn't hurt her, but we became passionate and my fang pierced her skin. Please, Lucia. You must know a spell to help me control this."

Her great-great-grandmother was not a vampire like the rest of the family, but she was their cornerstone, a witch her great-great-grandfather Cosimo had fallen in love with. Lucia had helped Cosimo introduce the Debrek rule of blood by consent. Everything they had was because of a spell Lucia had cast long ago.

"Do you have the item I asked you to bring?"

Byron reached into her suit pocket and brought out a hairbrush. "This was hers. She left it in my bedroom."

Lucia held the brush and closed her eyes for a moment. She grasped the arm of the couch. "She's here. At last."

"What? Who's here?"

Lucia put the brush down. "You need to go to her. She is the only one who can help you."

"Why?" Byron was confused.

"You must have nicked more than her skin. She already is your Principessa. You are bound in blood and spirit for all eternity."

Byron's stomach dropped. She looked right at her great-great-grandmother. "She shared my blood? How—" Then Byron remembered. During their last fevered lovemaking, she had clashed teeth with Amelia, and she must have sustained a cut. Some of her blood must have transferred when they kissed.

Lucia nodded. "You must protect her at all costs, Byron." From her pocket, Lucia took a silver ring with ancient writing inscribed on it, a blood-red ruby set in its centre. "Give her this, and bring her to me when you can. She has an important future."

❖

Byron sat in the silence of her conference room on her flight home. Her mind was reeling from the information Lucia had given her.

"Principe?" Alexis walked into the room. "Would you like to talk?"

"Sit." Byron pointed to the chair beside her.

"Did the Grand Duchess help you?"

Byron laughed ruefully. "It depends what you mean by help, Duca. She explained what was wrong, what I need to do, and how we need to act, but it's going to be a painful, difficult experience."

"Are we still heading back to Monte Carlo?" Alexis asked.

"Yes, but just briefly to pack. We need to move the household to London."

"Why? I thought you were determined you couldn't see Miss Honey again?"

Byron rubbed her face in her hands and gave a long sigh. "She showed every sign of being compatible with me, with my blood, she could have been my Principessa, but I decided to walk away to protect her. Things are a bit different now."

"What changed, Byron?"

"Computer, display picture of Amelia Honey," Byron said.

The conference screen displayed a picture of Amelia and her the night they had dinner on the beach.

"We are bound in blood and spirit for all eternity."

Alexis eyes went wide with shock. "She's had your blood?"

Byron nodded. "I was so determined that she would not be my Principessa for her own safety, never knowing all this time she already was. It was an accident—it happened on our last night together, I think. I would never knowingly have shared my blood with her, but it happened. She is my Principessa, and we need to protect her at all costs."

"Good God. A human was compatible?" Alexis said.

"It seems so. Lucia was…It was strange. I think my great-great-grandmother knows more than she is saying for the moment."

Byron noticed her hands start to tremble again, and clasped them tightly. The intense hunger was starting to return, and she had fed as soon as she had gotten on the plane.

"Well, at least we know how to help you, Byron. You need to feed from the Principessa."

Byron laughed. "What am I meant to do, Alexis? Turn up after six months and say, Sorry about breaking your heart and everything, but can I drink your blood?"

"I take your point." Alexis got up and poured them both a drink. "One thing is for sure, Byron, you need her blood or you will begin to lose who you are."

Byron took the glass of whiskey and sipped it. "I need to handle this carefully. I don't know if she will even talk to me. Bhal says she has been very hurt these past months."

Alexis said, "We should take Katie to London. She and Amelia bonded well, and if there's one thing Katie can do, it's talk. Maybe she could help pave the way."

"Good idea. This stays between you and me, Duca. If Victorija was to realize Amelia's extra importance—"

"It wouldn't be good," Alexis finished for her.

"We'll reopen the Debrek London mansion, and base ourselves there," Byron said.

Alexis looked at her with shock. "Are you sure?" It had been a long time since they had set foot in there, and a lot of terrible memories lived in that house. It was there that, by Victorija's hand, both Byron and Alexis had lost women they'd cared about.

"Yes." Byron put her hand on Alexis's shoulder. "I know it will be hard for both of us, you more than anyone, but it's time to move on, and we need somewhere secure for Amelia to come to, if she'll see me."

Alexis gulped hard, but said nothing. Byron knew she had shut down her emotions a long time ago, after that fateful night at the London house. Maybe this would be good for all of them.

CHAPTER FOURTEEN

The next day Amelia was excited for the first time in ages. After work, an attractive woman was taking her out. It was nice to feel optimistic for a change. Victorija had arranged to meet her straight from work, so Amelia was getting ready in one of the changing rooms, while Daisy helped tidy up.

Amelia realized she'd need Daisy to zip her into her dress. As she looked in the mirror, she remembered the last time she had worn a dress like this. It was in Monaco, and Byron had been the one to do the zip.

She closed her eyes and remembered Byron, who had just gotten dressed, but with her tie still hanging loose around her neck, walking over to her with that hungry look she always had on her face.

How could Byron have felt that way about her and just left? Amelia had tried to work it out in the months that had passed. Had it been an act? Did she really not have that desperate need for her?

Amelia felt breath on her bare shoulder, and opened her eyes. She looked behind her with her heart pounding in her chest, but saw no one. She turned back towards the mirror, and she jumped in fright when she saw Byron behind her, as she had been that night.

"This isn't real."

Byron stepped into her space and trailed her fingers down Amelia's back, making goosebumps break out all over her body.

"Mia cara, you are simply stunning. Why do you wish me to zip you into your dress, when I want to see you out of it."

Amelia couldn't believe what she was seeing, but that was exactly what Byron had said that night.

It can't be real, it can't be real, she repeated to herself but then began to groan as Byron kissed her shoulder and neck.

"Oh God. You're not real."

She grasped her neck when the burning hot, needy pain returned to her injury. She closed her eyes tightly, and tried to make sense of the urges inside of her. It was pain, but at the same time not. Her sex ached and her nipples hardened and all she could think about was Byron, and her deep need to give herself to her, like they were connected.

"Amelia? Are you okay?" Daisy's voice interrupted her thoughts.

When she opened her eyes, the image of Byron was gone, and Daisy was there instead. She tried to calm her body and catch her breath.

"I'm sorry, Daisy I was just thinking."

Daisy zipped up her dress for her and smiled. "Thinking about Byron?"

"How did you know?"

Daisy took her hand. "It's your first date since your relationship ended. You've got to be thinking about what you're leaving behind."

But had she left her behind? All the time she was getting ready she had this feeling of betraying Byron, which was ridiculous. Byron had left her, broken her heart. She was sure Byron had not given her a second thought over the past six months, as she slept her way around Europe.

The thought of Byron sleeping with someone else killed her, but she couldn't live this way for the rest of her life.

"Maybe this is too soon," Amelia said.

Daisy took her hands. "Listen, you are just going for dinner—you're not going to marry this Victorija. She saved your life yesterday. There's nothing wrong with that. You're just getting yourself back out there. Forget bloody Byron."

Amelia laughed at Daisy's turn of phrase. "You're right. It's just dinner. Is my hair okay?"

Daisy took the brush and hairspray, and walked all around Amelia making the final adjustments to her hair. "There's only one person I feel sorry for," Daisy said.

She knew exactly who Daisy was talking about. "Wilder." Amelia sighed. "I know. I didn't get coffee at her truck this morning because I felt bad. I tell her every day that I'm not ready to go out with anyone, and then I go out with someone else. I mean, she's sweet, just my type, butch and really good looking, but—"

"But what?" Daisy said.

Amelia couldn't quite put it into words. "There's something about Victorija, I don't know why or how, that I recognize and connect with."

Daisy gave her a smile and a friendly squeeze. "I can't wait to see this Victorija. She sounds delicious."

"How do I look?" Amelia asked.

"Gorgeous. Oh, did you watch the YouTube videos from my channel last night?"

Amelia smiled. She had gone to sleep watching Daisy and her team's investigation into witchcraft in Britain, and vowed to watch more. Daisy was engaging and interesting, just as she was at work.

"Yes, it was great. I'd love to watch some more."

Daisy rubbed her hands together. "Excellent. I'll send you some links."

Amelia heard the bell on the shop door and shuddered. *I shouldn't be doing this.* Something inside her was trying to tell her this was wrong.

"Introduce me to this woman who saved your life," Daisy said.

They walked out to the front of the shop and Victorija had her back to them, checking her appearance in one of the many mirrors dotted around the shop. As they approached, Victorija turned around and a broad smile erupted on her face. "Mademoiselle Honey, you are a vision."

Amelia felt red heat burn her cheeks. "Thank you. You look very nice too. Very dapper."

When she said that, Byron's image filled her mind. *Don't do this.*

There was a long silence while Amelia was frozen with her thoughts. Victorija eventually said, "Will you introduce me to your friend?"

"Oh yes—sorry. Victorija, this is my friend and apprentice, Daisy MacDougall."

"Pleased to meet you, Mademoiselle Daisy." Victorija took Daisy's hand to kiss it, and Daisy recoiled as if she got a shock.

Daisy rubbed her hand while looking intently into Victorija's eyes, and then to Amelia's neck. There was another awkward silence, and then Daisy eventually said, "Nice to meet you."

Victorija looked suspiciously at her, then directed her attention to Amelia. "Mademoiselle Amelia, shall we?"

"I'll just get my bag and I'll be with you."

Amelia and Daisy walked into the staff room, and Amelia grabbed her bag. "You sure you can lock up yourself, Daisy?"

"Sure…no problem," Daisy said with a worried tone in her voice.

"Are you sure? I can call Uncle Jaunty if you like," Amelia said.

"No, no, it's fine. Honestly." Daisy gave her a forced smile.

Amelia took Daisy's hand. "Is there something wrong?"

"Just be careful tonight, okay?"

"Why?" Amelia was totally confused.

Daisy sighed. "You might not believe me but I get feelings about things, and I get a bad feeling about Victorija."

Amelia narrowed her eyes. "She saved my life, Daisy. Why would she harm me?"

Daisy shrugged. "I can't explain…Just be careful."

The niggle that told her not to go out with Victorija, the part of her that felt guilty, like she was betraying Byron, got louder. She shook it away and said, "I need to do this, Daisy."

"Principe, what should we do?"

Bhaltair's and Wilder's concerned faces gazed at Byron from her office monitors. Byron could feel her rage, and her desperate craving for her Principessa's blood, clouding her judgement. She was breathing hard and was quite sure if she looked in the mirror her eyes would be blood red.

Bhal had called to alert them that Victorija had made contact with Amelia, while the whole household was in the middle of decamping to London. Clothes, supplies, and staff were being packed and taken to the Debrek plane. They would be leaving within a few hours.

Byron felt so out of control. If Victorija hurt Amelia or touched her in any way, she knew the monster within her would take control. Victorija was right—they were the same fundamentally. Perhaps if she had been brought up by Gilbert Dred, she would be exactly like her

cousin. The same vicious monster who valued humans as simply food and prey.

"Duca?"

"Yes, Principe?"

Byron looked at her shaking hands and closed her eyes to take a moment to calm. When she opened them, Alexis had a glass of blood ready for her.

"Drink this, Principe, until you can feed on an attendant."

"Thank you."

"Duca, my instincts are to hold back until we get to London and talk to Amelia. Victorija seems to have her own agenda, and is not going for a full-out attack. Do you agree?"

"Yes, she could have compelled Amelia and either taken her or killed her, but she didn't. She must have a plan to use her," Alexis said.

Byron nodded. "Bhal, hold your distance, so we don't force Victorija to do anything stupid."

Wilder said with frustration, "Principe, we can't. The Principessa is alone with a vicious, bloodthirsty vampire."

Bhal gave her warrior a hard stare. "Hold your tongue, Wilder. I apologize, Principe."

Byron almost growled and slapped her hand down on the desk. "Do not presume to say anything about Amelia, *my* Principessa. I say what is right for her. I say what is the best way to handle her security. Do you understand, Wilder?"

"Yes, Principe. Forgive me."

Clearly Amelia's goodness and charm had had an effect on the young warrior, by the jealous glint Byron saw in her eyes. When she thought of her shining girl bestowing her smiles and innocence on Victorija, who would rip her heart and throat out on a whim, she wanted to rip Victorija apart.

"Alexis, let's get on the plane now. We have to get to London."

❖

Victorija Dred was charming, and Amelia's apprehension soon dissipated. Amelia looked around the expensive restaurant and said, "This is a beautiful place."

The intimate, exclusive eatery had a line of people waiting at the door, but Victorija seemed to have the same sort of influence as Byron, and they simply walked past those waiting and were taken to the best table in the house, overlooking a roof garden.

Victorija topped up Amelia's champagne glass, and smiled. "A beautiful woman deserves only the best."

She felt her cheeks heat up, and said, "Hardly."

Victorija covered Amelia's hand with hers, and said sincerely, "Believe me, Mademoiselle Honey, you are a truly special woman."

"It's hard to believe that."

"I know someone has broken your heart. Like I said before, I recognize every shade of pain. Tell me about your hurt, Amelia. Maybe I can help banish it?"

When Amelia gazed in Victorija's eyes, she saw something she recognized. A familiarity that made her feel safe to talk. "I was in a relationship for six months, and—"

The waiter chose that moment to bring their starters to the table. Victorija gave him a fierce glare and looked him in his eyes. "Thank you, waiter, you may go now."

"I will go now," he repeated.

Amelia looked up sharply from the salad the waiter had just delivered.

Had she seen compulsion before with Byron? Victorija wondered. That was something she'd need to be more careful about.

"Everything all right, Amelia?"

"Yes, everything's lovely." She picked up her fork and started to eat. Victorija had to relax her and get her to talk again with ease. Oddly, she didn't want to compel Amelia to talk, which was very unlike her. There was something in Victorija that wanted Amelia to open up to her willingly.

"Amelia, you must believe that I understand heartache and pain. If you don't talk about it, and exorcise it, it can fester in your soul and turn you into a cold-hearted, angry, uncompassionate dark soul." Like me, she added silently.

Victorija was not unintelligent. She knew the life and pain that shaped her, and Amelia was reminding her of a very short time in her young life when she did feel, before she learned to bury that pain so deep it would never see light again. The memory of feeling was faded black-and-white, and led to places she didn't want to remember.

Amelia put down her cutlery and took a drink of champagne. "It's hard. I haven't even told my uncle what happened. I was in love, and she told me she loved me, but then—"

"Then what?" Victorija asked.

"She left me. I woke up the next morning and she was gone, leaving me just a letter. Saying our lives were incompatible."

Oh, Byron, you were so scared I would get near her, you broke her heart and your own.

Victorija took her hand. "Who was this fool?"

Amelia gulped hard. She obviously still felt so very hurt. "Byron Debrek."

"Ah, I see."

Amelia narrowed her eyes. "You know her?"

Victorija nodded.

"You don't seem too surprised?"

The last thing she needed was Amelia to become suspicious. "No, I'm not. I mix in the same business circles as Byron, and well…she has a reputation."

"What kind of reputation?"

Victorija lifted Amelia's hand, caressed it between hers, and tenderly stroked her knuckles and fingers. She felt her relax into her touch, exactly what she intended.

"Byron is a businesswoman on the world stage, she's never in one country for too long, and she is known to have a woman in every port, as it were." She saw tears come to Amelia's eyes, and she tried to pull her hand away, but Victorija kept a firm grip.

"You deserve so much more than Byron, Mademoiselle Honey."

"Do I?" Amelia said in a hurt and angry voice.

It was strange, but Victorija did believe what she was saying. Amelia did deserve more than her cousin. Amelia's innocence and goodness reminded her of someone she once knew, who hadn't deserved her fate either. It was a shame that she would have to kill Amelia eventually, but she would love to taste every last drop of her pure, innocent blood. Amelia's death would be on Byron's shoulders, not hers.

"Yes, you do. I've only known you a short time and I can tell that. Why don't we enjoy a wonderful dinner and forget about Byron Debrek?"

Amelia appeared unsure, so Victorija smiled and said, "They do the most decadent chocolate dessert here. I say we get one each, and luxuriate in every unhealthy spoonful." Victorija raised an eyebrow. "What do you say?"

That brought a smile from Amelia. "Yes, let's."

❖

Victorija dropped Amelia home, and Amelia thought about their evening as she got ready for bed. She was surprised that Victorija, quite chivalrously, simply kissed her palm to say goodnight, and didn't expect anything more. It was a good first date, and Victorija was charming, engaging, interesting, and so polite, but despite all that something gave Amelia an uneasy feeling. Maybe it was her imagination, but it was as if Victorija was holding back part of herself, and there were two incidents that were reminiscent of Byron, and Sera.

First there was the way she had dismissed the waiter, and the way he had reacted, much like the club staff member had when Sera had spoken to him, all those months ago in Monte Carlo, and like what Byron had tried to do to her the night before she left her.

But one other thing made her shiver. She had gone to collect her coat from the cloakroom while Victorija paid the bill. She got her coat and saw Victorija on the other side of the room, then turned away to slip her coat on. In less than a second Victorija was behind her helping her put her jacket on. Byron had appeared from nowhere, several times during their courtship, making her jump, as Victorija did tonight.

There were some truths she had pushed to the darkest part of her mind for the past months, and now after meeting Victorija, they were demanding she address them again.

Amelia felt the cold through to her bones tonight. She made a hot water bottle and a hot cup of cocoa, and went to bed. She got under the blankets and picked up her iPad from the side table. She had a few messages and emails to check. Just as she opened up Facebook, she got an instant message from Daisy asking her if she got home safely.

She recalled Daisy's strange reaction to Victorija earlier that evening, and now she was checking to see if she was safe. It wasn't something she would normally do.

"Why do I feel like I'm the only one who doesn't know what's going on." Just like Monte Carlo.

She quickly typed out a reply, and checked her emails. There were at least five different messages from Daisy with links to her YouTube videos. Amelia clicked the first one and it happened to be about the legend of the New Forest witches' coven, in the south of England.

Her religious parents always made disparaging comments about the folk stories and rumours about them while she grew up. She could never quite believe why her parents were worried about an apparently harmless gaggle of witches casting imaginary spells, but they did believe that gay people were evil, and that women who wore make-up were harlots, so it was hardly surprising.

Amelia watched Daisy and her friends walk through the forest paths, which during the day were idyllic, but in the early evening took on a whole other feel. Daisy's presentation to the camera was so professional, and her group of friends so charming, that she found herself laughing often, until they emerged into a clearing with an old stone cottage. The place felt eerily familiar.

Daisy walked to an old stone circle in the grounds outside the cottage, where she explained legend said the witches gathered and performed their old traditional magic.

An uneasy feeling gripped Amelia, and her heart began to pound. Something wasn't right, but she didn't want to face it. She shut off her iPad and got up to draw at the drafting table in the living room of her flat. Drawing and designing always calmed her.

After drawing for twenty minutes, she realized the model in the suit she had drawn unconsciously was Byron. She threw her pencil down and crumpled up the design.

"Get out of my head."

Then the burning pain in her neck hit her hard. She gripped her head between her hands, and shouted, "What is happening to me?"

CHAPTER FIFTEEN

The intense pain subsided, as it always did, but came back with unnerving regularity. Amelia didn't want to go to a doctor, because deep down she knew it wasn't something that medicine could help her with. It was something that, like her broken heart, she would have to live with.

Amelia didn't want to think about it deeply, so she threw herself into her work for the rest of the week. It felt good to be back to her one love that never let her down and always occupied her mind in times of trouble—tailoring.

It was Friday, the end of the workweek, and she was conducting her last appointment of the day. It was a first fitting with the famous Hollywood actor, Joel Hawk. The fitting should have only taken an hour at most, but due to the fact that he had never worn a suit in his life, fidgeted and complained about almost everything, and tried to flirt with her constantly, they were now two hours in.

Finally finished with the suit adjustments, she was now unpinning the pieces of material from him. While she unpinned the arms Joel said, "How would you like to join me at a club tonight? I'm on the VIP list."

Joel swept his hand through his midlength sand-coloured hair, with a smug smile that wasn't expecting a no. Amelia knew millions of straight women who would give their right arm for the chance, but she was not straight and, to be honest, after having been the girlfriend of a flash and glam billionaire banker, a Hollywood actor didn't really excite any more.

"I'm sorry, but I have plans." She wasn't lying. Victorija was taking her out to a club.

"Honey, listen. Whoever else you're going out with is not Joel Hawk. Joel Hawk is the best offer you're going to get this lifetime."

Amelia took the pieces of material, turned away, and rolled her eyes at his arrogance. "I'm sure you think so, but you're not my type, Mr. Hawk."

She turned around and saw a look of astonishment on his face.

"I'm everyone's type."

"Sorry, but I'm gay. So—"

A sly grin spread across his face, and then he took a step towards her. "I could change your mind." Amelia found herself pushed up against the dressing room wall. "Turning lesbians is my special skill."

Panic started to set in at first, but then anger rose inside her. How dare this greasy little actor make her feel uncomfortable and try to aggressively pursue her.

She felt the anger spreading around her body, and when he tried to lean in for a kiss, Amelia put a hand on his chest and said, "Back!"

Joel found himself knocked back a few feet and landed on his backside. "What the hell did you do?" he raged as he jumped to his feet.

Amelia looked down at her open hand, wondering what had just happened. It felt like anger spread down her arm and exploded out of her palm.

Just then, Daisy appeared at the dressing room door. "Is everything all right, Amelia?"

Amelia just kept looking at her hand in shock. Joel grabbed his jacket, and said angrily, "No, it's not fucking all right. You can stuff your suit up your ass, bitch."

He stormed past them and out of the shop. Daisy came into the room, took her hand, and then recoiled from her.

That made Amelia come out of her stunned silence. "What's wrong, Daisy?"

"Nothing. Just tell me what happened."

Amelia couldn't even explain to herself. "I have no idea. He was chatting me up, and didn't take kindly to me saying no."

"What did he do?" Daisy looked really worried now.

"He got me up against the wall, and all I remember is feeling so angry and trapped—I put my hand on his chest, shouted *no*, and he flew back."

"Have you ever had anything like that happen before?" Daisy asked.

"I don't think so, I…" Amelia searched her memories and then it came to her. "Once that I can clearly remember. I was bullied at school. It went on for a whole school year. The last day of term, at the Christmas church service, one of the bullies tripped me up in front of the whole school. I felt so embarrassed, but my overwhelming emotion was anger. I shouted, *I hate you*, and she was knocked clean off her feet. I got into so much trouble at school and at home. My parents took me out of that school."

"I see." Daisy sighed.

"What do you think it means?"

Daisy shifted uncomfortably. "I'm not sure."

Amelia was sure Daisy knew more than she was saying. "You do investigations into lots of strange things. Are you sure you don't know?"

"Let me do some research. Why don't you get ready for your big date, and I'll tidy up these materials?"

"Thank you, Daisy." She was glad for Daisy's help. Amelia had been faced with lots of strange happenings this week, and she really didn't want to think about what it all meant. The wound on her neck started to burn, one of the other things she didn't want to contemplate. No, she really needed to go out with Victorija and forget. "Sounds like a good idea."

❖

Amelia was finishing up before getting ready to go out with Victorija again. Daisy was heading off to meet with her friends for another overnight vigil for her YouTube channel.

"Have a good time tonight, and be careful. You don't know what's out there," Amelia said to Daisy, and gave her a hug.

"I do know what's out there, Amelia, and that's the scary part." Again, Daisy's eyes went to the mark on her neck, which had been aching and painful a few times today.

The pain seemed to come in intense episodes. The achy need and discomfort would build and build to a point where she became dizzy and thought she might pass out, and then it would start to ease. She was sure it had something to do with Byron. Even though she hadn't seen her ex-lover for six months, she could almost feel her in every cell of her body.

Amelia had been so busy today she hadn't had a chance to talk to Daisy about the videos she had sent her. The YouTube videos had really disturbed her. She felt connected to them somehow, as if she knew something and just couldn't make sense of it.

"Daisy, those videos you sent me…about witches and vampires. I know it sounds crazy but—"

Daisy took her hands and said, "Tomorrow. Can we talk tomorrow? I really need to run."

Daisy was avoiding this conversation. Why? "Okay."

Twenty minutes later, Amelia was just retouching her make-up in the staff room when she heard the door open and ring the bell. Daisy must have forgotten something. She hurried back out to the front.

"Daisy, did you—"

She stopped dead and gasped. There standing by the door of the shop was Byron, with a large bunch of flowers. Amelia's heart was thudding in her chest, and she felt her bite mark start to ache.

"Hello, Amelia," Byron said.

This couldn't be real. Some days during the last six months she had daydreamed about Byron turning up again, but now it was happening, and all she felt was intense anger. She walked up to Byron and examined her closely before slapping her on the cheek.

Byron grabbed her wrist to stop her from slapping her again. "I deserved that, but don't do it again, Amelia. Please let me talk."

"How dare you, how *dare* you walk back into my life, just as I'm starting to rebuild it, stand there with your flowers and expect me to fall at your feet."

Amelia pulled out of her grip, and Byron dropped the flowers on a chair.

"I don't. I just want a few minutes of your time to explain myself," Byron said.

Even as angry as Amelia was, her body and her heart were drawing her to Byron, and she had to fight so hard against them. "Get out," Amelia said with as much coldness as she could muster.

Byron took a step towards Amelia, and held up her hands in surrender. "Please, give me five minutes. Just to talk?" She didn't want to spook her ex-lover and make her run from her emotionally and physically. Seeing the pain on Amelia's face and knowing she caused it was heart-breaking.

Amelia crossed her arms defensively. "What makes you think I have any interest in what you have to say?"

"Amelia—"

Byron reached out to touch her, but Amelia pulled away. "Don't touch me, Byron. I'm not the innocent little woman who waited patiently for you and swallowed your lies any more. When you've had your heart ripped out and thrown on the ground, you tend to toughen up."

Byron had known this wasn't going to be easy, but she couldn't even get as far as talking. "I'm so sorry I hurt you. Believe me, I've been hurting right along with you, but I had my reasons—"

"You were hurting? Oh, please, Byron. I'm sure you were hurting while you were sleeping your way around Europe."

Frustration was starting to make Byron's anger rise. She grasped Amelia's wrist and pulled her towards her. "There's been no one—I've touched no one else. You're in my blood, Amelia."

Amelia looked at her silently as if trying figure out her truthfulness, and then tears started to well in her eyes. "I have gone to sleep every night thinking about you, thinking about what I could have done wrong. Why you would tell me you love me and then run away the next day. Sometimes I can still feel your breath on my neck, your teeth as they grazed my shoulders and neck."

"That's because I'm part of you. Please let me explain," Byron pleaded.

"Why would I listen to anything you say, when you've hidden and lied about yourself for our whole relationship?"

How much did Amelia know? Had Victorija told her anything?

"I'm ready to tell you the truth, if you'll listen. Just please come with me and don't go out with Victorija tonight."

Amelia gave her a rueful laugh. "Oh, I see. That's why you're here, Byron. Your ego. The first time I've met someone else and want to go out with them, here you pop out of the blue. What a coincidence."

Byron could see how it looked. "Mia cara, if you'll just let me explain, you'll realize it's not like that. Victorija is dangerous. I cannot allow you to spend time with her."

Amelia's face went red with rage, and Byron could feel the anger boiling through their blood bond.

"One, I'm not your mia cara, and two, you don't have a say in my life any more. You gave up that right when you smashed my heart to pieces. You can keep your flowers for the next woman you use." The tears tumbled from Amelia's eyes.

Byron was running out of options. If she couldn't get Amelia to listen, she would have to take her by force to safety. She placed her hand on the bite mark on Amelia's neck, and Amelia gasped.

"You feel that? We are connected by more than you can ever imagine. You are my shining girl, and I have to protect you from my enemies. Victorija is my enemy."

The bell rang, as someone walked through the door. "Amelia, are you all right?"

Byron stepped away from Amelia quickly, and Amelia said, "I'm okay, Uncle Jaunty. Byron is just leaving."

Jaunty gave his former friend an icy stare. "Byron, I think you should go."

Byron had no choice. She had too much respect for Jaunty to cause trouble for him. She would have to get Amelia to safety at a later time. She felt the tremors in her hands start too. Byron hadn't fed for a while, but being close to Amelia, the only woman who could sate her hunger, made things so much worse.

Byron nodded and said, "I'll go, but I can explain everything if you let me. I'm never giving up on you, Amelia." She turned and walked past Jaunty at the door.

"You let me down, Byron."

Byron nodded and left.

❖

Victorija knew there was something different as soon as she laid eyes on Amelia that evening. She appeared confused and emotional. She suspected it was something to do with Byron. Her informants told her the Debreks had arrived in London this morning, and it was clearly because of Amelia.

You really have lost your heart, Byron.

This information didn't change Victorija's plans, just moved her timetable up a bit. In fact the idea that Byron was fully aware of what was going on and that Amelia had chosen to come out with her would make her conquest all the sweeter.

And now they were riding to The Sanctuary Club, in the back of Victorija's limousine.

"Is there something wrong, Mademoiselle Amelia?" Victorija asked.

"No…nothing."

Victorija grasped her chin and looked directly into her eyes. "Tell me, what happened to upset you, Amelia?"

Amelia's eyes softened as she fell under Victorija's compulsion. "Byron came to my shop with flowers, and wanted to explain why she left me and broke my heart. She said we were connected, that I was in her blood, and she in mine."

Bound in blood and spirit for all eternity? It couldn't be, Victorija thought. This was even better than she had imagined. Amelia and Byron were bound in blood, and Victorija now had the biggest bargaining chip she could ever hope to have. The Debrek Principessa.

"And what did you do?" Victorija asked.

"I told her to get out. I wasn't interested in her explanations after breaking my heart."

Victorija couldn't help but laugh imagining Byron's hurt, but she did wonder why Byron hadn't just taken Amelia by force.

"What happened next?"

"My uncle Jaunty came back to the shop and told her to go."

Victorija was curious, so she went further. "Did you really want Byron to go? How do you feel about her really? Tell me the truth."

Amelia might have been compelled but tears of emotion still spilled from her eyes. "No, I didn't want her to go. She is the love of my life, and I know I'll never stop loving her."

Victorija sat back and contemplated someone feeling like that about her, but quickly dismissed the thought as weakness. Love was weakness. That was what she had beaten into her, and what she would always believe.

"Drasas?" Her Duca turned around in the front seat of the limo, and said, "Yes, Principe?"

"We will move forward with our plans tonight. We have the Debrek Principessa." Victorija smiled and Drasas grinned right back.

"Excellent. Are we still heading for The Sanctuary?"

Victorija's ego was stroked at the idea of their paranormal community seeing her with the Debrek Principessa.

"Yes, why not enjoy a drink and a dance before we make our demands to Byron."

Victorija grasped Amelia's chin again and said, "You will forget about this conversation and we will go and have a wonderful evening together at the club."

"I will forget our conversation and have a wonderful evening at the club," Amelia repeated before shaking her head and coming back from the compulsion.

"You feel better, Mademoiselle Amelia?"

"Much. Thank you." Amelia gave her a bright smile.

Amelia was surprised when Victorija's limo stopped in front of a nondescript Victorian building in London's Soho district. It didn't look like any club she had ever heard of.

"Are you ready for some fun, Amelia?" Victorija said.

Amelia had considered cancelling her date, but in the end decided that it was better to go out and stop thinking about Byron. How dared she drop back into her life?

"Shall we?" Victorija was already at her car door and extending a hand to help her out, and they walked down some stairs into the bowels of the building.

Victorija stopped at the old wooden door at the entrance, and knocked. A voice from behind the door said, "Name?"

"Victorija Dred."

The door opened immediately, and the tall, lanky doorman bowed his head. "Welcome, Principe. Do come in."

Principe? That word again. Amelia also noticed how nervous and almost frightened the doorman looked. Was he frightened of Victorija? Maybe Byron was right about her. Suddenly going into this club she'd never heard of seemed like a very bad idea. "Victorija, it's been a difficult day. Maybe I should just go home—"

Victorija put her hand on the back of her neck, and gazed deeply in her eyes. "Calm down, and trust me."

Amelia experienced a woozy sensation wash over her brain, like she'd already had a few drinks. She followed Victorija meekly into the dark foyer of the club. Victorija took her coat and checked it into the cloakroom. She then offered her arm to Amelia, who took it immediately. As wary as she was, the light fog in her brain was making her comply. They walked down another set of stairs. At the bottom was the main room, and Amelia realized quickly that this was not like any club she had been to before, even compared to the last club she'd visited with Victorija.

The music in the background had a slow, pounding rhythm, giving the club an erotic eerie feel. The room was dark. Black walls with silver decorations and low lights, and dry ice vapor coming from the dance floor added to the dark atmosphere.

At the end of the large room sat the bar, with the dance floor off to the right. In front of the bar were booths and tables.

They started to walk further into the room, and they passed couples consumed with each other on couches, sitting in each other's laps, and generally being seduced by the erotic thrum of the music.

Why had Victorija brought them here?

One couple who were caught up in their passion for each other against the wall reached out to Victorija and said, "Come and join us, Principe."

Victorija smiled. "Not tonight, thank you. I am with a most beautiful woman, who I want all to myself."

The couple looked her up and down, and bowed their heads to Victorija. Amelia knew she should feel panicked, but she was just so woozy, she couldn't.

It was strange how people kept bowing their heads to Victorija, and calling her Principe. Just like Byron. What was the connection? She was sure she could work it out, if only she could think properly.

Victorija guided them to a table and said, "Excuse me for a moment and I will get us some drinks."

Amelia could only nod, and Victorija left without asking what drink she'd like. The clubbers were a collection of unique individuals. Some were impeccably dressed in high fashion, and others looked like they had walked in from a goth club. There were a few men and women who were incredibly tall, unusually so, but the overriding feeling was that these people were somehow out of step with Amelia's world. A relic from a darker, almost Victorian age, as strange as that sounded.

Why didn't I listen to Byron?

❖

Victorija walked to the bar and found Drasas already there feeding from a woman's wrist. She stopped when she realized Victorija was there, and said to the woman, "Go."

The woman gave Drasas the dirtiest of looks and said, "Not even a thank you? You're an arsehole, Drasas."

Victorija laughed. "You really do have a way with women."

Drasas wiped her mouth with a napkin from the bar. "British women have no respect for their betters. How is Mademoiselle Honey?"

Victorija looked back to their table. "Very calm and compliant, at the moment."

"When are you going to contact Byron?" Drasas asked.

"When I return to the table. Now that Amelia is her Principessa, she will have to give us the Debrek secret."

"I have people stationed all around the room and the outside, Principe," Drasas said.

"Excellent."

Victorija turned to order drinks, but the bartender, Slaine, was currently talking to someone at the other end of the bar. "Fairy, if you could serve me, that would be wonderful."

Slaine stormed over to her and leaned menacingly over the bar. "Watch your mouth, vampire."

Drasas jumped up with red eyes and fangs showing. "That's Principe to you, fairy."

Slaine was six foot eight of solid muscle, and half fae, half shifter. It was taboo in The Sanctuary to call Slaine a fairy, and usually got you a punch in the mouth and thrown out, but two vampires were too difficult for her to take on. Hence Victorija took great delight in teasing her every time she was in the club.

"I don't care if she's the Queen, no one calls me fairy." Slaine and Drasas were almost nose to nose across the bar, ready to fight.

Victorija said, "Now, Drasas, stand down. We all know Slaine feels inadequate because of her ancestry. Let her be."

Slaine took a breath and stepped back. "I am not ashamed of being a fae, and I will not have the fae reduced by you to the status of fairies. The Sanctuary was founded as a place for all of our kind to come together peacefully, a neutral zone where we keep all hostilities at the door, so just watch your language."

The sanctimonious garbage about The Sanctuary's policies made Victorija want to gag. She'd rather go to an all vampire bar, but there were none in the area.

"Oh, just get me two glasses of red, would you please?"

Slaine turned away and got her drinks.

Victorija returned to table. "Here you are, Amelia. Drink this."

Amelia looked at it and said, "I don't like red wine."

She wanted Amelia to drink it for the sake of the picture she was about to take. Victorija pulled her chair closer to Amelia, and told her, "You will drink this and enjoy it."

"I will drink it," Amelia parroted.

"Good girl." Victorija took out her phone. "Now, Amelia, I want you to look at the camera and smile for me."

Amelia complied, and Victorija attached the picture to an email. She then typed out:

I have something of yours, Byron. She's enjoying some blood with me at The Sanctuary. Now, if you want your woman back, you're going to have to give me that spell. It's my birthright, and I want it. You have one hour or—Well, I don't really have to explain further. Do I?

Once it was sent, Victorija gazed into Amelia's eyes and said, "There are a few more things I want you to remember."

CHAPTER SIXTEEN

F uck! I knew I should have gone to follow Amelia with Bhal." Byron was in her office at the London house. She had already been in a bad condition because of her blood sickness, but now she was frantic. She loosened her tie and started for the door.

Alexis stopped her. "Wait, Principe. Before we go rushing in, we need a plan."

Byron was finding it hard to think clearly, because her body was starved of the blood it needed. "What plan do I need? I walk in there and rip Victorija's head off with my bare hands, and leave," Byron said with fury.

"A good idea, but Victorija could kill the Principessa before we got close. She gave us an hour. Let's at least take a few minutes to think. Bhal, Wilder, and the rest of her warriors are outside waiting and watching, in any case."

Byron took a breath and closed her eyes. "You are right. I need you to be rational for me, Duca, because I can't be at the moment."

"Of course I will. First thing, can you give her the secret? Only the Principe knows it."

Byron poured a glass of whiskey, and downed it in one. "I only know so much. I couldn't give her the spell, but I've asked Sera to bring the object the spell is tied to." Byron dialled Sera's number. "Sera, are you en route?"

"Yes, we're in the air. We should land in an hour and a half," Sera said.

"Good, we may need your package sooner than we thought. Stay safe." Byron ended the call. "The object is on its way. Let's go."

She made her way out of the house followed closely by Alexis. When they got into the car, Alexis said, "If we go in for her, there will be a fight, and we'll break the covenant of The Sanctuary."

"When Victorija took my Principessa, she committed an act of war. We have no choice. Slaine will understand."

Byron looked down at her shaking hands, and clenched them shut. She needed to be strong for Amelia.

❖

Victorija leaned over and whispered to Amelia, "I have to leave you for a few moments, but I have eyes everywhere, and you won't leave this table. Will you?"

Why couldn't she think? Why couldn't she clear the fog from her brain? Amelia could do no more than echo Victorija's command. "I won't leave the table."

Victorija smirked. "Good girl. Do excuse me, I have people to compel to my will. You know how it is."

When Victorija walked away, Amelia just stared into the distance, unable to move as she wished. She swayed to the music being played in the club, as if she was drunk. It was a horrible feeling. After a few minutes, she heard a distant voice behind her.

"Amelia? Amelia, it's me. Turn around."

She used all her concentration and turned her head. Through the fog of her brain—or was that dry ice?—she saw Daisy, dressed in a beanie hat and black clothing to try to disguise who she was.

"Amelia, are you okay?" Daisy whispered.

Amelia tried to make her brain work, but she just couldn't. "I can't think…"

Daisy reached out to her and said, "Touch my hand."

Amelia stared at her hand but didn't take it.

Daisy repeated, "Take my hand, Amelia. You can do it."

She pushed and pushed and her hand moved to take Daisy's. At the contact, she felt a jolt, and the fog started to lift.

"What? What's going on?" Amelia said in a panic.

Daisy placed her finger to her lips, and showed Amelia her iPhone.

Amelia was starting to remember Byron's visit, then going to the club with Victorija—everything was hazy after that.

She read the note typed on the phone. *Don't say anything. They can hear us. Victorija compelled you to do as she says. She's a vampire.*

Amelia gasped and looked up, ready to say something, but again Daisy put her finger to her lips, so Amelia mouthed, *Vampire?*

Daisy nodded and pointed back to the phone.

What was going on here? Vampires?

They exist. Victorija and her people are vampires. You have to believe me and trust me. I can get us out of here. On my signal, walk to the bathroom. I'll meet you there and we can escape out the window. Nod if you understand.

Amelia looked back to Daisy. She felt overwhelmed. Could she believe this? Then she thought of all the strange behaviours that Byron and her sister exhibited. My God, was Byron a vampire?

She nodded to Daisy. It looked like she was the only one she could trust.

They sat and waited, and waited, and then there was a commotion at the door. Amelia saw Bhal, Alexis, and their people by the entrance to the club.

Daisy nodded and she slowly and quietly edged around the room, as tables and chairs went flying in an erupting bar fight. Victorija's people met Bhal's and Alexis's people in the centre of the room. Amelia held her breath and prayed she could make it to the bathroom too.

❖

Victorija had just ripped out the heart of one of Byron's turned vampires, when something caught her eye—a girl in heavy clothing walking hurriedly towards the back of the club. Then the face came to her. Daisy MacDougall.

She turned back to the throng of vampires and bar patrons fighting and caught sight of Byron rushing down the steps into the room, dispatching ten of Victorija's vampires in seconds, breaking their necks like twigs, and biting their necks. Byron was such a strong vampire. Victorija didn't want to face her here without a new plan, but she didn't have much time.

Victorija hurried to follow Daisy and watched her slip into the bathroom where she was sure Amelia now was too. She burst into the bathroom and found Daisy and Amelia embracing.

Victorija shut the door and said, "Ooh, can I watch?"

"Amelia, run! Get out the window," Daisy said.

Daisy ran at Victorija, who grabbed her by the throat, and pushed her up against the wall.

"Stay where you are, Amelia, or I rip your friend's throat out," Victorija said.

"Victorija, don't, please," Amelia begged.

Victorija grinned. "If you wish. Stand there and don't move, Amelia. I need to compel your little friend to cause a diversion."

"I can't be compelled," Daisy said matter-of-factly.

Victorija gave her an incredulous look, and moved to within inches of Daisy's face. "I doubt that, little girl." She stared at her and said, "Kiss me."

"In your dreams, vamp," Daisy shot back.

Victorija couldn't believe it. She could compel anyone. She held Daisy's hands together tight. Daisy started to struggle. "I'm ordering you to do everything as I say it. Understand?"

Amelia watched with bated breath the scene that was before her. Daisy was standing up to a vampire, trying to protect her. A vampire. *What has happened to my life?*

"When hell freezes over, vamp," Daisy replied with venom.

Amelia ran towards them, but Victorija batted her to the floor. "Let her go, Victorija," Amelia said. "It's me you want."

"I do, but this little girl is annoying me. I knew she was trouble when I met her."

The bathroom door burst open, and it was Drasas, the one she'd seen in Victorija's limo.

"The battle is lost, Principe. We have to leave now."

Victorija growled and turned her head to Amelia. "We may have lost the battle but not the war. Tell that to Byron when she's whispering sweet nothings to you."

"Principe, we have to go," Drasas said.

Victorija looked back to Daisy, and said, "Before I go, I'll drain every drop—"

Before Victorija could finish her statement, Daisy struck and bit Victorija's shoulder at the crook of her neck.

It must have been hard, because Victorija jumped in pain. She pushed Daisy back, and all her features changed. Her eyes turned red, like Amelia was sure Byron's had done, and she saw sharp fangs in her mouth. Amelia was terrified.

"Just for that, little girl…" Victorija sank her teeth into Daisy's neck.

"No!" Amelia got up and ran at Victorija, but Drasas kept hold of her.

"We don't have time, Principe," Drasas said again.

Victorija pulled back gasping, gazing silently into Daisy's eyes. She wiped her mouth and said, "Let's get out of here."

Daisy dropped to the floor clutching her neck, and then Victorija and Drasas were gone. Amelia crawled over to Daisy, just as another bloodstained vampire walked through the door.

"The new Principessa?" He snarled. "Just what I need—"

He stopped speaking when a hand burst through his chest, and pulled his heart out through his back. He dropped to his knees, and revealed Byron standing behind him, her shirt and chin covered in blood, and her eyes crimson red.

"Amelia? You're safe now."

Amelia watched as Byron threw the heart in her hand to the floor. She couldn't take any more. Her head swam, she heard a confusing mix of voices around her, and then she lost consciousness.

CHAPTER SEVENTEEN

A melia became aware of a pounding in her head. She struggled to open her eyes, but when she did the light streaming through the windows startled her. She pulled the pillow beside her over her eyes and heard someone close the curtains in the room. It was only then she realized she wasn't in her own bed.

She sat up quickly and found Katie sitting by her bed. "Katie? What...?" Amelia looked around the bedroom, trying to work out where she was. All the pieces of furniture had white sheets over them as if the room hadn't been inhabited in a long, long time.

"How do you feel, Amelia?" Katie said.

It was then that last night thundered through her head. Being out with Victorija, Daisy appearing to help her, Byron and her people bursting into the club, and the realization that they were not human.

Amelia pulled the pillow in front of her for some imaginary kind of protection from Katie.

"Please don't be scared, Amelia. You can trust me."

"What are you?" Amelia asked directly.

Katie smiled and sat on the bed. "Don't worry. I'm a plain old human. I just work for the Debreks. I'm your friend—I would never hurt you."

Amelia believed her and felt such relief that there was one person who wasn't hiding something from her. Katie opened her arms and she took the offered comfort willingly.

"I'm so glad to see you. Where am I, and what am I doing here?"

Katie pulled back and stroked Amelia's hair. "You are in the

Debrek London mansion. You'll have to excuse the sheets and dust everywhere. The house has been in mothballs for a long time. Why you're here? That's for the Principe to tell you. I'm just here to look after you."

"The Principe? You mean Byron?" Amelia asked.

Katie nodded. "I know you are angry at her, but please hear her out."

"She lied to me, left me, and broke my heart," Amelia said.

"I know, and I'm not going to say I would have made the same choices, but she was scared."

"Scared?" Amelia laughed. "Emotionless and in-control Byron Debrek scared?"

"Yes, she's controlled, but do you really believe she is emotionless? You're the closest anyone has ever gotten to her. Was she really emotionless?"

The times when Byron let her sexual hunger control their lovemaking ran through Amelia's mind. She was anything but emotionless. She was raw and passionate, and Amelia even encouraged her to bite and taste her. In those moments Byron's heart was on fire for her.

"No, she wasn't, but the secrets, the lies…Wait—where is my friend who was with me last night?"

"Daisy?"

Amelia nodded. "Yes, she helped save me. I don't want her out there if Victorija is trying to hurt people connected to me."

"She's downstairs, don't worry." Katie chuckled. "She refused to leave your side, and is annoying Alexis no end, which is always good."

"Thanks."

Katie stood and said, "Why don't I get you some tea and something to eat, then bring Daisy to see you?"

"That would be nice, thanks. And, Katie?" As angry as she was, all she could think about was Byron and what she might be. Her logical mind fought against what she had seen with her own eyes.

"Yes?" Katie stopped and turned back to look at her.

"Where is Byron?"

"She's in her office, I believe. Do you want me to give her a message?"

"I need to see her before I leave."

Katie looked uncomfortable all of a sudden. "Of course. Just relax, and I'll be back."

Just then the dull aching pain in her bite mark increased exponentially.

❖

All Byron could feel was bloodlust and pain. She leaned against the wall of her office bent over, fighting the pain.

"I need to feed, need Amelia," Byron said breathily.

Alexis and Bhal were the only two with her. Alexis touched her on the back, and Byron turned, snarling, fangs ready to attack. "Get me blood, or I'll take yours, vampire," she roared.

Alexis jumped back like she'd been slapped, and Byron dropped to her knees, shaking.

She was only dimly aware of her friends' conversation through the fog of hunger, but she heard Alexis say to Bhal, "She has to feed on the Principessa. That's all she needs to make her better."

"No," Byron replied. "Don't let me feed on Amelia."

"Alexis, go. I'll take care of the Principe."

Byron heard the door close and Bhal kneeled beside her.

"Byron, look at me."

Byron held her hands on her head hoping the pounding inside her skull would stop. The pain of hunger pounded in her head, her chest, her stomach, and her sex. She needed to drink from her Principessa, make love to her, and only then would every need she had be sated.

Bhal pulled her head up and looked into her eyes. "I'm here, Byron. Calm, take deep breaths."

"Please don't let me feed from Amelia like this. The monster inside me will take too much. It's taking control of me. She needs to ask me to feed—I won't take without consent." Through Byron's panic and pain, she could still feel the horror of the time the darkness had taken control and Bhal had found her, and helped Byron fight the monster that was inside her, waiting to take control.

"I won't. I promise, but I'm sure she would help you if you told her the truth. In the meantime, you will feed."

Byron groaned at another wave of pain hitting her hard. "I'll take too much…"

Bhal rolled up her sleeve, and presented her wrist. "You won't take too much from me. I'm strong enough to give you what you need."

Byron's mouth watered as she gazed longingly at Bhal's blood-filled wrist.

"Feed, Byron. My blood is so much stronger than an attendant's, and it will help, until you can try and work things out with the Principessa."

She couldn't hold back another second. Byron sank her teeth into Bhal's wrist, just as she had done a long time ago as a young vampire. Bhal's rich, powerful blood flowed down her throat and she felt the pain start to calm slightly.

After taking more than any human could give her, Byron pulled back, and tried to get her breathing under control.

"Better?" Bhal stood and offered her hand to Byron.

"Much." Byron took her hand and stood on wobbly legs. "Are you okay?"

Bhal looked at her bleeding wrist and said, "It will heal in a few minutes. From now on I will feed you. I can take a lot more than your human attendants."

Byron wiped the blood at her mouth with a handkerchief and went to pour them each a drink. "It won't work forever, Bhal. My body will demand my Principessa's blood and the monster inside me will take control."

Bhal took a glass of whiskey from Byron and said, "There is no monster inside you, Byron. I've told you that so many times."

Byron took a large sip of her drink and looked in her office mirror. "You know what I'm capable of, Bhal." She touched the rapidly drying blood on her mouth. "How can I expose her to this? She's so good, so untainted by our world, my shining girl."

From outside the door she heard a whispered argument between Alexis and Katie.

"Amelia wants me to give the Principe a message," Katie said.

"The Principe is indisposed. Go back to the Principessa."

"Then let me feed her. I can help," Katie said.

"No"—Alexis raised her voice—"it's not safe for you. You will not be required to feed or serve the Principe from now on. Go."

Byron could hear the worry in her Duca's voice. She wasn't letting Katie anywhere near her. Alexis was clearly worried about the human.

I'm not safe. Byron held her head in her hands.

"Alexis, stop this. Let me tell Amelia about this and she will help Byron—I know she will," Katie said.

"Don't breathe a word about the Principe's condition. That is an order."

She heard Katie walk off angrily. So angrily that the sound of her heels echoed around the Debrek entrance hall.

Byron looked up at Bhal, and said, "I'm not safe. I shouldn't be leading this clan any more. If I lost control and hurt anyone, any of the loyal people who have served my family for centuries—"

"Don't talk that way. That is not going to happen," Bhal said firmly.

Byron gazed fearfully at the tremor in her fingers, a symbol of her loss of control, and knew what she had to say.

"Bhal, no one in our family has gone this long without the blood of their bound partner. But it has happened in other clans, and you know what lies ahead—murderous insanity. The monster will turn this clan into something that makes the Dreds look like pussycats. Look what happened to Gilbert after he killed his wife. He grew more insane than he ever was."

She walked around to Bhal. "I need you to promise me something."

"What do you need?" Bhal asked.

"If the time comes, take my heart and take my head," Byron said.

Bhal didn't answer, but she walked over to the window, leaned her arm against the sill, and said, "You can't ask me to do that. I helped bring you up, taught you everything I know."

Byron walked over and put her hand on Bhal's shoulder. "That is why it has to be you. Alexis may be my Duca and best friend, but you are my mentor and my family. This is something only family would do for each other. I need you to do it. Please don't let me become what I've always feared."

Bhal was silent, so Byron said, "Bhal, I am asking you this as a warrior. You wouldn't leave a wounded comrade lying in torment on the battlefield. You would put them out of their misery. Wouldn't you?"

Bhal gave a huge sigh and turned around. "Yes, I would help them."

Byron held out her hand and Bhal clasped her arm in a warriors' handshake. "If the worst comes, then I will take your heart and your head. I give you my word of honour."

She knew how hard this was for Bhal, but Byron was also certain that she had the courage to do what was necessary. "Thank you. I know what your word of honour means."

Bhal bowed her head and walked to the office door.

"Oh, and Bhal?"

"Yes, Principe?"

"I know my family will take care of Amelia, but Sera will be lost. She will be faced with a new life. Will you guide her, protect her, and make sure she is safe?"

"Till the very end."

❖

"Daisy!" Amelia rushed to embrace her friend as soon as she walked into the room.

"Are you okay, Amelia? Those creepy vamps wouldn't tell me anything."

Amelia pulled back from the hug and sighed. "Physically, but my head has never been more mixed up in my life. Are you okay?" Amelia touched the bite on Daisy's neck.

Daisy jumped slightly and gave her a strange look. "I'm fine, I'm fine. They told me downstairs it would clear up in a few days. It's weird, isn't it. I've been searching for real proof of the paranormal all my life, and then a vampire just walks up and bites me."

"Thank you for going to the club, and helping to save me," Amelia said.

"I wasn't going to let you be alone with a creepy vamp."

"Let's sit." Amelia pulled her over to sit on the bed. "You knew Victorija was a vampire, didn't you?"

"Not a vampire, but something paranormal. I get these feelings when I touch a paranormal creature. My friends call it my Spidey sense. They don't seem to be able to compel me either. Victorija tried, and so did Alexis, the vamp downstairs. I think the Debreks are frightened I'll put this on YouTube." Daisy pulled out a silver locket that was hidden under her T-shirt. "My mum always said this would protect me from any spooks out there. It was my grandmother's."

Amelia covered Daisy's hand with hers and said, "I'm glad you came last night, Daisy. You put yourself in danger for me. I was so taken in by Victorija. I really believed she understood my pain, and even now I'm sure she was truthful, but yet she was willing to kill me. I think she's a very mixed-up person."

Daisy smiled. "Most villains are, aren't they? But is Byron the hero of your story?"

"Not a chance. She lied to me, made me think I was going slightly mad with all the weird things going on around me, and then just broke my heart."

"I know. I've watched your hurt over the last few months, but she did come back to save you at least."

Amelia shook her head in disbelief. "She's a vampire, Daisy. They all are. Sera, Alexis—my mind can't even process it."

"Amelia, how did that bite on your neck happen? Did she hurt you?" Daisy asked.

"No, it wasn't like that. It was a passionate thing—I told her to, but she didn't bite me properly like Victorija did to you. I think she was fighting her instincts." Amelia felt her anger rise again, and clenched the bedcovers tightly. "Why am I making excuses for her? She broke my heart."

"Because you still love her, don't you?" Daisy asked.

Tears sprang from her eyes on cue, and tumbled down her cheeks. "I love her with all my heart, but I'm so angry at the same time. I don't think I can ever forgive her for lying to me, and leaving me."

"What happens next?" Daisy said.

"I go and talk to her, get some answers, then leave this creepy house and never look back."

CHAPTER EIGHTEEN

A melia followed Katie down the corridor to the stairs. From first impressions, the Debrek London mansion was so different from the estate in Monaco. Where the Monte Carlo house was light, airy, and glam, this house was dark, and somewhat a relic of the past. They started to walk down the large dark oak staircase and she could quite easily imagine servants in traditional outfits walking these stairs and floors in the past. There were imposing portraits everywhere, and they all seemed to have an uncanny resemblance to Byron and Sera.

"Katie? Is Sera here?"

"Not yet, but she will be coming. She's collecting something very precious to the family, then travelling to London, so I'm told. Not that I'm told a lot."

As they passed various members of staff milling around the house, she noticed they all bowed their head to her.

"Katie, why are they doing that?"

"What?" Katie looked at her quizzically.

Amelia leaned in to Katie, as they passed a male member of staff, and whispered, "The bowing thing."

"Oh, that." Katie seemed to consider her response for a second and said, "I think I should let the Principe explain that."

Amelia was about to question her more when they arrived at the entrance to one of the drawing rooms.

"Here we are. Just knock and the Principe will tell you to come in."

Katie left her quickly, so she did as instructed. Her heart was hammering at the anticipation of seeing Byron again.

She heard Byron call, "Come in." That voice still sent shivers down her spine.

Amelia entered the drawing room and found Byron standing by the window. The room's decor was aged and faded, like it had been frozen in time a hundred years ago. Aged, dark oak filled the room, and over in the corner a white sheet covered what looked like a piano.

When Byron turned around and smiled, Amelia had to remind herself that she was angry, because every part of her wanted to run and jump into her arms. *She hurt you, she lied to you.*

"Good morning, Amelia." Byron indicted for her to sit down by the coffee table. "I had tea served. Would you like a cup?"

Amelia nodded, but said nothing. Byron sat down and poured the tea from the china teapot. It was an absurdly normal scene and it made Amelia's anger bubble again.

"How very civilized," Amelia said sarcastically. "So, are we going to have tea and crumpets, and ignore the fact that you and your family are some sort of supernatural creatures, and that you lied to me since the moment we met?"

Byron remained cool and put her cup in front of her, before using the sugar tongs to add two lumps of sugar to Amelia's cup. She noticed Byron's hand tremoring, and wondered why. Byron didn't do nervous or scared, so what was having that effect on her?

"I always feel a cup of tea or whiskey helps with any conversation. For this conversation tea will suffice."

"Are we going to tell the truth in this conversation or are you just going to tell me what I *need* to know?" Amelia asked.

"I will answer anything you ask of me. There's no point in hiding any more. I've lost you anyway."

The sadness with which Byron said that sentence made Amelia want to take Byron into her arms and tell her she hadn't, but then her righteous anger and hurt kicked that sympathy away. "You've *lost* me? You were the one who ran, who left me with my heart crumbled on the floor after telling me you loved me."

Byron pinched the bridge of her nose, clearly finding this conversation uncomfortable. "I'm sorry. There's nothing else I can say but I'm sorry, and I did it to protect you."

"Protect me? That's a joke. Victorija might be your enemy, but at least she saved me."

Byron's eyes flashed red with anger. "She set that up to gain favour with you. I didn't leave you unprotected. Bhal and her people were watching over you from the moment you left Monte Carlo, keeping you safe."

The anger and emotion of Byron's reaction made her bite wound start to ache. She rubbed it and saw Byron's eyes gaze at it hungrily.

"You and your family…I can't believe I'm going to say this. No, I need *you* to say it."

Byron let out a breath. Amelia had worked out there was something paranormal about them, but not the full truth. She might as well get it all out at once.

"We—*I* am an immortal born vampire."

Amelia's face was full of confusion. "Immortal born vampire? I don't—"

"Vampires come in two kinds, humans turned into vampires and born vampires. Alexis is a turned vampire."

"Alexis? She was a human?"

Byron nodded. "Captain Alexander Villiers of the Household Calvary, Royal Dragoons, when I first met her a hundred and fifty years ago, but that's another story."

"A hundred and fifty years?" Amelia's voice registered her shock. "So what are you?"

Byron went to take a sip of tea, but her hand was shaking so much she put it down, and clasped her hands so the tremor wouldn't show so much. This blood sickness was gaining ground and would soon take hold of her. She had to get Amelia to understand.

"My family are born vampires. It's a long story, but the Debreks found a way to procreate, and produce more powerful vampires with each generation."

"Why was having children a problem?" Amelia asked.

"Because vampires are not alive, Amelia, and generally speaking only the living can produce life."

Amelia looked shocked. "You're dead."

Byron shook her head. "I am neither dead nor alive. I am vampire. I was born and would have seemed very much alive until I was eighteen, when I went through our ritual to become a true born vampire."

Tears started to fill Amelia's eyes. "You died when you were eighteen?"

"Yes, but I'm so much more alive in so many ways. I'm faster, stronger, than any turned vampire."

"So this banking stuff? It was all a lie?"

"No, that's our business, and has been since we first established ourselves in Venice, over six hundred years ago. I am everything you thought I was, a successful European banker, but the only thing you didn't know was that my family were vampires."

"Is Victorija—"

"She's a born, and my cousin twice removed, but her side of the family were expelled from the Debrek family a long time ago."

Amelia stood up and started to pace, holding her head. "I can't believe this. It's too much."

Byron went to her and tried to hold her but Amelia pushed her away. "Don't touch me, Byron."

That phrase hurt Byron so much, and the monster inside her whispered, *Why are you wasting time? Just take her blood. She's yours.*

Byron purposely walked away to get some distance, and found herself heading for the whiskey decanter.

As she poured, Amelia said, "The conversation has moved from tea to whiskey?"

Byron sighed. "It seems so."

"Why did Victorija want to hurt me?"

Byron walked back and put her glass on the covered piano. "To answer that, I need to tell you why Victorija's father and her side of the family were expelled. Since my great-great-grandfather's time, the Debreks have only taken blood by consent. It's our most sacred rule."

"Katie? All those people coming out of your office, they were feeding you?"

Byron sensed a tone of jealousy in Amelia's words. She did still care. "Yes, our staff feed us by consent, and we take care of all their needs, financially. They can leave at any time, no one forces them, but mostly the same families have served us through the years."

"And Victorija's family?" Amelia asked.

"They take. They see humans as food, and have no care for human life. Victorija's father was expelled from the family when he wouldn't keep our most sacred rule, and because of that, they were forbidden from the secret of how we procreate. Only each Principe knows what that is."

"And Victorija wants to have children so desperately?"

Byron gave a hollow laugh. "Good God, no. Victorija wants to build an army of born vampires. A family to rival our own. You can imagine the fate of the human population if that happened."

"I can't take any more of this," Amelia said angrily. "This is not my world. Yesterday I didn't know about it, and today I don't want to know about it. I'm leaving."

Amelia ran to the door, but of course Byron got there before her, blocking the door. "I can't let you leave, Amelia. Victorija will harm you."

"I don't want to be part of this world, Byron," Amelia said.

Amelia's anger drove Byron's hunger even harder. She grasped Amelia's face and threaded her hands through her hair.

Amelia touched her bite wound, and cried out in pain. "Why does this hurt all the time, and why won't it heal?"

Byron's mouth watered being so close to her Principessa, and the bite mark was calling her so strongly. "You're in my blood and I'm in yours," Byron replied.

Amelia touched Byron's face tenderly and gazed into her eyes. "Your eyes are red. I knew I saw that in Monte Carlo."

Amelia's softer gaze pulled Byron closer. She rested her cheek against Amelia, closed her eyes, and inhaled her scent. "I missed you so much, mia cara."

She felt Amelia's hands wrap around her neck, and her nails graze her skin. All Byron could hear was the thundering of Amelia's blood through her veins. Her mouth watered. She wanted it—she *needed* it.

Just take it. Take it now.

Suddenly Amelia pushed back from her, and said, "What do you mean, I'm in your blood and you're in mine? What does that have to do with this bite?"

Byron rubbed her face, trying to push away the effects of her hunger. Being with Amelia so close was tearing her apart, but she'd use every inch of control she had not to break down in front of her.

"We are bound in blood and spirit for all eternity," Byron managed to say.

"What the hell does that mean?" Amelia said suspiciously.

"Remember our last night in the Monte Carlo estate?"

Amelia wandered back over to her, and folded her arms

defensively. "How could I forget? It was the night my whole world started to crumble."

Byron said, "When I bit your neck, I tasted a drop of your blood, and I became so overwhelmed, our lips clashed—"

A look of realization came over Amelia. "We kissed, and I tasted your blood. What does that mean? Will I become a vampire or something?"

"No, not at all. When a vampire loves someone and their DNA is compatible, they can share blood and become bonded by it. You and I became that quite by accident. We are bonded by blood. You feel my need to feed. You can sense my feelings and I yours. In human terms it's a vampire marriage. You are my Principessa."

"Is that why everyone is bowing to me? I'm Mrs. Debrek without even being asked, not even so much as an engagement ring? I thought you people believed in consent?"

That comment hurt Byron. Little did Amelia know she was prepared to die so that Amelia wasn't forced into giving her blood to survive. "We do. It was my mistake, and I'm sorry."

"Did you know this when you left me?"

Byron shook her head. "No, I only found out recently, and when I did, I came back."

"Let me pass, Byron. I want to leave," Amelia said with a storm of emotions brewing on her face.

Byron tried to take her hand, but it was pushed away. "Please don't leave the house. Victorija knows you're my Principessa, and wants to use you as a bargaining chip."

"Funny. She wants to use me just like you did. Let me out the door, Byron, or I will run."

Byron stood back and sighed. "I'm sorry. I left because I loved you, and it destroyed me to do it."

Amelia walked out the door without looking back.

❖

To say Amelia was overwhelmed was an understatement. She retreated to her room, and apart from a text to her uncle to let him know she was safe and with Byron, she had lain on the bed and stared into space, trying to sort out her thoughts.

The bite on her neck was almost continually burning now, and every hour or so it became painfully intense, and her urge to go to Byron was almost uncontrollable.

Something had changed inside her.

There was a knock at the door and a voice said, "Amelia, it's Daisy. They're letting me leave now. I just wanted to check on you first."

Amelia sat up, and wiped her tear-stained face. She caught a glimpse of herself in the mirror, and her bite was burning red. It was like her bite and her heart were trying to tell her to do something. To act in some way that she just didn't understand.

She opened the door to find a concerned looking Daisy. "Are you okay?" Daisy asked.

"I'm okay."

"What did Byron say to you?" Daisy asked.

"She explained why I'm in danger, and there are also some things I need to come to terms with."

"Alexis the vamp says I can leave, if I take a guard. I don't know why they're worried about me. Are you staying?"

Amelia nodded. "For the time being. I need to work all this out in my head anyway. I'll walk you out."

As they walked downstairs, Daisy said, "If you need me, I'll be here in a second. You know that?"

"I know. I won't be here for long. I'll let you know," Amelia said.

At the bottom of the stairs Alexis, Wilder, and a couple of people she didn't know were waiting for them. Amelia made eye contact with Wilder, but Wilder quickly averted her gaze, and Amelia felt such a deep sense of guilt. For months Wilder had been the only one to make her smile, and yet she had gone out with Victorija, and now was apparently married to Wilder's boss. It was one big mess, and by Wilder's demeanour, she obviously hadn't just been doing her job. Wilder had genuinely liked her. She needed to talk to her, alone.

"Miss MacDougall—" Alexis started to say, but Daisy corrected her.

"Daisy—I'm no *Miss*."

Amelia smiled, and knew Katie would enjoy the look of displeasure on Alexis's face.

"Very well, *Daisy*. Wilder will take you home safely, and leave two of our warriors to guard your residence for the time being."

"Fine, and don't panic. You won't be all over YouTube tomorrow. At least not until I get the okay from Amelia." Daisy winked at her.

Amelia gave her a hug. "I'll be in touch, and I'll see you at work on Monday." Amelia heard Alexis sigh. They were determined to keep her here.

Once Daisy, Wilder, and the guards were gone, Alexis said, "Is there anything I can get for you, Principessa? I can have someone bring tea or—"

"I am not your Principessa." Amelia was immediately annoyed. They were trying to make her this Principessa thing whether she wanted to or not. "And no, I don't need anything. I'll go back to my room and try to get my head around this craziness."

Despite her words, Alexis still bowed her head before she left. As she walked off she hesitated and said, "She needs you."

Amelia didn't know what to say about that. Alexis had always just ignored her or scowled in previous meetings. Now she looked and sounded almost pleading. It was weird. She headed for the stairs, and stopped at the bottom when she heard piano music coming from the drawing room. The music was beautiful, and beautifully played.

Amelia couldn't help but follow the music to the drawing room doors. Instinctively she knew that Byron was behind the doors. She felt it in her blood, her bones, and her throbbing bite. Before she could stop herself she opened the doors and peeked through.

She saw Byron, eyes closed, and not just playing the piano but also lost in the music. Although the music was hauntingly beautiful, as was Byron whilst playing, she looked dishevelled. Her tie and jacket were off, crumpled on the floor beside the piano.

That was so unlike Byron. She was so careful, so smart, so dapper, and she never treated her clothes like that. Amelia also noticed the whiskey decanter on top of the piano, much less full than earlier. Next to it was a glass of whiskey, and another with dark red liquid like Byron had drunk in Monaco.

It hit Amelia then. Had Byron been drinking blood right in front of her, all through that holiday? If only she had opened her eyes, she would have noticed all these things.

She started to retreat, but jumped when in a nanosecond Byron was in front of her.

"Please don't leave. Come and talk to me?"

Amelia looked at Byron and saw worrying signs. Her eyes had red in them, her breathing was heavy, and her hair was messy. She almost looked ill somehow.

"Are you feeling okay, Byron?"

"Yes, now you're here. Come in." Byron took her hand and pulled her into the room. When the door shut behind her, she felt uneasy for the first time in Byron's company.

Byron lifted Amelia's hand to her lips and kissed it. "Please tell me you forgive me. I need you to forgive me, my shining girl."

This was not a side of Byron she had seen before. She was emotionally unstable and needy.

"No, you can't expect me to forgive everything overnight, if ever."

In a second Byron went from soft and emotional to angry. Her eyes shone deeper red, and dark veins appeared on the side of her forehead. She grabbed a vase from a side table and threw it across the room.

"Byron, what are you doing? What's wrong with you?"

"Why are you so angry with me. I did what was right," Byron roared.

"I'm angry because you never showed me who you really are. It would have been a shock but I could have gotten over that. Instead you lied and never showed me the truth."

Byron emptied her glass of whiskey and poured another. She strode over to Amelia angry, frustrated, and hungry. "Did you really want to know who I was? The signs were all there but you ignored them. You wanted Byron Debrek the mysterious international banker. You wanted flash and glam, not the bloodthirsty vampire I truly am."

Amelia's eyes started to fill with tears. "I wanted to know everything. I was so frightened of losing you that I didn't even tell you I loved you for the longest time. I walked on eggshells around you, worried about what little thing would make you run."

"Why did you think I'd run?"

"Because you'd never had a relationship before. Everyone kept telling me how you'd never done this or gone this far with a woman before. I loved you and I was convinced you'd leave me—and you did."

"I would have never left you if the Dreds hadn't become a problem again." Byron cupped her cheek and that one touch started to make the hunger for Amelia burn in her veins. She saw discomfort in her ex-lover's eyes. Apparently Amelia was feeling it too. "I sacrificed our love to save your life."

"How very noble of you to decide that for me, Byron. You always have to be in control, don't you."

Before Amelia knew it, she was across the room pushed up against the wall. Byron was inches from her face, her teeth had erupted, and she looked wild. Amelia felt an urge she couldn't explain, to pull Byron to her neck and let her feed. It was an impulse from her heart and her blood, and she had to use all of her control not to.

"Byron, what are you doing. I know you won't hurt me," Amelia said.

It appeared as if Byron was not quite present, and that part of her was in some other memory.

Byron looked down beside where they were standing and saw Rose bleeding onto the floor. "The last woman I cared about died against this wall, along with Alexis's wife-to-be. Victorija came here while we were out, and killed every one of my staff, and the woman closest to me."

Then Rose looked up to her and said, "Drink from her. You need her blood."

No, Byron realized. That was the monster speaking, not Rose.

She locked gazes with Amelia. "I vowed never to care for anyone again, but then this shining girl walked into my life and lit up my dark world."

Amelia touched her cheek in a gentle action, but the simple touch made her burn. She was so hungry.

"Byron, I'm sorry for what you lost, and maybe that explains why you were so protective, but it was my decision to make too. If I'd known…taking human blood is weird and knowing there's this other paranormal world out there is weird, but I would have gotten over it. I would have always been on your side, Byron, if you'd just shown me who you really were."

"You really want to know what I am?" Byron said angrily, and pushed away from her quickly. She went to the door and called in an attendant. "Jack, I need to feed."

"Byron, what are you trying to prove?" Amelia looked nervous and worried, as one of the young men on the staff walked in.

Jack unbuttoned his shirt without being asked, and Byron stood behind him. "Do you consent?"

"I consent, Principe," Jack said.

Byron sank her teeth into Jack quickly, and she heard Amelia gasp. As her attendant's blood ran down her throat, she opened her eyes and saw fear in Amelia's eyes. Byron didn't want to take too much or frighten Amelia too much, so she stopped quickly.

She pulled back and could feel the blood dripping down her chin. "This is the real me. Can you love this monster?"

Amelia turned around and ran out of the room.

That's why I didn't tell you.

"Thank you for your service, Jack."

CHAPTER NINETEEN

Amelia wanted to run out of the front door, but instead she went out to the back garden. It was a big plot of land for a London house, but it was long neglected, overgrown, and uncared for. She found a little bench and sat down. There was a chill in the air and she soon began to shiver.

What she had just seen in Byron's office was insane, and her brain just couldn't process it. Her hands were shaking and she went cold and shivery. A vampire? She'd fallen in love with a vampire.

At first Amelia felt fear, but then when Byron locked eyes with her, she felt something else. Her bite wound burned hot, she ached low in her stomach, and then a sensation she could only describe as hunger pangs began, and an urge to be where that attendant was. Amelia chastised herself for that, but rightly or wrongly, she felt it.

Maybe this urge was something…artificial, because of this bond she'd been forced into. But then she thought back to her time in Monte Carlo, before they shared blood, and she had craved for Byron to bite her neck. She'd encouraged it.

Amelia covered her face with her hands, and heard footsteps coming across the grass.

She opened her eyes and saw Bhal coming towards her. She had no idea if Bhal was a supernatural creature too, despite her modern military utility trousers, boots, and long black hooded cloak.

Bhal stopped in front of her and bowed her head. "Principessa?"

"Don't call me that. I didn't choose that title, nor this stupid bonded-by-blood thing," Amelia snapped.

"May I sit?" Bhal asked.

Amelia sighed. "If you like."

Before Bhal sat she took off her long black coat and wrapped it around Amelia's shoulders. "You look cold."

It was a sweet gesture, and she couldn't help but soften her attitude. She pulled the jacket tightly around her and began to warm.

Underneath the jacket, Bhal was every inch the warrior. She had a sword with an intricate hilt inlaid with green gemstone, strapped to her back. From the belt of her utility trousers hung a pair of dangerous looking daggers which were strapped to her thighs. Amelia was quite certain there were other weapons hidden from view.

"Did Byron send you out here?" Amelia asked Bhal.

"No. Not at all. She'd probably be pissed off with me if she knew." Bhal sat and took out a silver hip flask, and took a swig. "Would you like a drink?"

It wasn't quite lunchtime, but after what she had just witnessed, she guessed that it was allowed for shock. She wasn't a whiskey drinker, so the swig of alcohol almost made her gag, but then the burning warmth gave her a little comfort.

"Thanks."

"What brings you out here?" Bhal asked.

"I could list about fifty things, but I'd say seeing the woman you love feeding on another person would make you want to take some air to calm down."

Bhal turned around and faced her with her brows furrowed. "She fed in front of you?"

"Yes. Apparently to show me why she kept all these secrets from me. In her words, to show how I could never love a monster like her."

"You'll have to forgive her. She isn't feeling herself just now. She feels out of control, and frightened."

Amelia was surprised. "You are the second person to tell me Byron is scared, and I just can't believe it."

Bhal sighed and took another drink. "I shouldn't be telling you this probably, but Byron has been scared since she was eighteen years old. That is why she is so controlled."

Amelia turned and sat cross-legged on the bench. She had to know more. "Why?"

"She told you about the difference between turned and born vampires?"

Amelia nodded.

"Well, from birth born vampires are still part human, although the vampire blood from their parents makes them stronger, faster, and highly intelligent, but to become an immortal vampire—they have to lose their humanity."

"She told me that this morning, but I just can't…Wait—I just realized that I've never heard her heart beat. All the times we were close."

"It beats very rarely, yes. When the Debreks reach eighteen they are asked if they wish to become fully undead vampires. It's their choice."

"Everything seems to be about choice and consent, except getting married apparently," Amelia said sarcastically.

Bhal smiled. "Yes, it's what they live by. The Debreks are grateful for the gift of blood, but the Dreds believe humans are food. End of story."

Amelia pictured Victorija grabbing Daisy and feeding from her with a cruel smile on her face. "Victorija was so charming. I would have never guessed—"

"She is, most vampires are, but when you are brought up with no compassion it's hard to fight the natural urges they have. Hunt, feed, and kill."

"Byron isn't like that. She would never harm anyone," Amelia said.

"They all have that potential, but it depends how it's nurtured. I've known Byron and Sera since they were born, and they were brought up with good principles—"

"Wait." Amelia stopped Bhal in her tracks, with a hand on her leg. "Byron is three hundred years old. How old are you?"

Bhal started laughing. "Too old."

"But you're not a vampire?" Amelia asked.

"No, I am a Celtic Samhain warrior. Many, many centuries ago, my warriors were bound by honour to serve the Debreks."

Amelia squeezed her head between her hands. "All of this is just blowing my mind. Every time I think I know everything, I realize I know nothing."

"Our world is normal to us, but I understand that it is hard to comprehend for you," Bhal said.

Amelia took the hip flask and swallowed down some more burning alcohol. "You're not wrong." After a minute of contemplation, Amelia said, "Byron chose to become a full vampire?"

"Yes, she went through the ascension ceremony. They are reborn as a powerful born vampire. More powerful than any ordinary turned vampire."

"Like a super vampire?"

"Exactly," Bhal said. "They gain immortality, but lose the last of their humanity. Being born of vampire blood enhances their power, skill, strength, and speed. Byron as firstborn of two exceptional vampires is the most powerful vampire in existence, maybe the most powerful ever. No one can match her for speed and strength, not even Sera."

"Bloody hell." It shouldn't have come as any surprise to Amelia. Byron had a calm authority, characteristic of someone who had no equal, yet she was kind and compassionate and did not have an ego like Victorija.

Bhal continued, "The problem is all of her senses and needs are stronger than any vampire's before her. In her first year or so as an ascended vampire she struggled with her craving for blood, her needs to hunt and kill."

Amelia started to get a bad feeling. "What happened, Bhal?"

Bhal sighed and looked off into the distance. "She struggled with her cravings, she shook, felt ill, a bit like a drug addict desperately needing their next fix."

Amelia closed her eyes. Just like in Monte Carlo. Was she struggling that much then? Byron had run from her, and returned full of fire and passion.

"What's wrong, Amelia?"

"She behaved like that in Monte Carlo."

"That's because vampire emotions are more intense than humans', and when they are in love, even more so. They crave the blood of their lover."

"My blood?" Amelia squeaked.

Bhal nodded. "That's why—"

"Byron ran from me, and came back with fire in her veins," she finished for her.

"The Principe tried to protect you, even though it made you

suspicious, and caused her problems. Your safety was everything to her."

Amelia's mind was whirling with questions and answers and she couldn't quite fit them together yet. "What happened, in the past?"

"She was a young, green, powerful vampire caught in the lust for blood, and with no experience of how to control it. I tracked her down and found her in a cottage, covered in blood, crying and shaking in the corner of the room, with two bodies around her."

"Oh my God." She was shocked. The thought of Byron hurting anyone just didn't compute.

"She was distraught and had broken the Debrek clan's cardinal rules."

Amelia could see how that would tear Byron apart. Rather than anger, all she felt was compassion and empathy for the pain Byron lived with. "She's lived with this guilt?"

"Aye, luckily I managed to save the people before they passed on, and got Byron out of there."

"You saved them? Really?" Amelia was astonished. "What, can you bring the dead back to life?"

Bhal shook her head. "No, no one can do that. They weren't dead, and I helped them recover."

There was obviously more to Bhal and whatever powers she had than met the eye. Then a thought struck Amelia. "Wait, that's why she's so controlled, isn't it? Byron is frightened of losing iron control over her needs and hunger."

"You've got it in one. Byron thinks there is this monster inside her that she has to control at all costs. She fears being just like Victorija."

"Victorija would have never shed a tear over those people, would she," Amelia noted.

"Not at all. I've tried to teach Byron that there is no monster, but she won't listen."

"What happened after?"

"Byron was punished by the clan, and pledged to take care of the family she hurt in perpetuity. They grew to love her very much, actually, but that's a story for Byron to tell you."

When Amelia thought about all these anxieties and worries going through Byron's mind in Monaco, then being terrified that the Dreds would target her, she could see exactly why Byron left her so suddenly.

She leaned over and kissed Bhal on the cheek. "Thank you for telling me. You've given me a lot to think about."

Bhal blushed. She obviously wasn't used to that kind of affection or gratitude.

"Byron is my family, not by blood but I helped raise her, and I wanted to help you understand why she is like she is. She would probably never tell you."

"Thank you."

❖

Victorija paced up and down the living room of her London penthouse apartment. She was barely restraining her anger. Victorija turned back to Lillian, who was kneeling by the coffee table, with a map and a divining necklace.

"Mademoiselle Witch, you better get something quickly because you're starting to look like dinner."

"I'm trying, but whatever this object is that the Debreks are moving, it's well cloaked."

Victorija rushed over to Lillian, and grabbed her by the back of the hair. "Now, my dear Lillian. I need you to give this your very best shot, or your little coven of witches will be no more. Do you understand?"

Ever since Lillian's coven had helped take down her father, she had kept the witches under confinement. She couldn't risk Lillian using that group magic on her.

Lillian looked angry and frustrated. "I'm trying my best, Victorija, but your constant threat of death doesn't help my concentration."

"Very well. I will leave you to your work, and return with more threats of death later," Victorija whispered into her ear. "You better hope I'm not hungry."

The sound of Lillian's quickening heartbeat made Victorija smile. She walked over to the lift doors and Drasas joined her.

Victorija addressed the guards as they were leaving and said, "You guard her with your lives, or I'll have you walled up for eternity."

Once they were in the lift, Victorija said, "We're so close I can smell it, Drasas."

"Do you really think this witch is up to it?"

Victorija nodded. "She has incredible powers—she took down my father, after all. She'll do it with the correct encouragement. We have the Debreks on the run for the first time. Whatever this object is, it's the secret that allows them to procreate, and they are scared. The new Principessa is the key to this. I'm sure of it."

"If only we still had her. We could trade her for the object," Drasas said.

Victorija put her hand on her shoulder. "I told you to trust me, Duca. I have everything under control. Amelia Honey will be available to us if we need her."

The lift doors opened, and they walked into their clan's recreation room. The music was playing a deep beat, and there were vampires and humans in various states of undress, either feeding or enjoying each other.

A sultry blond vampire approached, and took Victorija's hand. "Come and help me feed from my human, Principe."

Victorija looked at Drasas, and smiled. "Everything will happen in good time, but for now, enjoy, Drasas."

Another female came and took Drasas's hand. "Do you think Byron has given in to her bloodlust yet?"

Victorija laughed as they walked across to a plush chaise longue on the side of the room, where two dazed and smiling humans were waiting for them.

"I doubt it. She's so ridiculously noble that she'll probably be losing herself to blood sickness. If she does, and kills her bonded Principessa, can you imagine? It would destroy her. When my father killed my mother, he was already a monster, and he didn't love her any more, but still, it affected him badly, even though he had Lillian replicate her blood as best she could. I think that's what destroyed the last of his sanity."

Drasas sat and pulled a human on her lap. "If Byron does that, Principe, she'll become one of us."

Victorija grinned, and pushed her blonde onto the chaise. "She always has been, Drasas, she just never admitted it, and now she can't deny it."

CHAPTER TWENTY

After eating some dinner in her room with Katie and Sera, who'd arrived earlier, Amelia lay down and fell asleep. She woke to the sounds of shouts, and her neck wound burning and pulsing like never before.

Byron needed her.

She got up and opened the door, and peeked out. She saw Bhal, Alexis, Katie, Sera, and Wilder outside Byron's bedroom. Amelia strained to listen and just heard Bhal saying, "My blood isn't working any more."

"She needs the Principessa's blood now," Alexis said with frustration.

Sera agreed but Wilder said, "No, you can't expose her to that."

Alexis grabbed Wilder by the neck and, more quickly than she had seen anyone move, pushed her up against the wall. "Mind your place, warrior. Your loyalty is to your Principe."

Bhal touched Alexis on the shoulder and said, "Let her down, Duca. We are all emotionally involved here."

Alexis let Wilder drop. "What do you suggest then, Bhal?"

"I gave Byron my word I wouldn't tell the Principessa that she needed her blood to survive. Byron insists she come to her."

Byron was willing to go through all this pain rather than make her feel obliged. Amelia was struck by the nobility of it all, and realized at that moment that Byron had been noble from the start. She loved her, and made herself walk away, simply to protect her from the Dreds, and now this? It all became quite clear what she had to do.

Amelia slipped on her dressing gown and walked out of the

bedroom, and along the hall. Bhal spotted her and said, "Please go back to bed. Byron is…feeling unwell."

Alexis said, "Your presence will just make her feel worse."

Sera took her hand. "It's probably best you go. Byron will be okay."

Amelia felt even more determined. This was her job, this was her task—to take care of Byron, the woman she loved. She stood a few inches taller and said, "I'm going in to her."

"No," Wilder said, "she'll hurt you."

Sera agreed. "We don't know if she can control herself with you."

Bhal and Alexis stood in front of the door.

"Both of you, move. I'm going to see her."

Alexis looked to Bhal and back to her. "No, the Principe doesn't want you near her like this."

Amelia took a step towards them and said firmly, "I am the Principessa of the Debrek clan, and I'm telling you to move."

They were all shocked at Amelia finally claiming her title, and after a few seconds, Alexis and Bhal stood back.

"Be careful," Bhal said. "We'll be here if you need us."

As strong as Amelia was trying to be, when her hand turned the doorknob, she was nervous and scared. Could she really handle this?

She walked into Byron's bedroom and closed the door. She gasped when she saw Byron curled in a ball, shaking in the corner. She was naked from the waist up, her shirt shredded a few feet away. All of her fears melted away. All that mattered was helping Byron.

"Byron?"

Byron looked up sharply and Amelia was shocked to see her eyes completely red and blue veins streaking across her temples.

Keep calm. It's just Byron.

She held her hand up and said, "It's okay, sweetheart. I'm here to help you."

"Get out," Byron snarled.

Amelia kneeled down in front of her, and took off her dressing gown.

"Get out now. I will hurt you," Byron pleaded.

Everything in Amelia ached for Byron, needed to give her what she needed. She reached out and touched Byron's face. Byron flinched away, but Amelia touched her again, and stroked her cheek.

Byron closed her eyes and groaned at her touch. "I'm so hungry for you. So hungry."

Amelia's heart was breaking watching Byron grimacing and in such pain. "Byron, you're in my blood."

Byron's eyes went wide as Amelia pulled off her nightdress, leaving her naked, apart from her underwear. "Don't, Amelia, I can't control…"

Amelia crawled forward, and Byron followed her up onto her knees, so they were face-to-face. She took Byron's shaking hands and placed them on her hips.

Byron groaned and Amelia felt an intense tug in her blood, in her heart, and in her sex towards Byron. She held Byron's face in her hands.

Byron said again, "I'll hurt you—I'm a monster."

"You won't hurt me. I'm your Principessa," Amelia said with complete assurance. She kissed Byron slowly with as much love as she could. "I love you, Byron. Finish what you started that last night in Monte Carlo."

Amelia presented her neck to Byron, and Byron squeezed her buttocks, pulling their pelvises together. She ran her lips over Amelia's neck making her shiver.

"Amelia, I shouldn't."

"You should. I love you, Byron. I consent. Take my blood."

Amelia heard Byron give an audible intake of breath. "I'm so hungry, mia cara."

She ran her fingers up the back of Byron's short hair, and pushed her head into her neck. "Feed."

No sooner had she finished speaking than she felt a sharp pain in her burning bite mark. She gasped and dug her long nails into the back of Byron's head. The pain soon gave way to a sense of light-headed exhilaration. Her muscles relaxed, but her need for Byron intensified exponentially.

She clawed at Byron's neck and back as her body demanded she get closer to her. It was as if Byron's blood was burning hot inside her veins. It was a sexual experience, but more than that, it was more intimate than any sex could ever be. They were in each other's blood, sharing their very life force.

But it was oh-so physical. There was unimaginable need, hunger, passion, and satisfaction that she was giving her lover what she needed.

Amelia's skin was alive with sensitivity, as if Byron's lips caressed every inch of her skin at once, and each time Byron sucked at her neck, she experienced the sensation of her lover sucking at her clit. The intensity caused Amelia to scratch her nails down the back of Byron's neck and back.

"Byron," she gasped, "touch me."

Byron reacted by sucking on her neck harder.

Amelia thought she might pass out, or her heart might burst, if she didn't get Byron to touch her soon. The walls of her sex were clenching and unclenching on the emptiness inside. Her body was demanding to be touched and filled.

Byron was lost to her blood, so Amelia took the initiative.

Amelia put her arms around Byron's neck and pulled her backward onto the floor. She opened her legs and Byron slipped between them. Byron started rocking against her sex, and her ferocious feeding had slowed, as if she was now slowly savouring every drop.

Amelia's sex was already wet and aching before Byron starting rocking against her, which made Amelia's desperate need so much worse. She pushed at the waist of Byron's trousers, and said with desperation, "Inside, I need you inside. Now, now."

Byron responded to her plea immediately and whilst keeping her teeth in her neck, unbuttoned her trousers and pulled her strap-on out of her jockey shorts.

Amelia felt the tip pressing at the entrance of her wet sex, and slide in with ease. She groaned. The feeling of her lover feeding from her, her teeth inside her body, while her aching sex was filled, was indescribable. The pleasure was so intense that Amelia threw her arms back behind her head.

"Yes, make me come. Make me come." Amelia could hardly find the air to speak.

Byron threaded her fingers through Amelia's and quickened the pace of her thrusts. She heard Byron mumble and moan as she drank, until she started to pull back. Amelia pushed her head back into place.

"No—come while you're feeding."

Byron nodded and her thrusts got even faster. With every thrust Amelia thought she was going to come, but her climax was just out of reach. She moved her hips slightly, and wrapped her legs and thighs around Byron's backside, bringing them closer than ever. Then it happened. The burning pleasure in her neck seemed to explode and travel all over her body, but most of all in her sex. She was coming and it was exquisitely almost painful, so intense.

Byron was everywhere. She was inside her mind, her body, and her heart. Now they were truly connected. Byron's hips thrust erratically as her orgasm washed over her.

Amelia was finally coming back to earth, when she felt Byron pull her teeth from her neck, but still she kept her face down.

Byron breathed heavily and said, "Thank you, thank you, mia cara. I love you." She had never experienced feeding like that. Byron had fed while having sex before, with other vampires, or willing humans, but the fact that they were bonded by blood was beyond sex, beyond pleasure. It was truly belonging to someone else and becoming part of them.

"I love you, sweetheart. I always did," Amelia said while stroking her head. "Don't run from me again."

Run? Byron would never leave her side again. Amelia was her world. "Are you okay?" Byron said as she tried to get her breath back.

"Byron, look at me."

She shook her head. She could imagine what her mouth and chin looked like, and she didn't want the truth of it to frighten Amelia. "No, I don't want you to see. You'll think I'm a monster."

She felt Amelia's hands stroking through her hair. "Sweetheart, look at me. You are not a monster. You're an immortal vampire who is moral and noble. You went through such pain just because you didn't want me to feel forced into giving you blood. Show me who you really are."

Byron wiped off the drips of blood from her chin with her hand, and raised her head. Amelia's eyes didn't show fear or disgust. Instead, they shone with love. It was an unusual response to Byron.

Amelia trailed her fingers down her cheek and over her bloodied lips. "Thank you for showing me the real you. You don't have to hide this from me. This blood on your lips is mine, and it's keeping you alive. Do you know what that feels like?"

Byron shook her head. "No, I've always been ashamed of it."

"I know, and we have a lot of talking to do, but this between us? I never want to change. I'm in your blood, and you're in mine. Tell me what you call it again?"

"Bound in blood and spirit for all eternity," Byron said while stroking her hair.

"That sounds about right to me," Amelia said, then pulled Byron down into a long, deep kiss, tasting the blood her lover craved.

❖

Amelia helped Byron wash in her bathroom and tucked her in to bed. She then went to the door to talk to Bhal and Alexis, who had discreetly moved further down the corridor. Wilder was gone, and she could guess why. She hated that she might have hurt her by rekindling her relationship with Byron.

"Principessa, how is she?" Alexis said while staring at her neck wound.

"She's settled now. I think she'll be okay. I'll be staying with her to make sure she rests."

Alexis didn't look totally convinced, but Bhal gave her a warm smile and said, "Are you all right, Principessa?"

Amelia touched her neck and was surprised that there was little pain, just a throbbing warmth. "I'm perfectly fine, Bhal. I'll give her what she needs from now on, so you don't have to worry."

Bhal bowed her head and said, "Our greatest thanks, Principessa."

Then Alexis followed suit, although not with the same warmth. She guessed that Alexis was somewhat unsure of her commitment and loyalty to Byron.

Once they left, she went back to the bedroom and slipped into bed beside Byron. She lay on her side and stroked Byron's head. It was wonderful to see her sleep so deeply and settled, so different to the Byron who had run from their bed every night they spent together. But now it all made sense. The secretive business meetings, urgent emails and telephone calls as soon as they were getting intimate. Byron had been hungry for her, and trying to protect her, but when she returned from feeding on someone else, her passion was intense and solely focused on Amelia.

One thing niggled in Amelia's mind since they'd finished making love. Did Byron feel that intimate, sexual experience with everyone she fed from? Was Amelia really special?

As Amelia's mind whirled with this and many other questions she needed answered, she drifted off into sleep.

A few hours later Amelia woke slowly, and her eyes flickered open to find a smiling Byron gazing at her, and stroking her cheek lovingly.

"Morning. You look better," Amelia said.

"I feel better than I have ever felt in my three hundred years, like I could scale large buildings in a single bound."

Amelia laughed. "That's my super vampire."

Byron cupped Amelia's face and whispered, "Good morning, my shining girl." Then she kissed her and had to force herself to stop. She was so full of energy, and feeling well for the first time in months, that she wanted to run, spar with Bhal, and make love all at once, but she tried to calm knowing that Amelia would have a lot of questions.

"Thank you for giving me your blood and saving me from my darkness," Byron said.

Amelia put her arms around Byron's neck and hugged her tightly. "You should have told me straight away what you needed. I would have helped you no matter what. Even if a relationship didn't work for us, I would have done anything to keep you healthy."

Byron pulled back and looked in Amelia's eyes. "It had to be your choice. I didn't want you to feel obligated to me. You already didn't get a choice about being bonded by blood with me, because of my mistake in the heat of passion."

"Whether it was an accident or not, last night I accepted who I am in your life, your Principessa. I was always yours from the first look."

Hearing Amelia say those words was more than she could have dared to dream in the past six months. "You have no idea what that means to me. I have never been happier."

Amelia playfully poked her in the chest when she went to roll Amelia under her. "No more secrets, though. It doesn't matter if you think I'll be upset, scared, or all of the above. I need to be an equal partner in this."

Byron held up her hands in surrender. "Okay, okay, don't poke me, Miss Honey. You must have a lot of questions."

"A million is a conservative estimate," Amelia joked, "but there's something I need to know."

Byron could see worry in Amelia's eyes, so she stroked her shoulder and arms. "Tell me. I'll answer anything I can."

"What we shared last night—you feeding and making love—is that what you feel when you feed from any human?"

"Has this been worrying you? How could you think anyone else could feel like you? No, when I feed it's like sating a physical hunger, but as the blood takes effect on my body, it heightens all my senses and needs, sex just being one of them."

"Is that why you came to me so hot and passionate and hungry for me?" Amelia asked.

"Yes, but that was because I was in love with you. When I feed, I don't need to have sex with the person I'm feeding from. But a lot of vampires seek out sex and feeding because feeding during sex heightens the experience."

"So you're not feeling like that for the other women you feed from?"

It touched Byron how insecure Amelia was, even though they had shared blood and she was now Principessa. She had to take such great care of her feelings and her heart because she had given Byron the precious gift of her blood and kept her alive.

Byron traced a finger over Amelia's beautiful lips. "Never. You are all I want, all I need. Think of feeding with other humans as necessary, but when I'm with you, you feed my heart and soul."

Amelia lowered her eyes and chuckled. "You're so sweet for a vampire, you know that?"

Byron placed a finger under her chin and gently lifted her head up. "It's the truth. Look in my eyes," Byron said, knowing they were becoming red with the need for blood building slowly inside her.

Amelia gasped. "They're getting red."

"Yes, for you. My heart burns for you, and I have a hunger for you that's never ending. You've seen the monster in me, and still love me."

She watched Amelia's eyes soften and lips part. "There is no monster inside you. Stop saying that about yourself."

She wished that was so. Byron felt like she had been fighting this battle her whole life. "If only that were true. I did some things in my youth that cause me great shame."

"I know what you did," Amelia said. "Don't be angry, but Bhal told me about the family you hurt, just so I would understand what you were going through."

Byron couldn't believe Amelia knew about her past. "Knowing all that, you came to me and loved me?" Byron asked with surprise in her voice.

"Of course, sweetheart. You made a mistake and lost control when you were young and couldn't handle your abilities and needs. Bhal told me you are the most powerful vampire to ever have been born, and that's got to be hard to handle when you're young."

Byron could still feel the terror of coming out of the fog of hunger, and finding herself with two people, apparently dead. "It was the worst moment of my life. I'd let my clan down, my parents down, and thought I'd taken the lives of two innocents. In that moment I believed I was just like my great-uncle Gilbert and Victorija, not a Debrek."

Amelia cupped her cheeks, and looked directly into her eyes. "You are nothing like them. Would they have felt guilt and shame at what they had done? No, you knew you were wrong, and have been making up for it ever since. Byron, you are the noblest person I know. You and your family do many great things for the human population that keep you alive. Bhal saved the lives of the two people you hurt—it's time to forgive yourself."

Byron cleared her throat nervously. She had no idea how much Amelia knew, so she asked, "Did Bhal tell you who the humans were?"

"No, she said they grew to love you, but she said who they were was your story to tell. Will you?"

"Yes. I'll tell you anything," Byron said smiling. "The family is Katie's. She is the newest member to join our staff. Her mother and father are travelling with my parents. We are very fond of them. The family gave me the gift of forgiveness, and I and my family pledge to look after them for all time."

Amelia smiled. "That makes perfect sense. Katie is so loyal to you, but also extremely kind. It must run in her family."

"It does, and I just hope that I never let that monster out again."

"It's not a monster. You just struggled and had to learn to control your powers," Amelia told her firmly. "The woman that Victorija killed, Rose, you said?" Byron nodded. "Did you love her?"

"I cared for her deeply, but I didn't allow myself to love. It suited us both. She was a witch in charge of a coven, and I had the business and the clan. But you know what?"

Amelia shook her head. "What?"

"She told me one day a woman would come into my life and not give me any choice but to love her."

Amelia kissed Byron's nose. "And here I am."

Byron laughed softly. "And here you are." She was starting to ache with hunger again. It was partly because they were newly bonded by blood, but also because Amelia understood her and her fears so well. "You know me without even being told. I can't explain how much that means to me. I've been alone for three hundred years."

"Not any more, sweetheart. I'll always be by your side, and on your side," Amelia whispered.

Byron couldn't stop her need any more, and rolled Amelia underneath her.

Amelia shivered. "When you're hungry, my blood burns and I ache inside."

Byron lowered her lips to Amelia's. "That's because you're in my blood, and I'm in yours. We're connected. Our souls are connected—"

"Bound in blood and spirit for all eternity," Amelia finished for her.

"I love you, mia cara." Their lips came together passionately and desperately.

Amelia opened her legs and Byron slipped between them. She kissed her way down Amelia's jawbone, and placed tender kisses over her healed bite mark.

"Byron, God, I need you."

Byron smiled and said, "I know. Patience." She kissed down her chest and moaned when she got to her full breasts. She kissed one while her hand squeezed the other.

Amelia moaned, "Yes," and placed her hand on top of Byron's, encouraging her to squeeze harder.

When Byron swirled her tongue around her nipple, both of Amelia's hands went to the back of Byron's head, grasping desperately. "Byron, please touch me now." Amelia grasped Byron's hand on her breast and pushed it down to her sex.

Byron didn't slip her fingers into the warmth she knew she'd find there. This was the first time she didn't have to hide her true nature, and she wanted to savour this. She didn't fight the fangs that wanted to erupt from her gums, and from Amelia's reaction, she knew her eyes were dark red.

"Don't be scared of me."

Amelia cupped her cheek, and let her thumb tenderly rub the skin around her eyes. "I'm not afraid of you, and I never was. When I see your eyes deeply red like this, they are red with passion for me. Drink from me again?"

Byron felt such liberation being able to be herself. Her mind cast back to the time they made love in Monte Carlo, when she had turned Amelia away so she would not see her vampire side.

"Do you remember the day I introduced you to Sera—we made love before going down to the beach?"

Amelia gave her a knowing smile. "I remember. We christened your antique chest of drawers."

"I did that because I couldn't control my vampire that day. I changed, my fangs, everything, so I had to change position so you wouldn't see me," Byron said.

"I'm sorry you felt you had to do that, but not any more."

"Not any more. I want to show you what I hungered to share with you that day. Do you trust me?"

"Always," Amelia said without hesitation.

Byron smiled, and quickly got up to get one of her ties. She knew how much Amelia loved to be restrained, and Byron adored to see her strain at her bonds as she made her come.

She held up the tie, and said, "Do you wish this?"

Byron got her answer from Amelia's broad smile, but she reinforced her desire for it by holding her wrists together above her head and saying, "Yes, please, Principe."

If she lived to be five thousand years old, she would never find someone as perfect for her as Amelia. After being so out of control for so long with the blood sickness, it was nice to exert some control again.

She tied up Amelia's wrists, and lay back on top of her again. "I'm so sorry I left you. I don't know how I survived without you."

"You did what you thought was the right thing, and you always do the noble thing, but never again, Byron. I have to know everything, and have a say in my future. I have to be your partner in everything."

"Of course," Byron said, then sealed her promise with a deep kiss.

She then began to kiss her way down to Amelia's breasts. As gently as she could, she grazed Amelia's nipple with her fang.

Amelia jumped in surprise, but then grasped the back of Byron's head. "Yes, again, sweetheart."

This time Byron sucked her nipple all the way into her wet mouth, and rolled it with her tongue, pressing it against her sharp fang.

Amelia seemed to love this. She gasped, "God, Byron. Yes, like that. Touch me, please, at the same time. I'll come."

Byron let her nipple go with an audible pop, and said, "I can do better than that. I want to show you something special."

Amelia could only watch her partner kiss her way down her body, using her fangs to trace their way over her sensitive skin. It was so much more exciting making love with Byron as a vampire, not only because she wasn't hiding anything and because she was with the most powerful vampire alive, a vampire capable of killing and ripping her enemy's throat out, but also because that same vampire was showing her so much gentleness and tenderness, because she loved her.

As Byron reached the fine hair just below her stomach, Amelia just had to say, "I love you, Byron."

Byron gazed up at her with passion and love, and replied, "I love you too."

Amelia had to lie back when Byron eased open her legs further and began to kiss intimately. Her hips were rocking and she ached to be filled. "Go inside."

Byron gave her clit one last lick and pulled back. She teased Amelia's opening with her fingers, never quite going fully in. Amelia moved her hips to try to encourage her, but Byron just smiled.

"Do you want me to feed from you?" Byron said.

"Yes," Amelia gasped. "You know you don't have to ask."

Byron kissed her inner thigh. "I do. I never want to do anything you don't want. Do you truly trust me?"

"Yes." That reply came from her heart.

Byron slid a fingertip inside her. Amelia's hips wriggled, and her wrists tested her bonds in frustration. She looked down and Byron was grinning.

"I love it when you get desperate, mia cara."

Amelia was about to reply with a pithy comment, when Byron slid two fingers deep inside her, and started to thrust. She gave a low groan. "Yes, sweetheart."

Byron was kissing her inner thigh while she thrust. All Amelia could think about was the orgasm that was building inside her. She needed to come so badly, and she wanted Byron's teeth to be in her as she came.

"Byron," Amelia said, "come up and feed from me when I come."

"I will feed. I told you this is what I wanted to do with you that day in Monte Carlo. I can hear your blood rushing through your blood vessels."

Byron licked a spot on her inner thigh, and then grazed it with her teeth. Amelia strained at her bonds to remind herself that she was helpless, and her orgasm got closer and closer, just as Byron's pace got quicker.

"God, Byron. Fuck me, drink from me, I'm nearly there," Amelia said.

"Look at me," Byron said.

She did look and her breath caught. Byron's eyes were a deeper red than ever, her teeth bared. It was so exciting. A vampire, her vampire was making love to her.

"Don't close your eyes," Byron said.

She was seconds from coming and Byron in a flash sank her teeth into her inner thigh. The most exquisite pleasure spread from her thigh across to her sex and her orgasm crashed over her, and each time Byron sucked at her thigh, a new wave of pleasure rolled over her, while Byron's fingers filled her at the same time.

Amelia shouted out her pleasure while her bound hands desperately clutched for Byron's head.

As Byron's ferocious feeding slowed, so did Amelia start to calm. Finally Byron pulled away, her breathing heavy and eyes still full of want. "Nothing and no one has ever tasted like you."

Amelia said, "I don't know what you just did, vampire, but you nearly blew my head off. Come here."

Byron wiped the blood from her chin, climbed up, and untied her. "Thank you for giving me your blood."

Amelia cradled Byron's head tenderly. "It's yours, always. You need to come. I can see the hunger in your eyes."

Byron nodded and positioned herself between Amelia's legs, so their sexes were touching, and began to thrust.

Amelia wrapped her legs around Byron, and thrust back against her. "I love you."

"It feels so good to make love with your blood inside me, keeping me alive, keeping me healthy. Oh fuck—"

Amelia on instinct guided Byron to her neck, and said, "Come with your teeth in me, feed some more."

"No." Byron groaned. "Taken too much."

"Just a little more, sweetheart. A little." Amelia pushed Byron's head down to her neck, and then she felt Byron pounce.

Amelia gasped, and Byron's hips thrust wildly into her, as Byron groaned into her neck. Then she pulled back and cried out, "Fuck, fuck."

Amelia knew then, as she watched Byron her rawest, most vulnerable moment, with her own blood painted on her lips, that she finally owned every part of Byron Debrek. There was nothing more hidden away. No more secrets. Byron the vampire was finally hers.

Chapter Twenty-one

Byron got up early, full of life and vigour. It was a wonderful feeling to be bonded by blood to her lover, wife, her Principessa. As soon as she woke she remembered what Amelia had said the first time she had explained about their being bonded by blood.

I'm Mrs. Debrek without even being asked, not even so much as an engagement ring?

That she was going to rectify. After showering and dressing quickly, she hurried downstairs to her office, got what she needed out of the safe, and returned to the bedroom.

When she walked in, Amelia was just stretching and opening her eyes.

"Did we not have a discussion about leaving me in bed all alone, vampire?" Amelia said.

Byron couldn't help but smile. They had their easy-going, loving banter back, something she'd missed terribly when Amelia was angry at her.

"I have a good excuse." Byron took her hand and gently pulled. "Up you get."

But Amelia remained a dead weight and didn't budge. "Isn't this something we could discuss lying down?" Amelia gave her a cheeky smile.

"No, I need you on your feet for this."

"I'm naked," Amelia said.

Byron quickly got her one of her shirts, and threw it on the bed. "Come on now, Miss Honey. Up, up."

"You know, I think you have too much energy now that you're drinking my blood." Amelia hid under the covers.

Byron crossed her arms, and said, "You do realize I'm a born vampire and could lift you out of bed with my pinkie?"

Amelia pulled the covers down just below her eyes. "Oh yes, super-duper vampire. You couldn't just be an ordinary vampire, could you?"

"Me? Never, mia cara. I'm Byron Debrek. Now if it'll make you feel better I have a gift for you."

"Presents?" Amelia pulled the shirt on quickly, and jumped up.

Byron laughed. "I knew that would get you up."

She pulled an ancient looking red velvet box from her jacket. "I remember you complaining that you were bound to me without so much as a ring."

Amelia slid her hands around Byron's neck, and smiled. "Well, a girl should expect a ring of some sort if she's going to be the wife of a super vampire, and Principessa to a clan of said vampires."

"You are quite right." Byron opened the box and revealed a silver ring, inset with a blood-red ruby. Amelia gasped.

"This has been in my family for over five hundred years."

"It's beautiful. Did your mother wear it?"

"No, she has her own ring that my father had made for her. This ring is different," Byron said. She took the ring from its box, and held it up. "This ring will protect you from danger, and help you heal from my bites more quickly."

"How can a ring do that?" Amelia asked, then said, "Wait, forget that. Of course a ring can protect me. I'm married to vampire royalty."

"Not quite," Byron said, lifting her hand.

"Wait, we're not married? I thought the whole blood bond thing meant—"

"Yes, it does. There's just a little ceremony we still have to complete, which is why I asked you to stand. Do you wish to complete the ceremony?"

Amelia caressed Byron's cheek. After all they'd been through, Byron still asked. She was the noblest person she had ever met. "Of course I do. I'm not going anywhere now I've got you back."

Byron lifted her own palm to her mouth and Amelia watched as the vampire in her emerged. Her fangs protruded, and she used them to cut a diagonal line down her palm, and it started to bleed.

She then lifted Amelia's palm to her mouth. "You are sure?"

Amelia couldn't deny feeling a little apprehensive. After all this was very different from wearing the big white dress and her uncle walking her down the aisle, but she was in a different world now, and in this world she was sure.

"I'm sure."

Byron ran her fang down her palm. She jumped at the cutting pain which was soon forgotten when the feel-good chemicals hit her brain.

Byron placed their palms together, so that their blood mixed together.

"Repeat after me. *Bound in blood and spirit...*"

Amelia took Byron's other hand, and looked directly into her eyes. "Bound in blood and spirit..."

"*...for all eternity.*"

"...for all eternity," Amelia repeated.

Byron took the ring and slid it on to her finger, whilst repeating the vow herself. Amelia felt a surge of heat and exhilaration run from the ring through her body. She staggered back from Byron, feeling light-headed.

"What was that?"

Byron grasped her, looking concerned. "What are you feeling?"

Amelia held her hand to her head, trying to process what she was feeling. "It was like something came from the ring—it was like heat, a good heat rushing all over me, and now all my aches and pains from last night are gone. I feel great." Byron didn't say anything and that worried her. "You mean this doesn't happen to everyone that wears this ring?"

"I don't really know. I wasn't around when it was last used. It is a magical ring, so anything is possible. Wait..." Byron brushed aside her hair, revealed her neck, and smiled. "Your bite mark is gone." She lifted Amelia's hand and kissed the ring. "This will protect you from harm, so we shouldn't be worried."

Amelia hurried over to the bedroom mirror, and for the first time in six months her neck had not a mark on it. She presumed the bite on her thigh was the same, because she couldn't feel any stinging pain.

Amelia looked down at her new ring. "Wow, my life is so strange now." She walked back over and put her arms around Byron. "So strange, but so full of love. I love you, Byron."

"I love you, Amelia Honey."

She rested her forehead against Byron's and said, "I think Amelia Debrek has a better ring to it."

A smile erupted on Byron's face. "Really? I didn't want to presume…"

Amelia cupped Byron's cheeks and said softly, "When you're traveling all around the world, doing all your banking stuff, I want every woman out there to know you have a wife. In fact, I'll have to get you a ring too."

Byron kissed her quickly and chuckled. "Of course, Amelia Debrek. I am very much taken, and I would love to wear your ring. In normal circumstances this blood bond ceremony would be more elaborate, and all the family and clan would be there to witness it. The tradition is that you don't share blood till the wedding day, but we jumped the gun a tad, as do most modern vampire couples."

Amelia sighed. "So Victorija robbed me of a big wedding day?"

"I promise you, once this is over, we'll plan something elaborate and wonderful."

Amelia lifted Byron's hand to look closer. It had a diagonal scar running down the palm. "You have a scar, but that's not possible. You're a vampire. You're supposed to heal."

"Not this wound. The blood bond remains a visible scar for always."

"So better than a ring?" Amelia asked with a smile.

"Exactly. Look at yours."

Byron lifted Amelia's hand, and she was shocked to find the same mark as Byron had.

"But I'm human. It shouldn't heal and turn into a fully formed scar in minutes."

"Your ring will heal you, remember?" Byron said.

A thought occurred to Amelia and she was almost scared to ask. "Byron? How long will I live?"

"As long as I do. We are one now."

❖

Byron left Amelia to dress and went downstairs to meet with Alexis and Bhal in her office. Now that she and the clan had a Principessa, their ways of doing things would need to change.

She sat down at her desk, and Alexis and Bhal bowed their heads.

Alexis said, "How do you feel, Principe?"

For once she could tell the truth. "More alive than I have felt in three hundred years, Duca."

Bhal smiled with pride. "I'm so happy for you, Byron. I knew you would find happiness one day."

Byron gave her old friend a mock glare. "I believe I have you to thank for helping Amelia to come to terms with what she was to me, and what we are."

"Well, you both needed a push in the right direction," Bhal said.

"I'm glad you did. I gave her the Grand Duchess's ring, so now I'm well and truly ready for whatever the Dreds have in store. They thought I was a difficult opponent before"—Byron slapped her hand down on the desk—"but now I have a Principessa to protect, and I will be relentless in keeping her and my clan safe."

Alexis nodded, and said, "We face a resurgent Dred clan at a time when our world is the most insecure. The Principessa's friend, Daisy MacDougall, has been exposed to our world, and she cannot be compelled. I've never seen anything like it, and she looks to expose the paranormal on the internet."

"I know there are lots of things we need to address, and that's why I've asked everyone here today, and why I've asked Amelia's uncles to join us. We have to ask the humans who know about us to help keep our world secure."

"Do you think they will do that? Daisy MacDougall is a loose cannon," Alexis said.

Byron took out one of her cigars and began to prep it. "I think through loyalty to Amelia, and to keep her safe, they will. Speaking of keeping her safe, did you ask Wilder to join us, Bhal?"

"Yes, she's outside, Principe," Bhal said.

"Ask her to come in." Byron lit her cigar and blew out a long cloud of smoke.

While Bhal got her, Alexis leaned over and said, "Are you sure this is a good idea, Byron? She is a warrior with a chip on her shoulder who doesn't respect the chain of command."

"Trust me, Duca," Byron said firmly.

Wilder walked into the office stony-faced.

"Bhal, Alexis—could you leave us?"

Once they left, Wilder said, "Principe, how can I serve?"

"I want to talk to you about the Principessa. She has now accepted her place beside me, and wears the Grand Duchess's ring."

She saw Wilder tense up. There was no doubt she had fallen for Amelia, but then everyone did fall for her sweet and innocent nature.

"Congratulations, Principe," Wilde said through gritted teeth.

Byron sat back in her chair and silently gazed at Wilder, making her shift uncomfortably where she stood. Byron had always been secure in her calm authority and used intimidation when required, but now that she had Amelia's blood in her veins, she was even more confident.

"Wilder, the Principessa's security is my top priority. Not only is she my partner, she is also the future of this clan."

"Yes, Principe."

Byron tapped her cigar into the ashtray and walked around to sit on the desk in front of Wilder. "I want you to be her guard, and work solely for her."

Wilder appeared panicked, probably at the thought of working 24/7 for the woman she cared about but could not have. "Are you sure that's a good idea, Principe? Wouldn't one of your vampires be better?"

"No, they wouldn't. You are uniquely qualified. You watched over her with Bhal for six months, so you know her habits, her way of doing things, her journey to work."

"She'll be going back to Grenville and Thrang?" Wilder said with surprise.

Byron crossed her arms. If it was up to her, Amelia would never leave her side, but she had made it clear this morning that she would be carrying on with her normal life. Byron had promised her wife she would be an equal partner in this relationship, and if she wished to return to work, then she had to allow it until things became too dangerous. Amelia had given her everything and Byron wasn't going to do anything that would jeopardize that.

"Yes, against my better judgement, but she insists, so I have to make her as safe as possible."

Wilder looked down at her shoes and nodded solemnly. Then she said, "I don't want to do it, Principe. I'm needed with Bhal—"

Byron decided to take a softer tone. She patted her on the shoulder and said, "I know why you don't want to do it. You care about Amelia. During the time you watched over her, you developed feelings for her." Wilder looked almost frightened. "Don't worry, I'm not going to kill you," Byron joked.

Wilder didn't seem to take the joke. She was still as tense as a board.

"Wilder, that's why I want you to head up Amelia's security, because there can be no better guard than one who cares about her. Besides, Amelia trusts you and is comfortable with you. That is my decision. Are we clear, Warrior Wilder?"

"Very clear, Principe."

Amelia walked into the drawing room and looked around. Some of Byron's most trusted vampires and Bhal's warriors were there. She spotted Daisy over on the couch and went to her. Daisy immediately got up to meet her, and gave her a hug.

"How have you been?" Daisy asked. "Byron's guards say you're together now. Wait, your neck is healed."

Amelia felt her cheeks burn remembering the bites and the passion they'd shared last night. "It healed up when Byron gave me this ring. It has some sort of mystical properties that help me heal more quickly. How is yours?"

Daisy held her hand to her neck and appeared nervous. "It's fine, it's fine. Your vampire friends say it will clear up in a few days."

Something seemed wrong with Daisy. "Are you sure you're okay?"

Daisy smiled and took her hand. "I'm okay. It's just a bit shocking and hard to take in. Even though I've been chasing after paranormal stories and creatures like this since I was sixteen, it's still a shock to come face to face with them, and then to be bitten? It's a bit crazy."

"I know—it's overwhelming for me too. Apparently, Byron and I are married and I didn't even get to pick a dress," Amelia joked.

"What?" Daisy pulled her down onto the couch. "How could that possibly happen?"

"It's a long story, but vampires become bonded by blood

apparently, their version of marriage or mating, when they share blood. We accidentally shared blood in Monte Carlo, and since then we have been bonded. That's why my bite didn't heal."

"Wait. How do you accidentally exchange blood?" Daisy asked.

Even though Daisy was her friend, it was hard explaining what had happened. The way Byron and she made love was very personal, so she fudged it.

"Oh, cut lips and deep kisses…Anyway, since then Byron became progressively sicker without my blood. She needs my blood to survive."

Daisy looked shocked, and quickly scanned the room, before whispering, "Are you sure you are okay with this, Amelia? I know they are superhuman and everything, but if you don't want to be here, and you need out, I could get you out with the help of my friends."

It touched Amelia so much that her younger friend was looking out for her, and willing to stand up against a clan of immortal vampires.

"I'm very okay with this. I love Byron, and there's nowhere else in the world I'd rather be."

"Wonderful to hear," Sera said, coming to sit beside them. Sera leaned into Daisy and teased, "You know, it's pretty pointless whispering among a room full of vampires. We can hear you plotting to steal Amelia away from us."

"Good point," Daisy said, "but I had to ask. Amelia is my friend."

"And I really appreciate it," Amelia said.

Sera reached over Daisy and lifted Amelia's hand to inspect the ring Byron had given her. "It's nice to see this on your finger. You are all I've ever wished for my sister, Amelia, and I'm glad to call *you* my sister."

"You too. I was an only child. It's nice to be part of a family, and one that doesn't find fault with everything I do. Can I ask you something, Sera?"

"Sure, I'm an expert in all things Debrek." Sera smiled.

"Does every Principessa wear this?" Amelia asked.

"No, our mother didn't because she was a vampire. Only mortals, so they have protection against injury."

That was interesting. So she wasn't the first mortal, as Sera put it, to marry into the clan. "Who was the last person to wear this?"

"My great-great-grandmother, the Grand Duchess Lucia Debrek, but I better leave Byron to tell you about her."

Now, that was intriguing. She sounded so grand, and a little intimidating. It was just one more thing to add to her list of a million questions. It was going to be hard being a human and entering a world she never even knew existed. At least Daisy had been researching this world for a long time.

Amelia looked up and saw Wilder filling a whiskey glass from the decanter. She had to talk to her. "Excuse me for a minute, will you? I need to talk to Wilder."

Sera grasped her hand as she stood and said, "Be careful with her. I think she's a little heartbroken."

Amelia nodded, and again felt guilty. She had never led Wilder on or made her believe there could be anything between them, but it didn't stop the guilt. She had to make this right again.

"Wilder?"

She watched Wilder tense at the sound of her voice, then turn around slowly, with a large glass of whiskey. There was an awkward silence. Then Wilder said, gesturing to the ring on her finger, "I hear congratulations are in order, Principessa."

"Yes, thank you. Wilder, I—"

Wilder stopped her. "You don't have to say anything. The Principe came back into your life, and no one's going to turn her down. But, then again, she never really went out of your life, did she? All these months you carried her with you everywhere you went, even though she hurt you."

"Yes, I did, because I couldn't equate the person I knew with what she did. Now I understand why she left me—because she loved me, and that's all I've ever wanted."

Wilder gave her a sad smile, and Amelia took her hand. "You know the only bright spot in the darkness over the past six months? It was you making me laugh and smile, Wilder. Thank you."

Amelia leaned forward and kissed Wilder on the cheek. Wilder jumped back when Byron walked into the room, flanked by Alexis and Bhal. Wilder looked visibly nervous as she waited for Byron's reaction to being kissed by the Principessa, but Byron smiled and held out her hand for Amelia to join her.

Byron stopped in front of the stone fireplace, and when Amelia came into her arms, she gave her a soft kiss. Neither was expecting the intensity that came in the slightest touch between them since they were blood bound, and Byron knew from Amelia's response that she was bound to Byron as much as Byron was bound to her. They craved each other. Byron's gaze dropped to Amelia's neck and she smiled.

"Everything okay with you and Wilder?"

"We had a chat, and I think we'll be good friends," Amelia said.

"That's what I like to hear, mia cara."

Amelia slipped her hand inside Byron's suit jacket, and whispered, "That's Mrs. Debrek to you, vampire."

"Quite so. Mrs. Debrek. My Principessa."

They were interrupted by a disturbance at the drawing room door. Katie walked through the door backward. "Please just give me a minute to announce you."

Amelia was surprised when she saw her uncle Simon barging into the room, followed by Jaunty. Uncle Simon was exuberant, flamboyant, much more of a social butterfly than the slightly reserved Jaunty, but they shared one trait. They were ferociously protective of Amelia.

"Where is this Byron? I'll have a few strong words for her." Simon strode angrily over to them, and then realized who Byron was. He wasn't a tall man, and he had to look up to Byron. "Oh my, you are very tall…Well, anyway, what are you doing keeping our girl captive?"

"Uncle Simon, it's—"

"Six months my Amelia was breaking her heart, crying over you, and now you reveal to her you're a bloody vampire, and lock her away in this dusty relic."

Jaunty put a calming hand on his back. "Simon, let Amelia speak."

Amelia furrowed her brow. "Uncle Simon, you knew Byron was a vampire?"

Simon waved his hand dismissively. "Jaunty knew about Byron and her father for years, and I told him not to let you date her. It would only end in trouble for you, sweetie."

Amelia couldn't believe it. "You knew, Uncle Jaunty? Why didn't you tell me?"

Jaunty stepped towards her, and took her hand. "It was just suspicions, sweetheart, until I confronted Byron about it before you went to Monaco. I warned her not to let me down—"

"And I did." Byron stepped into the conversation and put her arm around Amelia's waist. "But only for the best of reasons, to keep

Amelia safe, and Amelia is not captive here, Simon. She can leave anytime she wants."

"I do want to be here, Uncle Simon." Amelia gave her uncle a hug. "I promise."

"Why don't you and Simon take a seat, Jaunty. We can talk about the situation calmly," Byron suggested.

Jaunty took a reluctant Simon's hand and guided him over to the couches. Everyone else took a seat, leaving Byron and Amelia standing by the fireplace.

Byron cleared her throat, and put an arm around Amelia's waist. "Thank you for coming, everyone. I asked you here to tell you that Amelia has now accepted her role as Principessa of the Debrek clan."

Most of the faces smiled at that statement, apart from Wilder, Simon, and Alexis. Amelia knew it would take time for Uncle Simon to come around, and maybe longer for Wilder. Alexis on the other hand never seemed to smile, so she didn't take it personally.

Byron continued, "As we make this transition in our clan, we face a threat from the Dreds. Amelia is in danger because she can be used to gain our secret, and to that end I ask you, Daisy, if you would keep the knowledge of our world to yourself, not for my sake but for Amelia's. The chaos of outing our world would make protecting ourselves so much harder."

Both Amelia and Byron looked hopefully to Daisy. She looked like she was thinking hard, and Amelia was quite sure she wouldn't stop her investigations, but was certain she would never expose them.

"Daisy?" Amelia said.

Daisy sighed. "Of course I won't. I would never put you in danger. Typical, I've been searching for this world all my life. Now I'm in it, and I can't tell anyone."

"Thank you," Byron said. "And Jaunty and Simon? Can I rely on you to keep this quiet?"

"You and Amelia can always rely on us," Jaunty answered for them both. "Just make sure you put Amelia first, Byron."

Byron put her hand on her heart and said, "You have my word of honour, sir."

Amelia felt totally loved and adored, something she'd looked for her whole life. Byron had proved her nobility, and she knew Byron would keep the declaration she had just made till her dying day, if a vampire could have a dying day.

Byron took a few steps forward. "This will be a difficult and dangerous time. Amelia will be returning to work, at her request. Wilder will be her personal guard, and I have complete confidence that she will keep the Principessa safe, but the rest of you, keep alert, and remember we're not just fighting for us, we're fighting for the human world's safety."

Amelia imagined a world with many born vampires sired by Victorija, and it just didn't bear thinking about. They could not afford to lose this war.

Chapter Twenty-two

Amelia's eyes fluttered open as the alarm on her phone rang. It was Monday morning, the start of another workweek, but this was a very different Monday morning than she was used to. It wasn't grey, lonely, and devoid of love. No, she was loved and sharing a bed with the love of her life. She reached for the alarm and set it to snooze. Byron lay contentedly beside Amelia, her arm draped across her middle.

Amelia stroked her brow. It was wonderful that Byron didn't need to run and hide from her any more. She knew Byron's truth.

She scooted closer and began placing soft kisses on Byron's face. "Sweetheart, wake up. I have to go to work soon."

Byron stirred, stretched, and then wrapped her arm around Amelia. "No, stay in bed. Why do you have to work? You're the wife of a multibillionaire banker."

Amelia knew she was only half joking. She knew Byron would be happier if she didn't take the risk of going to work with the Dreds' threat hanging over them.

"Because it's my life, my family business, and who would make your suits and keep you dapper if I didn't? Besides, I'm not sitting around getting my nails done while you manage the world's banking industry."

"If you insist, but I was thinking. Would you like to have this house renovated and make it our home, or get something new? My penthouse isn't really a warm family home."

Amelia loved that idea. That meant she could live with Byron but still remain close to her uncles, and the shop.

"That's a great idea, and it would be somewhere for Sera to stay when she's with us."

"Exactly," Byron said, rolling on top of her. "Why don't you take charge of the project and make it the house you want."

Byron could see the excitement written all over Amelia's face. It felt wonderful and warm to share these moments with Amelia. It just reminded her that she wasn't alone any more, and the darkness inside her had Amelia's light to keep it where it belonged.

"I might bring down your bank and all the financial markets with the shopping and purchases we'll need."

Byron chuckled. "I doubt it. I have very deep pockets."

"Lucky me, then. What a good catch you are. A billionaire banker, super vampire"—Amelia tenderly stroked her face—"and a heart that will love me for eternity."

Byron could feel her morning hunger grow with every second she looked into Amelia's eyes.

"You're hungry, sweetheart?" Amelia asked.

"It's not that bad," Byron lied. She didn't want to disrupt Amelia's morning.

"Don't, Byron, we promised we would be honest and open, no matter how it would affect me. I know you're hungry—your eyes are red, and I can feel you in my blood," Amelia said.

"I can't hide anything from you now that we're bonded by blood, can I?"

Amelia gave her a soft play-hit on the arm. "Exactly, so don't even try, vampire."

"Fair enough. How long do we have?" Byron lowered her lips to Amelia's, and started to kiss her chin and cheeks.

"An hour. It's plenty of time. Remember, I've got a car and driver now, no more running to catch the Tube for me. One of the perks of being married to a rich international banker."

"Are there other perks?" Byron said before kissing Amelia's jawbone and down her neck.

"Oh, a couple." Amelia reached down and grasped Byron's solid buttocks.

Byron's rate of breathing increased and her eyes became a deeper red. She broke away from her neck kisses and said, "You know you could feed me without having sex, don't you?"

Amelia laughed. "What? You get the pleasure of feeding and I get nothing else? Not likely, vampire." Amelia stroked Byron's hair. "I want this always to be special between us, never routine, not like the way you feed from your attendants. This is different. It's you and me with no barriers between us, no lies or half-truths, just Byron and Amelia, Principe and Principessa bonded by blood, heart, and soul."

Byron simply gazed at her with awe. "I don't know how I survived three hundred years without my shining girl, never mind the last six months. It was…lonely."

"I know, sweetheart, but you don't need to be alone now. I'll always give you what you need, and this will always be special."

Byron's hunger was getting more desperate, and she said, "May I feed, Principessa?"

Amelia pulled her down into a kiss. "Always, Principe."

Byron smiled and felt her first ripple of pleasure. Amelia was not only perfectly attuned with her DNA, her blood, but sexually too. They fulfilled a need in each other that needed no explanation.

As hungry as she was, she wanted to kiss Amelia, and show her how much she loved her. Feeding from Amelia wasn't simply about being hungry for blood and sating that need. It was about tasting her lover's lips, tasting her body, and savouring every last part of her, before losing herself in the sweet ambrosia of her Principessa's blood.

Amelia moaned into her kiss, and Byron couldn't wait any longer. She reached down between Amelia's legs, and found the wetness that showed her how much her lover wanted her.

The hunger for Amelia's blood grew too intense. She slipped two fingers deep inside Amelia, and then sank her teeth equally deep into her neck. The taste was so intensely rich and delicious, that she wondered how she'd lived so long without it.

Amelia gasped, and dug her nails into her back. Amelia was right, this would always be different special. Nothing could compare with feeding from her Principessa.

❖

Victorija awoke from her slumber with two of her female vampires beside her, and three human bodies strewn across the floor. She rubbed her head to soothe it. It had been a long night, where human blood just wasn't enough. She craved the taste of something more than human, and drank heavily from her two vampire companions.

The last thing she wanted was them in her bed the next morning. She pushed them both and they began to stir. "Get out of my room by the time I get back from the bathroom."

One of the women traced her finger provocatively across her shoulder. "But we could have so much more fun, Victorija."

Victorija couldn't be bothered with wasting time. She grabbed her by the throat and compelled her. "You'll get out of my room now before I rip your pathetic turned vampire heart from your chest."

"I'll get out of your room before you rip my pathetic heart from my chest," the female vampire repeated, while her companion was quickly gathering her clothes.

"Don't worry, Principe. I'll take her."

Victorija got up and walked to her bathroom, but before she went through the door, she pointed to the human bodies on the floor and said, "Oh, and get someone to clean up the mess."

She slammed the door and quickly splashed water from the sink onto her face. Victorija looked at herself in the mirror, gazing at the bloodstain still visible on her mouth and chin. Last night her hunger was ferocious. She guessed it was frustration at making no progress with Lillian and the Debrek secret. Lillian was the most powerful witch she knew. If she was struggling to find the item, the spell, whatever it was, then there must be some powerful magic at play.

There was a knock at the bathroom door.

"What? I don't wish to be disturbed."

"Sorry, Principe." When she heard Drasas's voice she opened the door.

"What is it, Duca?" Victorija took a towel and wiped her face.

"One of our people was at The Sanctuary last night, and there was a drunk warrior crying on her shoulder."

"And why should this interest me, Drasas?" Victorija said.

"The warrior was Wilder, from the Debrek clan."

Victorija threw the towel down and folded her arms across her bare chest. "And why was a warrior from the wonderful, perfect, noble house of Debrek crying into her ale?"

"The one she loved had chosen to reunite with her lover."

She had an inkling who that love would be. Wilder spent a great deal of time watching over Amelia, and had obviously fallen for her. It was inevitable that someone as beautiful, as gentle, as innocent would ensnare the heart of a warrior.

In the short time she had spent with Amelia, even she, a bloodthirsty vampire with no human feeling left inside of her, had started to open up to her. She closed her eyes and remembered.

Someone hurt you, Victorija? Amelia asked.

Victorija shook off the memory. Amelia had an aura of empathy and it was easy to fall to her charms. "So Byron has finally grown some teeth and taken her woman?" Victorija said.

Drasas shook her head. "No, the way I was told it, Miss Honey went to her willingly. Byron the pious was willing to die before taking the blood she needed."

"Byron's desperate desire to keep her last shred of humanity never fails to amaze me. She is pathetic, and not worthy to carry on the royal born vampire legacy. So the Debreks have a new Principessa? No matter, I'll still get what I want. My plan was not dependent on them."

Drasas bowed her head, and left.

Victorija clapped her hands together. "If I can just get Lillian to get her bloody arse in gear and find this item, everything would be perfect." She turned and looked into the mirror. She smiled and said, "Byron, I'm coming for you, and everything that it means to be a Debrek. You better be ready."

Byron walked out of the shower room with only a towel around her, and the sight that greeted her took her breath away. Amelia was half dressed in her underwear and silk blouse, one leg up on the bed while she pulled her stocking up.

She leaned against the wardrobe and simply watched, just to convince herself this was real. In the time they spent apart, she'd imagined many times what it would have been like to have followed her sister's advice, and her heart, and not cut things off with Amelia. She dreamed about her that whole time, but then opened her eyes, and there was nothing there but an empty room.

"What are you gazing at so intently?" Amelia said with a smile.

Byron walked over to her and pulled her into her arms. "You,

you're so beautiful, and I can't believe you're here. I was thinking about how I dreamed of you like this all the time we were apart. It nearly killed me to stay away from you."

"I know, but that's all in the past now. We're together, and we still have so much to catch up on, and talk about. Maybe once this Victorija thing is sorted out we could go on holiday, just you and me."

"I'd love to. Where would you like to go? You name the place, and I'll make it happen."

Amelia wrapped her arms around Byron's neck and said, "Hmm… somewhere hot, with white sandy beaches and blue sea."

"I think I know just the place, I own a nice little island in the British Virgins Islands."

Amelia chuckled and shook her head. "Of course you do. Flash and glam as always, sweetheart. It's going to take some getting used to being married to a billionaire banker."

"I'm sure you'll soon get the hang of it when my sister starts taking you shopping," Byron joked.

Amelia looked down and sighed.

"What's wrong?" Byron asked.

"Nothing, really."

In Byron's experience of three hundred years, a woman saying *nothing, really* meant there really was something wrong. She grasped Amelia's chin lightly and met her eyes.

"Tell me."

"I was just thinking. I mean, it's silly really, but I always had this dream that when I got married I'd have the white dress, Uncle Jaunty giving me away, cake, and dancing, the whole fairy tale, I suppose."

"Instead you got a vampire and a blood bond," Byron said.

Amelia gave her a smile and a quick kiss on the cheek. "I wouldn't change it for the world."

Everything had happened so fast that she hadn't given Amelia anything she should have. They were bonded by blood for eternity, yes, but she hadn't honoured Amelia's human world, or her family. She needed to fix that as soon as their very real vampire problems were dealt with.

Amelia looked at her watch and gasped. "I'm so late." She ran over to the bed and slipped into her skirt.

Byron walked over to the wardrobe and took out one of her suits.

There was a knock at the door, so she quickly put on a dressing gown. "Come in."

Katie walked in with a huge tray laden with food. She smiled and bowed her head to both Byron and Amelia. "Principe, Principessa, cook thought you might enjoy breakfast in bed."

Amelia looked greedily at the delicious looking food, coffee, and juice. "That looks so good, but I'm just going to have to run out the door."

"I'm sure your uncle won't dock your wages just for being a few minutes late. Eat some breakfast with me, please?"

Amelia was torn.

Katie started to pour out two cups of coffee for them, and said, "I'm sure Daisy will hold the fort for you."

"Okay, okay, give me a minute." Amelia picked up her phone and walked off to her dressing table to call into work.

Katie brought a cup of coffee over to Byron, and said, "How are you feeling, Principe?"

"Perfect, now that I have Amelia."

"Congratulations, I never got the chance to say that," Katie said.

"Thank you, and thank you for being such a good friend to Amelia and a support to us both. Now, there was one thing I wanted to ask you, Katie."

"Anything, Principe."

Byron took a sip of coffee and set the cup down on a side table. There was something she'd been mulling over ever since they had arrived back in London. A phone call to Katie's parents had confirmed her thoughts.

"Now that Amelia is Principessa, things are going to change. She will have her own way of doing things, her own ideas for the running of the household. We plan to make this house our home, our base, and travel from here."

Katie smiled warmly. "That's wonderful. The Principessa will want to be near her family."

"Quite," Byron's said. "I had a conference call with my parents and your parents in New York. They are very happy with my mother and father, and we all feel it's time for everyone to move on. Make way for a new generation."

"What do you mean?" Katie asked.

"Your parents wish to stay with my mother and father, and I would like you to take your mother's place as my head of household."

Katie looked shocked. "But there are lots of staff and attendants a lot older than me that would expect the job."

Byron cupped her cheek and smiled. "They don't have your enthusiasm, intelligence, or close relationship with Amelia. She counts you as a friend, and she needs a friend close to her as she embarks on her new life." Katie stared in silence for a few moments before Byron said, "Well? Is that a yes or a no?"

Amelia came over to join them and Byron naturally put an arm around her waist.

"I can stay and have breakfast. I don't have my first client till twelve o'clock." Amelia looked between Kate and Byron and said, "Wait, what am I missing?"

"I told Katie we were making London our home, and offered her the job of head attendant of our household."

"Oh yes, please say you'll do it, Katie," Amelia said excitedly.

Byron watched on happily and the two women shared a hug, and immediately began talking about house plans.

"We need to redecorate this whole house, and make it something less like Dracula's castle," Amelia said.

"Exactly! We need to bring this place into the twenty-first century," Katie said, sitting on the bed with Amelia. "I can't wait to tell Alexis. She's going to hate it."

Byron couldn't help but chuckle along with them. Alexis's feathers did tend to ruffle when Katie was around. She walked to her dressing room. It was a strange but oddly comforting experience to hear them chat and plan her life.

Amelia said goodbye to Katie, then opened the dressing room door and walked in. She saw Byron trying to choose her suit for the day.

"I thought you were busy changing the house with Katie?" Byron said.

"No, she had to go, and I thought I'd like to help you dress," Amelia said.

Byron raised an eyebrow. "Oh, really? I thought you were pushed for time."

Amelia looked through Byron's collection of ties and tried a few against the suit. "I'm already late. Besides, I'm your personal tailor."

"How true. Then I am at your disposal. Dress me, Mrs. Debrek." Byron took off her dressing gown, and Amelia's eyes roved all over her body.

Amelia was lost in her gaze, until Byron said, "Amelia? Underwear is in those drawers."

Amelia shook herself and took a breath. She loved Byron's body, and could look at it for hours. She walked over to the drawers and picked out jockey shorts and a vest. She knew there was one more thing that made Byron who she was, but should she ask?

Byron decided for her when she said, "Bottom drawer, mia cara."

She opened up the drawer, and quickly picked out one of the strap-ons. Byron had them made to measure so they could be worn under her suit.

Amelia had never used a strap-on with any other lover before. She'd always fantasized about it, but never asked for it. That was part of the reason she and Byron were so sexually in tune. She didn't have to ask. The strap-on was such an essential part of Byron's sexuality that it was just natural to her. Amelia remembered the first time she'd measured Byron at Grenville and Thrang.

Amelia moved around in front of Byron with her pencil in her mouth. This would be the difficult part—being in such close proximity to someone who radiated a heat that drew her in and made her want things she had only thought about in the privacy of her mind.

She took what she thought was the safest option and kneeled by Byron's legs. When her eyes naturally went to Byron's fly and she saw a slight bulge there, her heart started to hammer.

Oh my God. Does she? She couldn't wear—

Just like her fantasy?

She held up the tape to Byron's inside leg and couldn't help the small groan that escaped her lips. Byron wore a strap-on.

It was her fantasy, Byron was her fantasy. She looked up when she felt Byron's hand stroking her head.

"You see why I need discretion, Amelia?" Byron said.

"Yes," Amelia croaked. "I can give you discretion, I can give you anything you want, Byron."

"I know."

She was pulled from her thoughts by Byron's touch. "Amelia? What are you thinking?"

"About the first time I measured you. I thought someone had seen into my fantasies, and sent you to me."

Byron smiled, took the strap-on, and underwear, and quickly put them on. "I think I was made for you three hundred years ago."

Amelia chose a shirt and tie and held up the shirt for Byron to slip into. Then she wrapped the tie around Byron's neck and held it there. "Byron, what was it like for you, living through those different time periods? Did you always wear suits and look—"

"Dapper?" Byron finished for her.

Amelia nodded, and she felt Byron wrap her arms around her waist.

"I always presented as male. It was easier for me, easier to express who I was at times in history when women were generally pretty ornaments with pretty dresses. Although Sera happily tried to push those boundaries."

Amelia smiled. "I could quite imagine, but you are different. The thought of you in a dress just doesn't work. Your energy is so different."

"Yes, and Alexis was the same. As times slowly changed I revealed who I truly was, but it seems fashion has only started to catch up with me in the last few years. I was dapper back when the word was first invented, but now lots of gay women embrace the dapper gent inside of them." Byron winked at her.

Amelia grinned, and started to fix her tie. "You are just perfect, but I think if I'd met you back in the 1700s or the 1800s, I'd have still known who you were."

Byron pulled her closer, and whispered, "Who am I?"

Amelia stroked Byron's cheek softly. "A vampire, someone who is noble, thinks of others before herself, a Principe, a leader, a sister, a daughter, a woman, but a very special kind of woman who expresses herself in a more masculine way, and the person I love with all of my heart."

Byron was silent gazing into Amelia's eyes.

"Your eyes are getting red."

"They're red because I want you. Every time I think I love you as much as I can, you say something, and I realize I love you more."

Their lips came together softly, and Amelia felt Byron's fangs had erupted, but she didn't recoil. This was who Byron was and she loved every part of her. She pulled back an inch or so, and ran her tongue slowly around one of Byron's fangs. Byron seemed to find this seductive because she moaned low and deep, and grasped her backside firmly.

Byron's moans made Amelia want to hear more, so she lowered her hand and caressed Byron's strap-on through her underwear.

She was rewarded with more moans, and Byron said, "How late can you be?"

"Enough time for me to do what I wanted to do when I was measuring you that first time."

"What was that?" Byron asked.

Amelia smiled and took her dressing gown off, leaving just her bra and stockings. She licked her lips, and lowered herself to her knees. She looked up at Byron, who was breathing heavily. "Measure your inside leg and make you come."

CHAPTER TWENTY-THREE

Victorija had spent a frustrating afternoon in the gym, helping train her newly turned vampires. She was fighting one in the centre of the gym, while the others watched around them in a circle.

Victorija blocked several punches and kicks with ease. These new recruits were meant to be cannon fodder, true, but she still had to impart some skills to them for the fight ahead. She was becoming bored with the pitiful attack from this vampire, though, and with a sigh snapped his neck. He fell to the floor of the gym with a heavy thud.

"You have to be better than this," she thundered at the turned vampires circling the floor. She stalked around the circle and saw the fear in their eyes. She couldn't lead fearful vampires into battle.

There had to be a cull.

"Those of you who wish to be immortal and live extraordinary lives, and have the courage to fight in battle with me, take a step forward. If not, then I will free you from my service."

Tension was high in the room, and the vampires looked to each other, trying to figure out what to do. Finally, some started to step forward, a few at a time, until just under half had chosen to serve her.

"Very well, we have our answer, then." She stood in front of one man who hadn't stepped forward, put a hand on his shoulder in a friendly fashion, and smiled at him. "I always keep my word, so I will free you from my service."

Victorija looked over to the back of the room, where her seasoned vampires stood waiting and watching. She nodded, and in a flash they moved at incredible speed around the room, and the newly turned vampires started to fall to their knees, their bloody, crushed hearts dropping beside them.

The man in front of her was the only one left standing, and was shaking with fear. "I'm sorry, I've changed my mind, Principe. Please?"

Victorija rubbed her chin as if considering it, but then thrust her hand into his chest, and squeezed his heart. "You know, I actually thought about it for a second, and then I remembered I dislike weak cowards."

She pulled his heart out and crushed it in front of his eyes. He fell to the floor and Victorija turned to the remaining new vampires.

"This is a lesson to show you what happens to the weak, and the feeble. You have immortality by my say so, you keep breathing by my will, so toughen up and get stronger!" Victorija roared.

She strode to the back of the gym where the lift was.

The doors opened and Drasas was there. "I have a report on the Debreks, Principe."

Victorija stepped into the lift. "Ride with me up to my apartments. The stench of cowardice is making me feel sick." The doors closed and Victorija said, "I think these humans we turn get softer with each passing century."

Drasas handed her her phone. "This might cheer you up, Principe. Amelia Honey is back at work, although with a wall of warriors and vampires around her."

Victorija gazed at the pictures of Amelia getting out of a Debrek car and walking into Grenville and Thrang. There was something about Amelia that stirred a shadow of feelings once brutally destroyed in her. She ran a finger over her beautiful face. If only she had gotten to Miss Honey first—or Mrs. Debrek, as she now was. Amelia Dred sounded much better.

"May I, Principe?" Drasas took the phone back and zoomed the picture in to Amelia's hand. "Look closely at her hand."

Victorija couldn't believe what she was seeing. "The Grand Duchess's ring? Why does she have it?"

"We have no idea, Principe," Drasas said.

Victorija ran her hands through her unruly hair. "That ring has not left her finger since she married my grandfather."

It had been over two centuries since she had spoken to the Grand

Duchess, her own grandmother. She was yet another family member who had found her wanting and rejected her.

Victorija redirected the lift to take her to Lillian's rooms. The lift opened and she pushed open the door without knocking and found Lillian writhing on top of one of her vampires while the vampire fed from her wrist.

"I can see you're hard at work trying to work out the Debrek spell."

"You could knock, Victorija." She slid off to the side, and the nervous vampire under her fixed his clothes and hurried past Victorija and Drasas, saying, "Excuse me, Principe, Duca."

"You could find out the Debrek spell or I could rip your head from your spine."

"I'm trying to uncover the item twenty-four hours a day, but I need a little recreation."

"Look at these pictures." Victorija handed Lillian the phone. "Look at her hand—she's wearing the Grand Duchess's ring."

Lillian looked at the pictures and then back to Victorija. "She gave it up?"

Victorija nodded her head. "That ring is her protection. It's what kept my father from killing her to get the spell. Why just give it up to Byron simply as a wedding ring?"

"Lucia is the most powerful witch I've ever known," Lillian said. "She wouldn't have done it lightly. Maybe she is protected in some other way."

"Drasas," Victorija said, "send two of your best people to Venice, find out what's going on, and take her prisoner if they can. Meanwhile, Mademoiselle Witch, get back to your spells and incantations, before I start to think you are useless to me."

She could hear the fear in Lillian as her heart thudded and her blood rushed. Lillian hurried back to her table.

Victorija couldn't believe her luck. Lucia, her grandmother, was unprotected. If she could kill her, then she would have killed the two people who had hurt her most.

❖

Over the next few weeks, life started to settle down for Amelia. They heard nothing more from Victorija and the Dreds, and Amelia was slowly coming to terms with a new world of vampires and other paranormal creatures.

Amelia and Daisy were just finishing up with her second client of the afternoon, a rather elderly and rotund member of the House of Lords who appreciated her talent for designing a flattering suit for his size.

Amelia took the last measurement and Daisy wrote it down. "I think that's all we need for size. So, it's the grey houndstooth fabric, and the dark blue herringbone, Your Lordship?"

"I wish you'd call me Dickie, young Amelia."

Amelia looked at Daisy and winked.

"Okay, Dickie, when can you come back for a fitting?"

Dickie started to chuckle as Daisy helped him back on with his jacket. "Anytime you like, my dear. It's a delight to be helped by two such pretty girls, although I see you are spoken for now." Dickie pointed to her ring, and Amelia couldn't help but smile.

The last few weeks had been the happiest of her life, apart from a team of vampires and warriors following her everywhere.

"Yes, I am. Very happily taken."

"I hope the young man is worthy of you, my dear," Dickie said.

Before Amelia got a chance to say anything, Daisy piped in, "Yes, her young man is a billionaire woman banker."

Dickie looked confused and gave Daisy a withering look.

"Yes," Daisy continued. "Byron Debrek. You might have heard of her?"

Realization dawned on him and he seemed to understand. "I see. I understand. Very powerful woman she is indeed, could bankrupt Britain on a whim," he joked.

Amelia's phone started to ring, and she checked it quickly. It was Byron. "I'm sorry about that. I thought I had it on silent."

"Don't worry, my dear. On you go, and I'll finish up with the delightful Daisy." Dickie waggled his eyebrows suggestively.

"Thank you, Dickie."

Daisy whispered as she passed, "I'll get you for that."

She hit Call Back and walked down a corridor to the storeroom for some privacy.

"Good afternoon mia cara. How are you?"

"Hi, sweetheart. I'm fine, can't wait to see you tonight. Where are you?"

"I'm in Paris, but I'll be back in time for a dinner. A nice quiet dinner, in the drawing room, and then we could eat dessert in front of the fire, hmm? I'll have something brought in for us."

As wonderful as things were between them, it was starting to feel like Monte Carlo again, being cooped up, never going out. It couldn't be that way again.

"Byron, while you're running the world today, try to find a moment to think where you're taking me out on Saturday night. I'm not going to be cooped up every night. This can't be like Monaco all over again."

"But Victorija—"

"No, Byron, I'm not going to live my life waiting for some vampire to attack us. You're all immortal—it could be centuries."

Amelia really had changed in the time they had been apart. She had gained a strength she hadn't had before, and was only too willing to call Byron out, but she suspected Byron liked it.

"You are right, of course. I will plan something nice for you. I promise I won't make the same mistakes again," Byron said, and Amelia believed her. Things really were different now.

❖

Byron waited at the bottom of the stairs for Amelia. Sera and Bhal were talking, while the staff milled around helping people with their coats.

"Try not to get into any trouble this time, Sera," Bhal said to Sera.

"Why, thank you, Bhal. I'm so glad you like my new dress. Can you ever say anything nice to me or just criticize me?"

Byron heard footsteps on the stairs and turned around expecting it to be Amelia, but instead it was Katie, and she looked beautiful. Alexis stopped midconversation, and she heard her Duca's heart thud loudly.

Alexis immediately marched over to meet Katie at the bottom of the stairs.

"Where do you think you're going, Katie?" Alexis said sternly.

"Out, to have a life. You know, that thing you don't have?"

Byron heard Alexis almost suppress a snarl. "It's not safe for a human at The Sanctuary."

"The Principessa is going," Katie replied.

Alexis took hold of Katie's arm and pulled her over to the side of the staircase. "She has a multitude of vampires and warriors to protect her. You don't, and I can't be in two places at once. I need to concentrate on the Principe, and her wife. Your place is here."

Katie yanked her arm away from Alexis, and said angrily, "Since when is it your job to keep me safe? I keep myself safe. The Principessa invited me and I'm going. Besides, I'm sure I can pick up some strong vampire or...something...to look after me."

Alexis leaned into her and said coldly, "When you find yourself drained of blood, and in need of rescue, don't come running to me."

"At least one vampire will like the taste of my blood," Katie said.

Byron was continually surprised at the venom between the two. They seemed to always be at each other's throats.

"Duca? Come here," Byron said.

Alexis approached her angrily, and Byron noticed the red in her eyes. "Principe?"

"Leave Katie be. She'll be perfectly safe with us there."

"The Sanctuary is no place for humans."

Byron was about to answer when she caught sight of Amelia. She was so beautiful. To Byron it seemed like Amelia floated on a cloud down the stairs. She wore an off-the-shoulder red cocktail dress that accentuated her curvaceous figure.

Everyone standing in the entrance hall stopped to look at her.

Byron walked over to meet her and kissed her hand gently. "You look absolutely stunning. I will be the envy of every vampire out there."

Amelia looked down at her dress as if she wasn't totally confident she could pull it off. "I thought red to match the ruby in my new ring. I wasn't sure, but Katie said I should wear it."

"She was right. Are you ready to meet your new world? Let us make up for your first visit to The Sanctuary. Tonight, you shall be the belle of the ball."

❖

"Mademoiselle Witch? I need an answer now," Victorija demanded of Lillian.

Lillian sat on her knees at the coffee table with the map of London spread out on top, and all her magical objects spread out, trying desperately to find the Debrek item.

She held her hands over her face and said, "I can't. It's impossible, Victorija. The Grand Duchess's magic is too powerful. There's no way I can break it. It's taken all my energy. I just can't."

Victorija kicked the coffee table so hard it flew across the room. Her anger was partly panic. If she couldn't get hold of the spell, or the magical object, she would never be Principe to a strong clan. One born vampire could not compete with the other older turned vampire clans, far less the Debreks.

She grasped Lillian by the neck and pushed her up against the wall. "You must know of some way to replicate the magic of my grandmother."

Lillian pulled at the hand around her throat, and struggled. "I've told you—no witch has ever known how to create life from the dead. It should have been impossible."

Victorija leaned in close to her and said, "And yet my grandmother did. She created a spell that allowed my family to have offspring, so it *is* possible. Maybe you're not up to it, hmm? Maybe your usefulness has run out, Mademoiselle Witch."

Lillian wriggled in fear as Victorija's teeth erupted ready to tear her throat out. "I can help, if I had the power of my other witches—"

"Do you think I'm ever going to let you anywhere near your coven?" Victorija sneered. "What you did to my father, you could do to me."

"You promised my coven—" Lillian gasped.

She whispered in Lillian's ear, "You don't want to listen to my promises. I do what I wish, what I want, anything and everything to suit my needs. You are under my control, and you will do what I say." Victorija let go of her and she dropped to the ground gasping. "I'm sick of waiting."

"Principe?" Drasas came striding into the room.

"What?" Victorija snapped.

"The Debreks have left their house. Our people watching the house say they are on their way to The Sanctuary."

Victorija smiled. "Really? Well, my cousin is really under the human's thumb. There's no way this was her idea."

"What are you thinking, Principe?" Drasas asked.

"I think it's time to put these new recruits of ours to the test, Drasas, and call in our bargaining chip."

Victorija walked over and picked up Lillian, and said softly, "I think you may be useful after all, mademoiselle. I'm going to need a protection spell of my very own."

❖

Their entrance to The Sanctuary was very different from when Amelia came with Victorija. Under a spell of compulsion, she'd seen everything and everyone through a blur or a cloud of smoke. Now everything was clear and real.

As they walked further into the club, on their way to a table, all the patrons stood and bowed their heads.

Amelia, who had her hand looped through the crook of Byron's arm, whispered, "What are they doing?"

"Welcoming the new Debrek Principessa. You're part of vampire royalty now." Byron smiled and winked. Byron led her to a booth at the back of the club, next to the bar. Sera and Katie sat with them, and their entourage of security people took their places at strategic tables around them.

Amelia looked around at all the bar patrons staring at her and whispering. "I suppose it's big news in the vampire world that Byron Debrek got married."

"You're not kidding. Only took three hundred years," Sera joked.

"Thank you, Sera," Byron said, and lifted Amelia's hand to kiss it. "Love gave me no choice."

Sera and Katie laughed, and Sera said. "Very smooth, Byron."

But Amelia didn't laugh. She felt the warm glow of love in her heart, and experienced the pull of Byron's blood inside her.

Sera nudged Katie. "I think we should go and get the drinks before they get too lost in each other."

"How long have you been coming here?" Amelia asked.

Byron slipped her arm around Amelia's waist, and smiled. "Since a few years before my ascension ceremony. I was too eager to sample life at The Sanctuary, believe me. I had my eyes opened. The Sanctuary was here long before I was born. It was built to be somewhere for all paranormals to come together in peace."

Amelia looked out over the club and wondered who was who. "Are they all vampires?"

"No, no, everyone comes here. Witches, shape-shifters, fae, werewolves, vampires."

Amelia gasped, "Shape-shifters and werewolves?"

"Well, not so many werewolves. They are family people and generally too busy at home with their mates and pack to bother coming to a club."

Amelia didn't know what to say. Every time she thought she'd gotten a handle on this new world, something else came along and knocked her off balance.

Byron pulled her closer and said softly, "I know this is a lot to take in, and a world which you've only read about in books and seen in films, but this is normal to us, and it will be to you soon. You can see why we keep it secret. Humans would be distrustful of us, they would see us as a threat and try to destroy us, and believe me, we have enough turf wars in the paranormal community without adding humans into the mix."

Amelia let out a breath. "I can understand that."

"Here in The Sanctuary, the golden rule is we leave our grievances at the door, and it's mostly worked well, apart from the night Victorija had you here. But it's been a wonderful place to come over the years. The twenties were a whole lot of fun." Byron winked at Amelia.

She could quite imagine the dapper Byron in her dinner jacket and bow tie, charming and dancing with all the ladies. How many women had Byron known in her long life? The thought of Byron with someone else made her feel queasy.

Byron must have noticed her subdued mood because she asked, "What's wrong? Did I say something?"

Amelia felt silly and childish even saying this out loud, but she had to be honest. "You've lived for a long time."

"Yes, I have." Byron furrowed her eyebrows, obviously not quite understanding what Amelia was trying to say.

"Um…you must have known and been with a lot of women." She felt her cheeks flush as she said it.

Byron nodded in understanding. "Oh, I see." She could imagine the impact of Amelia realizing Byron must have had centuries of other sexual partners. Byron knew she would feel exactly the same in Amelia's place. Amelia had lowered her head, feeling a bit embarrassed, Byron imagined. "Amelia, look at me."

Amelia looked up and Byron cupped her cheek. "I have lived a very long life, and I have met many women, but there was only one I cared for, and only one I loved."

"Rose?" Amelia asked.

Byron nodded. "I cared for Rose, but you are the only one I have ever loved, mia cara." She moved inches from her lips, and smiled when Amelia's lips parted for her.

"You, Amelia, are the one who captured my heart, my soul, and the only one I want as my Principessa. I love you."

Their lips came together softly, and they kissed slowly for a few seconds.

"All right lovebirds," Sera's voice interrupted them, "cool it down a second. Look who we've found."

Byron pulled away with a sigh. She was really enjoying that kiss. She looked up and found a grinning Sera, Katie, the bar manager, Slaine, holding a tray of glasses, and one of her bar staff behind with an ice bucket of champagne.

Slaine bowed her head. "Principe, Principessa, it's an honour to have you here."

Byron stood up immediately and smiled, delighted to see her old friend. "Slaine, wonderful to see you again."

Slaine set the tray of glasses on the table, while her companion placed the ice bucket at its side.

Byron offered her hand, and Slaine shook it warmly, while Sera and Katie took seats.

"We haven't seen you for a while, Principe, but I can see why." Slaine smiled at Amelia.

"Forgive me, Slaine, this is Amelia Honey—sorry, Amelia Debrek, my wife and new Principessa. Amelia, this is Slaine, the ever-present bar manager of The Sanctuary."

She watched Amelia's look of awe at the sheer size of Slaine. "Nice to meet you, Slaine."

"You too, Principessa. I can only apologize for the last time you were here. If I had known you were here under compulsion I would have—"

"I should have been here," Byron interrupted.

Amelia put her hand over Byron's. "That's all in the past now. Let's just enjoy the present."

Slaine picked up the bottle of champagne and said, "Thank you, Principessa. Please enjoy this champagne on the house."

❖

Amelia rested her head on Byron's shoulder as they swayed together on the dance floor. It was heaven to just be together, relaxed, with no worries or secrets between them. She let out a contented sigh.

"What are you thinking?" Byron asked.

Amelia lazily hung her arms around Byron's neck. "Just how happy I am. The last time we danced together, there were so many secrets between us, and now we are equal partners in this relationship."

"I promise you, I will never hide anything from you again. Secrets very nearly cost me your love, and I will never risk losing you again."

Amelia smiled and kissed Byron softly. Out of the corner of her eye she saw the table where Bhal and Alexis were sitting. Alexis appeared tense, and almost angry. She followed her gaze to the dance floor where Katie was dancing with a woman dressed in black leather.

"What is it?" Byron asked.

"Alexis seems to be very annoyed at something in Katie's direction," Amelia said.

"Something in Katie's spirited character doesn't seem to sit well with Alexis," Byron said.

"Or maybe it does?" Amelia smiled.

Byron raised a questioning eyebrow. "What do you mean?"

What Byron saw as annoyance, Amelia was beginning to see as electricity. Amelia dragged her nails teasingly down Byron's neck causing a spark of crimson in her eyes. "Just that sometimes, those that anger you the most, you want the most."

Just as the song finished, Byron turned around, and looked from Alexis back to Katie, whose dance partner was kissing her hand in thanks for the dance.

"I doubt it. Alexis would never love again—I know that. Especially a human."

"We'll see." Amelia smiled.

The next song started and it was a fast number. "Shall we sit? This tempo isn't quite my thing," Byron said.

"Even in the twenties?" Amelia joked.

"Even then," Byron replied.

Sera and Katie appeared at their side, and started to pull Amelia away. Katie giggled, a little tipsy. "We're here to take the Principessa to dance."

"Yes," Sera said, "we'll take care of her."

Amelia was almost giddy as they pulled her away. She wasn't used to this type of family. Uncle Jaunty and Uncle Simon were the best stand-in parents ever, but she'd never had siblings, and that's what Sera and Katie felt like. Not only did she have Byron, she had a whole new family now.

❖

Victorija's car parked at the back of The Sanctuary. She sat in the back seat with Lillian, who appeared extremely nervous.

"Victorija, you're not going to try to take the Debrek Principessa from under their nose, are you? Remember what happened the last time you fought with them here."

Victorija leaned into Lillian menacingly. "Do you think I'm a complete idiot? I'm not my father. Amelia will come to us. A little fail-safe I built in the last time I was in her company. I just need you to put a spell of protection around this car, when I have her."

Lillian was silent, obviously considering her options. Victorija grasped her neck in a flash of speed and pushed her against the back of the car. "Are you quite clear on your role, Lillian?" Victorija drew a finger down her cheek. "I would hate for you to be of no use to me any more."

"I'm clear. I'll do what you want," Lillian said, gasping.

As soon as she said that, Victorija loosened her grip and smiled. "Thank you, Mademoiselle Witch. I knew you would see it my way."

Lillian caught her breath and they both sat back against the plush back seat. "So, what now?" Lillian asked.

Victorija dipped her hand into her jacket and pulled out her phone. "Wonderful machines these portable telephones, aren't they?" Victorija grinned. "The mischief I could have gotten up to if I had one of these through the ages."

❖

Amelia, Katie, and Sera had danced for about twenty minutes before they decided a toilet break was needed. Wilder left her position near the dance floor and tried to follow them, but Amelia said, "I'm sure I'll be perfectly safe with Katie and Sera, Wilder."

Wilder looked unimpressed, but with persuasion from Sera she finally pulled back to her original position.

Amelia was out of the stall first, and began to reapply her make-up. She shook her head as she listened to Sera and Katie talking, laughing, and joking between their two stalls. Both were clearly feeling the effects of the alcohol they had consumed.

She put her lipstick away and noticed her phone screen flashing. She had put it on silent before their night out so she wouldn't be disturbed. Amelia saw the name Victorija flash on the screen and even though she knew she shouldn't answer, somehow, she just couldn't stop herself.

"Hello?"

"Hello, Amelia. It's Victorija here. You will walk to the back door, without alerting anyone, and come to me. Do you understand?"

In her mind a memory of her last encounter with Victorija came to the surface.

"The next time you hear my voice, Amelia. You will do exactly as I say," Victorija said while gazing into her eyes.

"I will do exactly as you say," Amelia repeated.

Even though every fibre of Amelia's being was fighting against it, she couldn't help but reply, "Yes, I understand, Victorija."

Amelia quietly walked out of the bathroom and down some steps to the back door. She pushed them open and found Victorija and another woman standing by Victorija's limo.

Run, Run! Amelia screamed inside, but she just couldn't.

Victorija opened her arms in welcome. "Ah, Amelia, I have you at last. Come here."

She walked to her, and Victorija held on to her wrist. "Right, let's get her in the car, and you can cast your spell, Lillian."

Lillian went to take her other wrist, but as soon as she touched Amelia's skin she recoiled sharply, making Victorija drop her hold.

The moment she felt the jolt, Amelia realized she once again had control of her mind and body, but she couldn't just run from a super-fast vampire.

"What is wrong with you?" Victorija bellowed at Lillian, who was staring at Amelia and rubbing her wrist.

"She's, she's—"

"Just grab her—Drasas, help us."

When Victorija and Drasas launched for her, quite by instinct she pushed out her hands and shouted, "No!"

As she shouted, a force of white light knocked both vampires to the ground, unconscious. Amelia gasped, staring at her hands, then turned her gaze to Lillian, shaking by the car.

"You're the one," Lillian said.

"What?" The doors behind Amelia burst open, and Wilder pulled her back into the club.

CHAPTER TWENTY-FOUR

Byron heard a commotion at the back of the club. She rushed over and found Wilder cradling Amelia. Bhal and Alexis followed Byron, and Sera and Katie soon joined the group surrounding Amelia.

"What happened?" Byron demanded as she fell to her knees, and took Amelia from her.

"I don't know exactly. The ladies were in the bathroom, but they were taking too long and I just went for the back door on a hunch. Victorija and Drasas were there with Amelia and another woman I didn't know."

"They were trying to take her from me?" Byron said angrily.

Wilder nodded.

Byron looked to Bhal and Alexis. "You two, check the back door—Victorija is there. Wilder, Sera, Katie, follow me out." Byron lifted Amelia in her arms and started to walk out of the club.

Amelia started to come to. "Byron, Victorija is—"

"I know. You're safe now." Byron kissed her brow.

When they got outside, Byron's driver opened the Daimler's doors for them. Byron set Amelia down and they all climbed into the car.

"What happened?" Byron said to Sera and Katie.

Sera answered, "I have no idea. We were in the bathroom, and when I got out of my stall, she wasn't there."

Katie added, "We never even heard the bathroom door open and close."

Byron turned to Amelia, who was silently gazing at her hands for some reason. "Amelia, do you remember what happened?"

"I…I was putting on my lipstick, then my mobile rang. It was

Victorija. I don't know why I answered, but I did. She told me to walk to the back door of the club."

Amelia leaned into her for support, and Byron put an arm around her, cradling her against her chest.

"What happened then?" Byron asked.

"I don't know why, but I did what she asked. I used all of my strength but I just couldn't fight it. I went to the back door, and Victorija took hold of me."

Byron tensed with anger. The thought of the bloodthirsty Victorija touching her wife was horrifying. At least the ring had been some protection. She turned to Sera and said, "Compulsion. She must have implanted those instructions in Amelia's mind the last time they were together."

Sera nodded. "Sounds like Victorija. Then she had an ace up her sleeve when she needed it. I wonder why she couldn't get Amelia into the car."

Byron stroked Amelia's hair. "What happened next?"

"There was another woman there. I heard Victorija saying something about a spell of protection. Anyway, she touched me and jumped back like she had been burned or something, and then I could finally control what I was doing and—"

Amelia went quiet as if something was going over and over in her mind. "What?" Byron asked. "What happened next, Amelia?"

Amelia sat up, and rubbed her forehead. "Nothing. Wilder got there and got me away."

The car door opened and Alexis popped her head in. "They've gone, Principe. No sign of them at all."

"Right, let's get home, and we can work out what we do next."

Just as the door shut, Byron heard her phone signal a text message. She took it out and tapped the messages icon.

"Victorija," Byron spat.

I may have lost my bargaining chip, but I will never stop, Byron. I will be relentless until I get hold of my family birthright. Give me what I want or I will never stop. Remember 1850?

Byron felt all the blood drain from her face. "Alexis," she shouted to the front of the car, "get us home, and fast."

❖

Byron looked around the entrance hall to her home with horror and simmering rage. All around her, loyal members of staff, attendants whose families had worked for her for decades, some for centuries, lay dead and bloody. Those vampires who had been left at the house were tending to the bodies with care.

As soon as Byron got that text she knew what would await her at home. Alexis ran in first, her memories surely making her relive the most painful time in her eternal life. Then they all followed and could only look on in shock.

Bhal checked the rest of the house, while they stayed in the entrance hall. Amelia began to weep at the sight before them. Sera walked around checking the bodies and shook her head to Byron.

Victorija had taken from her again. Had attacked at the heart of her clan, and killed the people under her protection. Alexis walked back from the other first floor rooms and shook her head. Her rage was palpable.

Byron watched Katie, who had been very quiet, walk forward and kneel by one of the bodies. His face was bloody.

"It's Jack," Katie gasped. "I—he helped me get ready. He loved doing nails and hair and…he's gone."

Alexis walked to her and said, "Katie, you can't help him now. Stand up. You're upsetting yourself too much."

Katie looked up at Alexis and said, with tears rolling down her cheeks, "I would have been lying here with my throat ripped out if I hadn't gone to The Sanctuary tonight."

Byron could see the what-ifs running through Alexis's mind as she stood there. Her jaw was tense, her rarely beating heart was thudding, and her knuckles were white she was clenching them so much.

Alexis had lost everything the last time the Dreds had attacked, and if Amelia was right that there was some sort of spark between her and Katie, she'd nearly lost someone she cared about again, and would have done if Katie had followed her instructions.

Alexis held out her arms to Katie, as if to offer comfort. Katie stared at her for a long moment, then turned and walked to Bhal, who took Katie in her arms and hugged her.

Byron knew she had to take command and get everyone under control. She would have to summon her forces from Monaco to replenish her London guard, but in the meantime she had to get everyone safe, and protected.

Amelia squeezed her tightly and said, "What are we going to do, Byron?"

"We are going to a stronghold that the Debreks haven't used for a long, long time, but there we will be protected."

She looked over to Sera. "Sera, go to the safe house, and prepare to move our secret. We're going to the Debrek castle in Scotland."

❖

The smaller Debrek private plane landed at Inverness Airport, and waiting blacked-out cars drove them and their staff on further.

Amelia held Byron's hand with an iron grip. "How long till we get there?"

"Two and a half hours approximately. The castle is on the very tip of the north of Scotland."

Byron put an arm around her. Amelia laid her head on Byron's chest and was reassured by a single thud of her heart. Although Byron's heart seldom beat, it always seemed to when she lay close.

"Are you sure Uncle Jaunty and Uncle Simon will be safe in London? If Victorija is willing to hurt anyone connected to you..." Amelia didn't finish the sentence.

"They'll be perfectly safe. I've left some of my people to protect them, and besides, Victorija's attentions will be on finding us, not harming your uncles."

"She killed all your staff just to get a spell. It's senseless."

Byron kissed her head. "Not for Victorija. She wants to sire an army of born vampires, a threat not only to us, but to the human population. They already have a blatant disregard for human life, and if they became more powerful with each generation, we would be overrun."

Something that had been bubbling under the surface between them came to Amelia's mind. "Did you always plan to have a child?" Amelia said.

"I honestly never thought about it. I never even thought I'd have a Principessa. When you're immortal, time is not really of the essence.

I thought Sera would have children, and I suppose I thought I might eventually have to pass on my genes but—"

Amelia sat up quickly at that comment. "Pass on your genes? Is that what you think having a baby is?"

"No, I didn't mean it like that. It's simply that I never thought I would be married and in love. I might have been obligated to create the next strong generation of vampires eventually, but it wouldn't have been out of love."

"And now?" Amelia asked.

Byron smiled and caressed her cheek. "Now things are quite different. Now I have you."

It was a big, overwhelming thought that she could play a part in creating the next generation of Debrek vampires. "How do you know I would be able to have a baby with you—maybe the spell wouldn't work with a human."

"My great-great-grandmother, Lucia, is a powerful witch. When I was seeking answers to what I thought was my blood sickness, she connected to you by holding a hairbrush of yours, that you had left in our bedroom in Monaco."

"What did she say?"

"That we were blood bonded, and I had to protect you at all costs. It was more what she didn't say."

"What do you mean?"

"It's hard to explain. She appeared to know more than she was saying. The first thing she said was, *She's here at last*, and gave me the ring."

Amelia sat back in the seat and remembered the flash of power that had come from her hands, and knocked Victorija and Drasas off their feet. She still hadn't told Byron. She was frightened to face what it might mean. "My life has become so strange."

Byron laughed. "That's nothing. Wait to you meet the BaoBhan Sith."

"The *Baavan* what?" Amelia said.

"It's Gaelic. They are a relic from an earlier time, living in our world."

"Are they vampires?"

"They are vampires, but with a deep connection to nature and magic. Vampires with a great deal of fae in them. An ancient kind of paranormal being."

Amelia sat up quickly. "Fae? Like fairies?"

Byron smiled and raised an eyebrow. "I wouldn't say that to their face. People with that heritage in their blood, like Slaine, prefer the term fae."

"Slaine is part fairy? She's like seven feet tall or something."

Byron laughed softly. "She's only part fae—her father was a shape-shifter, hence the big build."

Amelia held her hands against her cheeks. "So let's just recap. I'm bound by blood and in love with a super vampire. A super vampire clan that has secrets every other clan would kill to get hold of, and we are going to seek refuge with a band of Scottish fae vampire people?"

Byron leaned over and kissed her lips and whispered, "You still have the Debreks' greatest treasure to meet, my great-great-grandmother, the most powerful witch in the world—the Grand Duchess."

The castle came into view, and it was as beautiful as Byron remembered. She hadn't been here in a century, but it never seemed to change. The road they were on led across a stone bridge with a gatehouse, the only access to the castle on the island. Remnants of the ancient Caledonian Forest, which used to cover most of Scotland and down into England, surrounded the loch.

"Byron, this is gorgeous," Amelia said, her face pressed up against the car window. "It's like something from a film about medieval times."

"It certainly hasn't changed since then. It's so far away from the nearest town that it's unaffected by modern living."

They drove across the bridge and slowed to a stop at the gatehouse.

"Byron, look." Amelia pointed to an owl sitting on top of the gatehouse. She'd never seen an owl up close, and it was a real surprise to see a bird of prey just sitting there.

"I see her. She's a long-eared owl. You'll see all sorts of birds and animals around here."

Byron never seemed to be surprised about anything they encountered. The gatehouse barrier lifted and the owl flew off. Amelia followed its flight up to the castle turrets where she saw an assembly of large birds of prey. An eagle and an owl were the only ones she recognized.

"This place is seriously strange."

"You haven't seen anything yet," Byron said with a smile.

The car pulled though the gates of the castle wall and drove over to what seemed to be a main entrance. Byron got out and walked around the car to help Amelia out.

Amelia took her hand and stepped out. The place looked deserted, and there was no one there to meet them.

"Where are they?" Amelia asked. "Those BaoBhan…people."

"BaoBhan Sith," Byron corrected her, and pointed up to where the long-eared owl was sitting on the castle turret. It left its perch and flew down to sit in front of the large castle doors.

Amelia gasped, and held Byron's hand tightly as the bird started to transform before their eyes. In a matter of seconds the bird had grown and morphed into a woman wearing a long green gown, embroidered with gold with a gold tassel tied around her waist. She had long ringlets of the most beautiful copper hair.

Amelia forgot to breathe. How could this even be happening?

The woman held out her arms and had a warm smile on her face. "Byron Debrek, after all these years. Welcome."

Byron walked forward and embraced the woman, something Byron seldom did with people. Had they been lovers?

"Wonderful to see you, Hilda, and thank you for helping us again," Byron said.

Hilda waved her hand and the other birds of prey flew down from the turrets.

"This is your castle, Byron," Hilda said, while behind her the other birds transformed into women wearing the same green dress, each with a different appearance.

Hilda continued, "You have let us use this as our home, and we will always be in your debt. Now introduce me to your young lady before she faints with shock."

That's exactly how Amelia felt. Light-headed, confused, and liable to faint at any second. How else would one react to birds transforming into women before one's very eyes?

Byron took her hand, and she felt more grounded. She led her over to Hilda and said, "This is Amelia, my wife and new Principessa. Amelia, this is Hilda, clan leader of the BaoBhan Sith."

Hilda held out her hand in welcome, and Amelia took it with trepidation. "Pleased to meet you."

Hilda gave a little jolt when they touched, but not to the same extent as the woman with Victorija had. Amelia watched her search her face, and then Hilda said, "Yes, I can see why she is the one, Byron. You are most welcome, Principessa. Welcome to the Scottish Debrek residence."

"You people do have a lot of houses," Amelia joked.

Byron smiled and said with a wink, "We are vampire royalty after all."

Hilda's gaze went behind Amelia's shoulder. Amelia turned around, and followed Hilda's gaze to Alexis, who was leading Bhal and Katie from the second car.

"Alexis, are you well?" Hilda said with a tone that suggested a lot of history.

"Quite well, Madam Hilda," Alexis replied in a monotone.

"Ever the talkative soldier, I see." The she turned her gaze to Bhal. "Bhal?"

She came striding forward with a broad smile on her face, and gave Hilda a bow. "Hilda, so good to see you again."

Hilda embraced Bhal warmly. "You too, you old warrior."

It was still so strange when anyone invoked the age of Bhal, or any of the vampires, when they looked twenty-one at worst.

"And who is the beautiful girl lingering at the back?" Hilda asked.

"Katie, the new Debrek head of household," Katie said, with an edge to her voice that Amelia didn't expect.

Hilda never showed annoyance, if she felt it. "You are all most welcome. I and my sisters are at your service. Please follow me. My sisters will set up a protective circle around the castle. No one will get through."

Byron took Amelia's hand, and asked, "Are Sera and our special package here in one piece?"

"Yes, perfectly safe, and resting upstairs. I'll let you settle in, and take you to them."

❖

JENNY FRAME

They were taken to a bedroom which in decoration was not dissimilar to the London house, except for the ancient stonework in amongst the aged oak. The castle interior was like many Amelia's mum and dad had dragged her around as a child. Large tapestries hanging on the walls, swords, shields, and armour all over the place. Medieval swords that she noticed very much resembled Bhal's sword, only in better shape. Bhal couldn't be that old, could she?

Katie was helping her unpack while Byron was sitting on the bed fighting with her tablet and internet signal, or lack thereof.

"Bloody thing!" Byron threw her tablet across the bed.

Amelia shivered at the ripple of intense feeling she felt in her blood. It was not unpleasant—in fact it was exciting.

Byron rose and Amelia met her at the end of the bed. "Is everything all right?"

"I'm trying to hand off all my day-to-day business duties to my American cousin, Angelo. She's in charge of the North American side of Debrek International, but she'll need to take my place until we can sort out our current problems."

Byron lifted her phone, and Amelia saw there was no signal. "Looks like I'm going to have to do this the old-fashioned way, and find out if we still have a landline in this place."

Amelia pulled Byron to her and they kissed. "Don't be too long."

"I won't. I'll come back and take you to meet someone very special," Byron said.

Once Byron left Amelia gathered a few pieces of clothing and went over to the wardrobe, where Katie was. Katie had been really quiet, not her bubbly self. "Katie, are you okay? You haven't said much since we left London."

Katie placed a jumper into the wardrobe and covered her face with her hands, and started crying.

"Hey, hey, don't cry. Come here." Amelia hugged her and rubbed her back trying to soothe her. "What's wrong? You can tell me," Amelia said.

"I can't stop thinking about what happened in London. If I hadn't gone with you, I would have—"

"Don't think that way. Maybe it was meant to be that you came with us."

"I lost so many friends." Katie wept even more.

Amelia squeezed her tighter. "I think Alexis feels guilty, and scared that we could have lost you if you had listened to her."

Katie pulled back and went to get a tissue. "Alexis feel guilty or scared? She doesn't feel emotions like that. She's icy cold."

"I don't think so, Katie. I saw her with her eyes glued to you at The Sanctuary while you were dancing with that other vampire," Amelia said.

"Really?" Katie said with surprise. She wiped her tears away and then shook her head. "There's no way. She hates me."

"Hate and love are very closely linked. I should know," Amelia told her.

Katie, now calmed down, went back to Amelia's suitcase, and continued to unpack. "Alexis wouldn't know the meaning of the word love," Katie said angrily.

Amelia sensed Alexis and Katie both had feelings they had never explored, which was manifesting in frustration and anger. She decided to change the subject.

"So, do you know anything about these Baa—ugh, I can't say it. These bird women vampires?"

"The BaoBhan Sith? It's Gaelic. Yes, my mum told me about them. She said that they were vampires who became crossed genetically with fae, through their history. They are very old."

"Wow, why the bird thing?" Amelia asked.

"It's their spirit animal or totem. Mum said they think that's where the myth of vampires turning into bats comes from. They are an all-female clan and don't drink the blood of humans, only animals, to keep their connection to nature strong," Katie explained.

"Why do they live in the Debrek castle, then?"

"That I don't know. The Debreks have a long history, and have made lots of friends over the years. A bit like Bhal and her Samhain warriors," Katie said.

"Yet another mystery. I don't suppose you know that story, do you?" Amelia said.

"No, that one is a mystery to me too. Bhal never talks about her past."

They carried on unpacking and chatting for another twenty minutes, before Byron returned and said to Amelia, "Are you ready to see the Debrek secret?"

Byron escorted Amelia to a sitting room on the second floor. She knocked on the door, and opened it. "This is our secret."

Amelia looked into the room and saw Sera sitting on a couch, and a frail looking old lady standing by the windows. "This woman is your secret?" Amelia whispered.

Byron smiled. "This is the Grand Duchess."

The old woman turned her head, and smiled. "Ah, you're here at last. Come in, my dear."

CHAPTER TWENTY-FIVE

They all sat on intricately carved, but old and threadbare, red damask covered couches, next to a big open fireplace, while the Grand Duchess poured out some tea. The room was silent and Amelia felt nervous.

The Grand Duchess handed Amelia a cup, and said, "Help yourself to milk and sugar, my dear."

Amelia took the cup and tried her best not to shake. "Thank you, Grand Duchess."

"Call me Lucia. Grand Duchess makes me feel very old, which I am, I suppose."

She handed Byron her cup, and started to poured Sera's. "It's such a long time since I've been here, but nothing much changes, does it?"

"No, it's still dusty, and cold," Sera said.

Lucia chuckled. "You are too used to the good things in life, Sera. Amelia? Give me your hand."

Amelia nervously held out her hand, and Lucia smiled and let out a breath of relief when she touched her.

"I knew it was you. I've been waiting for you for a very long time," Lucia said.

Amelia looked at Byron and Sera before saying, "What do you mean? I don't understand."

"To answer that I need to explain to you the secret of how the Debreks produce new generations of born vampires. The thing that all other vampire clans covet. The secret is *me*."

"You?" Amelia said with confusion. "What does that mean?"

Lucia continued holding Amelia's hand and said, "Everyone who covets our secret thinks it is some special incantation, and they have spent centuries trying to work it out for themselves. Gilbert, Victorija's father, used the best witches he could find, but he never could work out the simple truth."

"Which is?" Amelia said.

"Vampires are neither dead nor alive, and to allow them to procreate, they need someone whose life force is so strong it will allow them to make the next generation. As the matriarch of the clan, they draw life from me."

Dead vampires, and vampire babies. Amelia felt like her brain was at its limit of what she could grasp from this new world. "So there is a spell tying your life force to every Debrek?"

"Quite so, my dear. A very, very long time ago, I was a young witch and I met a brash vampire named Cosimo Debrek, Byron's great-great-grandfather. The Debreks were very different back then. All they were concerned with was feeding off humans, both by blood and financially, through their burgeoning banking dynasty."

"They didn't believe in consent then?" Amelia said.

"Not at all," Lucia said. "Cosimo pursued me relentlessly. I have no idea why, but I was not going to have a relationship with a vampire who used humans as food, and killed on a whim."

"No one could push you into anything you didn't want, Lucia," Sera butted in, "even an ancient powerful vampire."

Byron chuckled, and looked at Amelia. "Quite like someone I know and love."

"Yes indeed, and quite like you, Byron. Cosimo didn't give up on me until I fell in love with him. Through our conversations and his love of me, he realized the wrong his clan was doing by taking blood without consent. He promised me the Debrek clan would always take by consent, as long as the clan existed, if I would marry him," Lucia said.

Amelia smiled. "And you did. That's so romantic."

Lucia took a sip of tea, and said, "It wasn't as easy as that at the time. My coven was horrified that I married into a vampire clan, and Cosimo faced resistance about taking by consent, but we proved them wrong."

"And how did you have your children? Did your coven know?" Amelia asked.

"No, that was something no one knew. We searched the world over trying to find an answer because we both wanted a child so desperately, but how can you create life from death?"

"But you found a way."

Lucia nodded. "A way, but a painful one at that. My ancestors, who give my coven power, made us an offer. The Debreks could procreate and grow stronger with each passing generation, on two conditions. One, that they never waver from taking by consent, and respecting human life…"

Lucia's voice wavered with emotion, and Amelia saw tears in her eyes. "And two?"

"Cosimo, the love of my life, would give up his immortality, and live out a normal human life as sacrifice, and I would live on as the life force, the matriarch who would allow each new generation to procreate."

Amelia grasped Byron's hand. "What a heart-breaking choice." She couldn't imagine having to choose Byron's life over a child.

"It was. There had to be a sacrifice, you see, to create life from death. What bigger sacrifice than for a vampire to give up immortality?" Lucia said. "I refused to contemplate it, but Cosimo wanted us to have children like any normal family, and agreed to their terms behind my back. I was so angry, I left him."

Amelia looked at Byron and thought of the long six months they'd spent apart, how painful it had been. "I can understand how hard that was." Byron squeezed her hand in reply.

"Finally, I just couldn't live without him, and came back. Nine months later, Byron's great-grandfather Antoine and great-uncle Gilbert were born. You see, Amelia, that is what this clan is all about, love. Love is what allows those Debreks who wish it to have children. When I lost my husband, I was distraught, but I knew I'd had a lifetime of love with him, and he would be waiting for me when my time came."

Byron suddenly sat up. "What do you mean when your time came, Lucia? You are our life force. You are immortal."

"There are secrets even you don't know, Principe," Lucia said. "I was promised that a time would come when my replacement would arrive. A witch chosen by birth to fulfil my destiny as the matriarch of our clan. That is why I gave you my ring, my dear. Without it I'm vulnerable and await death willingly."

Byron saw Amelia's hand start to shake, so she put her arm around her. "Lucia, Amelia is not a witch. This can't be true."

"She has witch blood in her, and she knows it. Don't you, dear?"

Amelia nodded, and Byron cupped her cheek. "What does she mean?"

"Daisy and Victorija's witch have all gotten some kind of shock when they touched me, and when Victorija tried to take me, a bolt of light came from my hands and knocked them out. I was scared to tell you. I'm sorry."

Byron pulled her into her arms. "It's all right. I understand."

Sera stood up and started pacing. "Do you know Amelia's past? Why doesn't she know of her heritage?"

"I wasn't shown that. You'll have to do your own digging to find out, but I do know that the ring triggered the powers that have been hidden her whole life."

Byron said with more calmness than she felt, "So Amelia is the new Debrek matriarch. What happens to you, Lucia?"

Lucia smiled and took another sip of tea. "I get to live for eternity with my love, Cosimo, and for that I must face my destiny."

They heard the slamming of car doors and shouts from outside the castle. Lucia put her cup down and said, "It looks as though my destiny has arrived."

Alexis knocked and came straight in. "Principe, Victorija and her vampires are here."

Byron rushed over to the window. "They're here, but they can't get in."

Lucia pushed hard on her stick to stand up, and said, "But I can go out to her."

❖

Everyone had now gathered in the sitting room—Bhal, Alexis, Hilda, as well as Byron, Amelia, and Sera.

Victorija had made her position clear from the shouts they had heard. She wanted the secret, and if she didn't get it, she would go to the nearest village and massacre every living thing.

Byron had been pacing up and down for the last half hour. "There is no way I can let you do this. You cannot go out to face her, Lucia."

Lucia walked slowly over to the window, needing her walking stick more than ever. "Victorija is my granddaughter, Byron."

"That means nothing. She killed her own father for power," Byron said.

"Byron, you often wondered if you had the same monster inside as Gilbert and Victorija do. The answer is yes."

Byron felt her heart sink and looked over to Amelia and Sera with resignation.

"Not because you are that way, but all vampires have that in them—the heightened emotion, desperate hunger for blood, and instinct for hunting down your human prey. But you have free will, and of course born vampires are nurtured by their upbringing. Cosimo made a choice to change this clan for good. You, Byron, follow in his stead."

"And Gilbert and Victorija?" Sera asked as she walked over to join them.

Lucia sighed. "Gilbert was selfish and egotistical from childhood. We tried our best, but he couldn't fight who he was. Victorija was different. She was a normal child when she was with us but deeply affected by fear of her father. When he was banished from our family, Victorija was only a small child, and I believe she is a product of her upbringing."

Byron was losing patience. "Whatever made her who she is doesn't matter. She's now a murderous born vampire threatening us and the world."

"Which is why I must go to her. I let her down when Gilbert took her away—we all did. I can't fail her now. This is my destiny, and you will not stop me."

Obviously feeling her anger and frustration, Amelia came to Byron, and placed a calming hand on her back, trying to soothe her.

"Give me your hands," Lucia said to Byron and Amelia. They held out their clasped hands, and Lucia covered them with hers. "I might be the secret, but Amelia is the life force now. My burden has been handed on. I must face Victorija, and you must not interfere, no matter what you see. I have your promise?"

Byron did not think she could keep that promise, but they both nodded.

❖

Victorija was becoming more and more frustrated. Her repeated threats were falling on deaf ears, and Lillian's attempt to break the protection spell were fruitless.

Lillian put her hand to the invisible barrier one last time and was thrown back to the ground. "It's impossible, Victorija. I can't get through."

Victorija lifted her up, and call out, "Give me the secret or I start my massacre with this useless witch. You know I will, Byron."

Drasas, who was standing behind by the cars, said, "She's not going to care about a witch who's been helping us. Let me go and gather up some humans, Principe."

Victorija dropped Lillian when the huge wooden doors to the castle started to open. "Put the witch in the car, Drasas. I knew Byron would see sense—" She stopped midsentence when she realized who was walking out. "Lucia is here? What does she have to do with it?"

Victorija tested the barrier and it was down. She stepped through, and started to walk to meet Lucia halfway. "Hold your position, Drasas. Lucia and I have things to talk about."

Lucia, although old and out of breath, seemed calm and confident. "Victorija?"

Victorija inclined her head politely. "Grandmother. It's been such a long time."

"My door has always been open to you, if you came in peace," Lucia said.

Victorija rolled her eyes. "Let's skip the pleasantries. Give me the secret. I have a dynasty to build."

"What did your father tell you of the Debrek secret?" Lucia asked.

"That you created the spell and it was tied to a magical object, and when we were banished the spell was removed from our line."

"That is somewhat correct. I created the spell, but it was connected to my life force, a burden I have carried for a long, long time, but now rests with Amelia."

Victorija laughed. "I should have guessed, and all this time my father was looking for a magical object. You were in front of our noses. Tell me the spell, *now*."

"Why do you want it?" Lucia said.

Victorija felt all her resentment and fury racing to the surface. "Do

I not deserve the same rights as Byron? Do I not have a natural right coming from the line of Debreks to have children? Put the spell back on me. It is my right—"

The Grand Duchess touched her cheek and Victorija fell to her knees. All of Victorija's memories from when she was younger ran through her head. Every friend she'd ever made, her father killed, her first and only love as a young vampire, who made her heart feel again, whom her father compelled to suicide in front of Victorija. The pain of losing her, and a childhood of mental abuse, taught her to shut off her feelings, exactly as Gilbert wished.

A tear ran down Victorija's face, and Lucia said, "There is no special incantation I can tell you. The spell was never taken from your family, Victorija, but it only works when you truly feel love for another person, someone who you would die to protect. That is how I devised the spell, and how your grandfather and I planned the future of the clan. Your father once loved your mother, and had you, but after his brother inherited the clan, his heart grew dark and his soul blackened. The light died inside him, and he became the most vicious vampire there has ever been. He could have no more children, because he couldn't feel love, but you can, Victorija. There is a glimmer of light in your dark soul. I can see it."

Victorija plunged her hand into her grandmother's chest and grasped her heart. "Shut up! I don't want to feel. At least I can kill you like my father never could. You and your perfect Debreks left me with that monster, and guess what? He created another monster. Me."

Lucia gasped and breathed heavily. "The chink of light? It is in there. Even if you kill me here, Victorija, there is still hope. Never give up hope."

Victorija tightened her grip on Lucia's heart. "My soul is drenched in blood because of my father and because my grandparents, aunt, and uncle abandoned me to him. Even when my mother was killed, no one cared about little Victorija, did they? No, you were all too busy living your perfect life, and running the world."

"Victorija, I'm sorry. We couldn't—"

"You're over five hundred years too late, Grandmother. That chink of light is dead, and what's left is a bloodthirsty monster who would kill her own grandmother."

Victorija pulled the heart from Lucia's body and crushed it in her hand. She heard Byron shout, and knew she would be upon her in seconds.

"Retreat, now!" Drasas shouted.

❖

Byron ran as fast as she could, but as she neared Lucia's body, she had to choose to pursue Victorija or stay by Lucia. She stopped, fell to her knees, and cradled her great-great-grandmother in her arms. "Lucia? You shouldn't have done this. We would have found a way."

Lucia gasped and blood ran from her mouth. "My time...has passed. Amelia is the lifeblood of this family now. Protect her, and our bloodline will continue in love, forever."

Byron heard Alexis and Sera arrive by her side, and kneel in respect beside her.

"I promise you, I will protect her, and we will make you proud."

Lucia reached up and touched Byron's cheek. "Victorija is damaged." She gasped. "I am partially at fault for her. If she had been brought up with us—we should have done more."

"We all make our own choices, Grandmother."

"I told her the secret she has been seeking. The secret spell is love. It was never taken from the Dreds. They abandoned love."

Lucia's skin started to go greyish blue.

Byron heard Amelia's voice cry out, "Byron, Lucia!" In a few seconds Amelia was beside them. She looked at Lucia and then to Byron and Sera. Byron shook her head and tears started to spill from Amelia's eyes.

"Listen," Lucia gasped. She grasped Amelia's hand, and said, "Byron, Sera."

They both laid their hands on top of Amelia's, and Byron felt the icy cold from Lucia's skin.

"You three are the future of the Debrek clan. Always live by blood, family, and love, just as Cosimo and I wished for."

"We will, Grandmother," Byron said.

Sera, who had tears streaming down her face, said, "We'll miss you so much, and never forget you. Great-great-grandpa is waiting for you."

Lucia eyes started to flutter closed. "Amelia—be strong for what's ahead, and, Byron…help Victorija if you can—"

Then her breathing stopped, and the light went out of her eyes. Amelia jumped in fright as a light spread from her ring throughout her body, then disappeared, and Lucia's body crumbled to dust.

CHAPTER TWENTY-SIX

Amelia kneeled by the fire in the drawing room of the castle, desperately trying to get the warmth into her bones. Byron, Sera, Alexis, and Bhal were enjoying a drink while Hilda explained what she knew about Lucia and her legacy.

Hilda took a sip of hot tea before placing it on the coffee table in front of her. "As Lucia told you, when she created the spell that allowed her and her descendants to have children, her spiritual ancestors gave her two conditions and a prophecy. One condition was that her husband"—Hilda looked to Byron and Sera—"your great-great-grandfather, Cosimo, would sacrifice his life as a vampire, and live out his natural life, while Lucia lived on as the life force that would allow more children to be born."

Byron walked over to the decanters on the sideboard and filled her glass. "And the second condition being that we keep our word to take blood by consent."

"Yes. Your great-great-grandmother was from an ancient coven of witches that practised an old craft. Much older than ours, and although we study it we don't understand it all."

Amelia's mind was beginning to crack under the pressure of everything that was apparently her destiny. Not only did she have a family heritage she knew nothing about, she was now, to all intents and purposes, immortal. "And the prophecy was that a witch would come along to replace Lucia one day?"

"Yes, that's right," Hilda said. "Lucia told me that when she touched the hairbrush Byron brought to her, her ancestors told her you were the one. The one to release her from this earthly bond, and to breathe new blood into the Debreks and their sacred covenant with the witches."

"So I have magic in my blood, except I'm from a human family. Or so I thought. So they were lying to me?" Amelia said angrily.

An uneasy silence fell over the room, and Byron quickly put her glass down, before saying, "Would you excuse us?"

Once the rest of the group had left, Byron walked over and touched Amelia on the shoulder. "Mia cara—"

Amelia stood up quickly, and began to unbutton her blouse. "You need to feed. I can feel it."

Byron took hold of her hands. "Amelia, stop. You're upset. I can see that."

"I'm *upset*?" Amelia said angrily, making air quotes. "I'm apparently not completely human, so my family history is a lie, and I'm now an immortal who gives life to each new generation of Debrek vampires…Forgive me if I'm a little *upset*."

Byron tried to pull Amelia into her arms but she struggled out and stormed over to the window. Amelia's confusion and uncertainty were ramping up her anger and there was only one person to take it out on.

"You know, a month ago, I was heartbroken, but I was a normal woman, a tailor with a career, something I made for myself." She turned around and looked at Byron with fury. "Then I find out I'm bonded by blood and Mrs. Debrek, without so much as a proposal, and now a bloody uber mother to the Debrek clan of vampires without asking. The life I built for myself is over, and now I don't even know if my family is really what they've told me. I've been lied to and press-ganged into being some sort of a chosen one by a bloody witch…vampire… whatever prophecy."

As soon as she finished talking and saw the look of hurt on Byron's face, she regretted her rant. Byron's walls slammed down before her eyes.

Byron buttoned up her suit jacket and said formally, "If that is how you truly feel, Miss Honey, then please, do feel free to leave. The Debrek clan believes in consent above all, and if you feel like you have been forced into a relationship with me, and my family, then you most certainly should leave us and return to the normal, single life you seem to crave. I'm sure we can come to some sort of agreement in exchange for your blood, so that you are not tied to me. Just remember you came to me that night in my bedroom, not the other way around."

Before Amelia could reply, Byron was gone in a flash.

"Bloody vampire super speed." Amelia smacked her hand to her head in frustration. "Why did I say that?"

❖

Victorija lay against a stone wall in a farmer's field, by the side of the road, sheep gently grazing and baaing in the background, and the bodies of two backpackers she had come across, lying dead beside her. Her confusion and hurt had erupted in a moment of blind rage and violence.

She stared at her bloody hand that had ripped out and crushed her grandmother's heart. The cascade of memories that Lucia had evoked in her had unlocked a part of her memory her father had conditioned her to forget existed. She remembered herself as a young child, running through her grandmother's garden in Venice. Victorija liked it there. She could be free to play and laugh without being scared her father would punish her. He never showed that side of himself in front of the Grand Duchess.

Victorija had a vision of sitting on her grandmother's lap, while she used her magic to entertain her as a small child. She saw in her mind's eye her favourite teddy bear floating before her, dancing in the air. That happy memory then switched to Victorija pulling out her grandmother's heart, and crushing it.

She felt tears roll down her cheeks, and when she wiped them away she saw the fresh blood of her victims all over her other hand.

"See what I've become, Grandmother?" Victorija shouted into the sky. "I'm a monster, and all because you abandoned me, because they all abandoned me. My so-called family."

A car pulled up and Drasas got out. "Principe? Are you well?"

She couldn't reply. Everything was black, and her hope to build the Dreds to something more than the Debreks was over. The secret to building her army was love, and that was something a Dred—something she—could never feel.

Victorija looked up and saw a worried looking Lillian in the back of the car. Her lip rose in a snarl. Lillian had outlived her usefulness. She picked herself up, and walked to the car.

Before she stepped in, Drasas said, "Where to, Principe?"

"Paris. There's nothing for us here now."

When she stepped into the car, she said, "Mademoiselle Witch, you are just what I need…"

❖

Amelia had to walk twenty minutes to get to where Sera said Byron had headed. "If only I had super vampire speed as well as immortality."

She spotted Byron standing on the beach at the back of the castle. It was an idyllic spot looking over the loch, and to the side was a little wooden harbour that led into a small boathouse.

As soon as Byron walked out on her, she knew she had to make this right. She loved Byron and that was all that mattered. Byron had already been hungry after the fight and Lucia's death, but after all the high emotion of their argument she could feel Byron's hunger becoming desperate.

The bond they shared made Amelia feel everything that Byron did, in her blood, in her bones, and in her heart, and that made her love for Byron all the more intense.

She stood beside Byron at the shore, but Byron never acknowledged her presence. Amelia sighed and looked down at the small waves of the beautifully clear loch water rolling up to her toes.

Amelia couldn't stand the silence any more. "Byron I—"

Byron turned her head and gave her a stony look. "You don't have to say anything. I will have someone take you back to London."

"Don't give me that stoic, controlled Byron rubbish," Amelia said with annoyance. She took Byron's hand and turned it over, and placed their wrists side by side. Their palms showed the scars of their blood bond. "We are in each other's blood. I can feel your hunger, your passion, your joy, and your pain. You can't hide from me any more."

"Oh, really?" Byron said coolly.

"Yes, and I know I hurt you with what I said. I was confused, hurt, and angry at everything. My life's been turned upside down, Byron, but I know I was not forced into anything. You were right—I did come to you in London, and not just because I didn't want to see you in pain, but because I wanted to be the one who gave you what you needed."

Byron let out a sigh and entwined their fingers. "But it's true—you had no say in our blood bond. It was my mistake in the heat of passion. I wasn't careful."

Amelia reached up and cupped her cheek. "Listen, if I knew that you were all vampires then, and you'd asked me that night to bond by blood with you, I would have said yes."

"You would?" Amelia could see the hope returning to Byron, and the red in her eyes intensifying.

"Yes, I would. I knew I loved you well before we left for our holiday in Monte Carlo. I wanted to tell you how I felt every second I was with you, but I was frightened of scaring you off. All I wanted was commitment from you, to know that when you went off around the world, that I was the only woman for you. So if you'd asked, I would have said yes, without hesitation."

Byron put her arms around Amelia's waist and pulled her closer. "You always were the only woman, from the first moment I saw you in your uncle's shop. I was destined to love you."

"You accept my apology?" Amelia said.

"Of course, I understand why you were upset." Byron slipped her fingers into Amelia's hair.

"Then don't call me *Miss Honey* again."

"Never, you are a Debrek now, and I promise you that we will find out the truth about your family, and I will give you the human wedding you missed out on. I will pledge myself to you, in front of our two families."

"Kiss me, vampire. Make everything feel better," Amelia said.

Byron leaned down and captured her lips in a passionate kiss. Her first taste of Amelia made her fangs erupt in her gums. She was already hungry but Amelia's passion always made her more desperate. She pulled back and looked into Amelia's eyes. "Can you feel what's in my blood now?"

Amelia rewarded her with a coquettish smile, and said, "Hunger." She then quickly led her by the hand into the small boathouse and Byron closed the door. When Byron turned around Amelia was standing dressed only in her lacy bra on top, and dropping her blouse by her side. "Are you hungry, vampire?"

Byron used her speed to take her in her arms and push her up against the wooden wall of the boathouse.

Amelia gasped. "That speed thing always makes me jump."

"I like to keep you on your toes," Byron replied, pulling off her jacket and throwing it to the ground.

Amelia caressed her temples, which Byron knew showed the veins of her vampire features, and looked at her with such want in her eyes. "I love it when I see you like this."

"Why?" Byron asked.

Amelia ran her finger down her cheek and teasingly and bravely down her vampire fang, showing absolutely no fear. "Because you are holding nothing back from me," Amelia said while Byron pulled her tie off and threaded it through her palms.

"You make me lose control, but only so much." Byron raised her eyebrows and gave her a wicked smile.

Amelia's heart started to beat with anticipation. Byron held up the tie, held taut between her hands, in question. As with everything in their personal and sexual relationship, it was about consent, and Amelia's absolute trust in Byron.

She let Byron wait for a few seconds, then presented her wrists to her. Byron smiled, and said, "Thank you, Amelia Debrek." She then kissed the scar of their blood bond with reverence. "Blood and family."

Amelia smiled. She truly did have the family she'd always dreamed of now. "Blood and family."

Byron tied her wrists together and led her over to the bench that ran down the side of the boathouse. Byron sat and pulled Amelia onto her lap, pulling off Amelia's bra at the same time.

Amelia moaned as Byron massaged her breasts. She could feel how desperate Byron was to feed and she ached to give it to her. She wrapped her tied wrists around Byron's neck, and offered her neck. "I love you, Byron. Let me give you what you need."

Byron ran her tongue along Amelia's collarbone and up to the artery that gave her life. "I'll hunger for you for eternity, mia cara."

Amelia felt Byron's two fangs pierce her skin, and her head swam. In that moment she knew she would always hunger for this just as much as Byron did. Everything around them might change, but this love and hunger between them never would.

About the Author

Jenny Frame (www.jennyframe.com) is from the small town of Motherwell in Scotland, where she lives with her partner, Lou, and their well-loved and very spoiled dog.

She has a diverse range of qualifications, including a BA in public management and a diploma in acting and performance. Nowadays she likes to put her creative energies into writing rather than treading the boards.

Books Available From Bold Strokes Books

A Call Away by KC Richardson. Can a businesswoman from a big city find the answers she's looking for, and possibly love, on a small-town farm? (978-1-63555-025-2)

Berlin Hungers by Justine Saracen. Can the love between an RAF woman and the wife of a Luftwaffe pilot, former enemies, survive in besieged Berlin during the aftermath of World War II? (978-1-63555-116-7)

Blend by Georgia Beers. Lindsay and Piper are like night and day. Working together won't be easy, but not falling in love might prove the hardest job of all. (978-1-63555-189-1)

Hunger for You by Jenny Frame. Principe of an ancient vampire clan Byron Debrek must save her one true love from falling into the hands of her enemies and into the middle of a vampire war. (978-1-63555-168-6)

Mercy by Michelle Larkin. FBI Special Agent Mercy Parker and psychic ex-profiler Piper Vasey learn to love again as they race to stop a man with supernatural gifts who's bent on annihilating humankind. (978-1-63555-202-7)

Pride and Porters by Charlotte Greene. Will pride and prejudice prevent these modern-day lovers from living happily ever after? (978-1-63555-158-7)

Rocks and Stars by Sam Ledel. Kyle's struggle to own who she is and what she really wants may end up landing her on the bench and without the woman of her dreams. (978-1-63555-156-3)

The Boss of Her: Office Romance Novellas by Julie Cannon, Aurora Rey, and M. Ullrich. Going to work never felt so good. Three office romance novellas from talented writers Julie Cannon, Aurora Rey, and M. Ullrich. (978-1-63555-145-7)

The Deep End by Ellie Hart. When family ties become entangled in murder and deception, it's time to find a way out... (978-1-63555-288-1)

A Country Girl's Heart by Dena Blake. When Kat Jackson gets a second chance at love, following her heart will prove the hardest decision of all. (978-1-63555-134-1)

Dangerous Waters by Radclyffe. Life, death, and war on the home front. Two women join forces against a powerful opponent, nature itself. (978-1-63555-233-1)

Fury's Death by Brey Willows. When all we hold sacred fails, who will be there to save us? (978-1-63555-063-4)

It's Not a Date by Heather Blackmore. Kade's desire to keep things with Jen on a professional level is in Jen's best interest. Yet what's in Kade's best interest…is Jen. (978-1-63555-149-5)

Killer Winter by Kay Bigelow. Just when she thought things could get no worse, homicide Lieutenant Leah Samuels learns the woman she loves has betrayed her in devastating ways. (978-1-63555-177-8)

Score by MJ Williamz. Will an addiction to pain pills destroy Ronda's chance with the woman she loves, or will she come out on top and score a happily ever after? (978-1-62639-807-8)

Spring's Wake by Aurora Rey. When wanderer Willa Lange falls for Provincetown B&B owner Nora Calhoun, will past hurts and a fifteen-year age gap keep them from finding love? (978-1-63555-035-1)

The Northwoods by Jane Hoppen. When Evelyn Bauer, disguised as her dead husband, George, travels to a Northwoods logging camp to work, she and the camp cook Sarah Bell forge a friendship fraught with both tenderness and turmoil. (978-1-63555-143-3)

Truth or Dare by C. Spencer. For a group of six lesbian friends, life changes course after one long snow-filled weekend. (978-1-63555-148-8)

Children of the Healer by Barbara Ann Wright. Life becomes desperate for ex-soldier Cordelia Ross when the indigenous aliens of her planet are drawn into a civil war and old enemies linger in the shadows. Book Three of the Godfall Series. (978-1-63555-031-3)